The Secret

Katharine Johnson

"In *The Secret*, Katharine Johnson brings Santa Zita
and its citizens to life. She weaves a seamless tale from
the period of struggles in Italy during the Second
World War to revitalisation of the village in the present
day. But it transpires that everybody in
Santa Zita has a secret."

**Val Penny, author of
The Edinburgh Crime Mysteries**

CROOKED
CAT

Discover us online:
www.crookedcatbooks.com

Join us on facebook:
www.facebook.com/crookedcatbooks

Tweet a photo of yourself holding
this book to **@crookedcatbooks**
and something nice will happen.

For Raffaella,
Anna and Leo

Acknowledgements

This book would never have been published without the help of my wonderful early readers: Eleanor, Shirley, Rosie, Jenny and Shani. I knew I could rely on them absolutely to give brutally honest feedback and point out howlers like a character changing their name halfway through the story as well as flagging up weak or unclear plot points.

My family including the dog have been especially tolerant this year as I've battled to finish a fiction and non-fiction book at the same time, so huge thanks to them, too.

I'm so very grateful to Stephanie and Laurence at Crooked Cat Books for taking on my third novel and helping to turn it into something publishable, and for assigning me to brilliant editor Christine McPherson.

I feel very lucky to be part of the Crooked Cat community - the advice, encouragement and humour of the other writers and readers has kept me going when I've thought about giving up.

But most importantly, I want to thank you, the reader, for taking the time to read this book - it means a lot to me. Feedback from readers is so valuable - in one of the reviews for The Silence someone said they'd love to know what happened to the baby afterwards, which got me thinking about writing The Secret.

I hope you enjoy it.

About the Author

Katharine Johnson grew up in Bristol and studied History at Cambridge before training to be a journalist. She's been a magazine editor and has written for over a hundred publications. Her passion is houses and the stories they have to tell.

She's lived in Italy and escapes to her home near Lucca whenever she's able. When she's not writing you'll find her playing netball, guiding people around a stately home (not her own!) or walking her dog around the lake near her house in Berkshire.

She blogs about her writing and shares her love of books at Katy's Writing Coffee Shop
(katyjohnsonblog.wordpress.com).

Katharine loves meeting readers so if you have a book club or are arranging a book event, please get in touch through her website, Facebook (@Katharinejohnsonauthor) or twitter (@kjohnsonwrites)

If you'd like to be kept up to date with her writing and receive special offers and other goodies, please sign up on her website for her free newsletter.

Other Books by Katharine Johnson

The Silence (a Villa Leonida story)
Lies, Mistakes and Misunderstandings

The Secret

Chapter One

SONIA

1992

A moment was all it took.

Sonia heaved open the door of the little church, taking in the familiar smell of polished wood, beeswax, and crumbling plaster. A shaft of sunlight crept through the window, spilling onto the centre of the milky white floor, leaving the corners in shadow.

She fumbled in her purse, pulled out a coin and put it in the slot. With a loud click, the painting behind the altar flared into life. Although she knew what to expect, she was still shocked by its intensity. From the shadows rose a fiery, wrathful Mary wielding her club above the head of a small child.

You're still here then.

As a child, the painting had struck terror into Sonia. That face so full of anger. But then, she'd reminded herself, mothers in a rage could be terrifying.

She lit the usual candle, placing it in the iron stand in front of the painting. Not that it would make any difference, not now.

You've never listened. And now it's too late.

It was years since she'd given up on her prayer. Now, her swollen stomach and the absence of monthly blood seemed like a final mockery of the state she'd longed for all those years when she was still young enough for it to bring hope.

But the ritual was a comfort. It had become so much a

3

part of her routine she barely thought about what she was doing. She watched the flame flicker and the smoke drift up, veiling the glowering Madonna. For ten, perhaps twenty, minutes she sat absorbing the quietness and coolness of her surroundings, savouring those few moments away from the world.

A scrunching of shoes on the stones outside brought her to her senses. Sonia felt a tightening in her stomach. Heard the grating of iron against wood, the squeaking of the rusty ring handle. She shrank back behind the font. The heavy oak door juddered. A shaft of light appeared. The silhouette of a small figure with plaited hair.

It was one of the English girls from Villa Leonida. They came here sometimes, got up to mischief, messing about with the candles, having water fights with the holy water, leaving screwed up chewing gum wrappers on the floor. She'd found the dusty prints of their trainers on the marble, empty drink cans under the pews, and once some disgusting words gouged into the panelling. She had also seen them down at the pool where she worked, chasing each other round and knocking over deckchairs while she was clearing the café tables.

But this time the girl was alone.

Sonia could seize the moment. She could rise up and accost her about the mess and the disrespect. This child would be easy to take on. The way her face flushed and she twisted her plaits around her fingers when people spoke to her, let alone raised their voices. She was pallid except when she blushed, which was often, and her eyes were wistful and watery. Her awkwardness reminded Sonia of herself as a child – in the days before she'd understood why people found it so difficult to accept her.

But the girl didn't speak much Italian and Sonia didn't speak English. She'd be wasting her breath.

The girl was carrying something. She seemed to be in a trance. That round face, so white and smooth, and the large, clear eyes – a lovely face, like the glazed terracotta cherubs on the altarpiece. But she was no angel. None of them were.

4

She laid the bundle down on the floor in front of the altar. Stood up, took a step back, staring up at the painting as though she might be about to make the sign of the cross. But instead, she slipped something from around her neck and dipped down to the floor again.

The ancient wood of a pew creaked. The girl whipped round, her eyes filled with light and fear. A choking noise escaped her. The trance had broken. Sonia should say something to reassure her, step out of the shadow, see if she was all right. But her breath caught.

The door banged. The girl was gone.

The pile of rags twitched. It bleated. Sonia's heart exploded. *How could this be happening?* The thing she'd prayed for so many times brought directly to her. Right here in this place where all her secrets were known. She must be mistaken, must be mad. If it was a trick, it was the cruellest yet. But no, as she got closer and peeked inside the bundle, she could see that this was no doll. It was a real baby – weak but alive.

She gathered it up, marvelling at the smallness and lightness, nuzzling her face against its soft head. The wonderful smell of its skin. The little face was red with crying, but the baby stopped just long enough to open one of its huge, unfocussed eyes.

"It's all right," Sonia whispered.

Outside, the air was damp and smelled of pine needles and sweet acacia wood. The colour had leached out of the sky but there was a residual warmth. The path was deserted in both directions – no sign of the girl. Sonia should go after her, call her back. She should, but she wasn't going to. If she did that, it would be like rejecting God's gift. Because surely that's what this was? A bit late in the day perhaps, but after all her prayers, how could it be anything else?

Chapter Two

CARLO

"The day I left Santa Zita, I said I was never, ever coming back," said Carlo.

The memory of that spring morning in 1965 stood out more than any other he'd formed in more than fifty years that followed. The piazza was bathed in a soft, liquid light, the church bell tolling its single, muffled note as he hurried through – twenty years old, with his hair newly clipped, a clean shirt, and all his belongings in a borrowed holdall.

Ghosts of buildings slipped past as he ran. A boarded-up restaurant, shops, and a *gelateria* – none of them had been in operation in his memory. Blown render, flaking paint, broken shutters, and faded signs that said *vendesi* or *affitasi*. For sale or rent.

An old man tethering his mule in front of the stone cistern at the end of the piazza waved and shouted something Carlo didn't catch. A small child wearing only a pair of grubby pants lay on his stomach across the wall of the fountain, trailing his skinny arm into the silty water for coins that might have been thrown in by people hoping for some luck. Carlo dug in his pocket and tossed the boy his last few lire. It would be no use to him any more. The child sat up, tucking his legs under him, turning the money over and over in his hand as if he couldn't believe his fortune.

"Carlo. Wait." An elderly neighbour, dressed in the floor-length black dress that was customary among the older women, ran out of her door and pressed some bread and ham into his hand. He protested, but she insisted, "You'll need it for the journey. God knows when you'll next get a decent meal." Thanking her, he squeezed it into the holdall.

Two shoeless children jumped down from the step outside their house. "If you meet Elvis Presley, will you get us an autograph?"

He laughed. "America's a big place, but if I do, I will."

Someone gave a shout. The bus was coming up the hill. He couldn't miss it. He broke into a run under the arch and out to the bus stop, under the umbrella pines where a knot of people was gathering to wish him luck and offer advice. Looking down over the precipice, he could see the bus lumbering up through the olive trees.

Carlo's mother took his face in her hands and planted kisses on his cheeks until he begged her to stop. He'd never seen tears in her eyes before, but she pushed him onto the bus, making sure he had everything, reminding him to be good-mannered and make himself useful in his uncle's business, and to remember to write.

"You'll come out and join me soon, won't you?" he said. He'd save up enough for her airfare. She assured him she would.

Sitting on the bus as it pulled away, he noticed Sonia with her mother Martina walking up the hill towards the village, arm in arm, eyes cast down to the floor as usual. They were always on their own, those two. Only three years older than he was, Sonia already dressed like an old woman. Her hair was scraped back behind her round ears so hard that it pulled the skin taut around her dark eyes, giving her a permanently startled expression.

As though she sensed him looking at her, she glanced up and gave a shy wave. Relief swept through Carlo as he waved back. The crazy thing was, if he stayed around here he'd probably end up marrying Sonia, simply because there'd be no-one else left.

With the new industrial opportunities springing up in the cities, girls in 1965 were looking for a better catch than boys from Santa Zita. Why marry a peasant when they could be living in town surrounded by new, shiny luxuries

7

and be free to wear red lipstick and mini-skirts?

Carlo's mother had evidently suspected the same thing about him and Sonia. Why else would she have arranged a new life for him in the land of opportunity? Well, he wasn't complaining.

As the bus started its descent, the two children who'd asked about Elvis chased after it for as long as they were able, but just before the first bend they folded onto the ground, arms raised in defeat.

Carlo's last image of Santa Zita – and the one he knew he'd carry with him into the future – was of the desolate grey fortress of Villa Leonida, where Martina and Sonia had once lived, rising up above the village as though to claim it.

As if it was saying: *Don't come back.*

***

2018

"And yet here you are," Cass said, handing her husband a glass of Prosecco.

The piazza was filled with chatter, laughter, the clinking of glasses, and the splashing of the fountain, the air scented with basil and garlic. Fairy lights, strung among the potted olive trees, glowed like fireflies as the sun dipped behind the mountains, turning the sky from rose to pale gold.

Yes, here Carlo was, back in the village he'd left behind, now the proud owner of the *Tre Fratelli* restaurant. If he hadn't been away all those years pursuing the American Dream, rising from humble reporter to owner of a newspaper empire, he'd never have had the means to buy this place and restore it, and Cass wouldn't have been able to start her Tuscan property business. Three years ago, friends had said they were mad to embark on these new ventures at their ages, but Carlo had given retirement a try and rapidly reached the conclusion that playing golf, pruning roses, and joining senior fitness classes, weren't ever going to be for him.

Cass took round the tray of complimentary Prosecco to mark the restaurant's anniversary. Laughter floated up as she weaved her way through the tables, receiving grateful comments and congratulations.

"Speech!" someone demanded.

Carlo protested, but they weren't going to back down. He spoke in Italian and then English, for the benefit of the foreigners.

"When I was a boy, I used to peer through the gaps in this boarded-up building and try and imagine what it would look like if it was brought back to life – the piazza full of people again. Well, now I know."

A murmur of appreciative laughter.

"Five years ago, when I was living in Manhattan, if someone had told me that I'd be back here today in Santa Zita – the village where I was born – running this restaurant, I'd have said they were mad. But it's turned out to be the best decision I ever made."

He moved aside to let a waitress past with a tray. "And its success is down to all of you sitting here. So, thank you for coming, and please keep telling people about it, keep leaving your reviews, and tweeting your photographs."

He raised his own glass. "And to my wife Cass, who always says to me 'Don't call it a dream, call it a plan'."

Applause broke out as he kissed her.

"So now, can you please stop thinking of yourself as the rat that deserted the ship?" Cass whispered in his ear during a brief lull.

He smiled. "I can't help feeling bad that I abandoned this place when it needed me, while others who stuck out the hard times aren't much better off now than they ever were. But I like to think the rat's come back in the nick of time."

Laughter erupted from a table behind him. A camera flashed, and a couple of small children broke out of their seats and chased each other across the piazza, their feet echoing on the stone slabs. Looking round, Carlo felt a swell of pride. Life was returning to the village, but he knew it was the restaurant that had the potential to turn

Santa Zita into a destination. It made the tortuous mountain drive worth it, gave people somewhere to stop and rest and enjoy the surroundings.

Moving here and helping him set up the restaurant had turned out to be a larger undertaking than Cass had expected or would admit. Nonetheless, she'd got stuck in, planning the kitchen and dining room, and ordering the catering equipment. Now the space was simple and welcoming, with sand-blasted beams, colour-washed walls, and a tiled wood-burning pizza oven. She'd sworn she wouldn't get involved in cooking, but she'd helped out until they could afford to take on staff.

"What about you?" he asked her. "Any regrets? About moving here, doing this?"

She laughed. "Oh, plenty. Sometimes I think it's a conspiracy to drive me mad – all the bureaucracy and those endless battles with the planning department. Not to mention the fact that your mum's a little hard to deal with at times." She stepped back to let a waitress pass and nodded over to where the sun had dipped behind the mountain, then broke into her familiar downward smile. "But then I come out here and look at that view and think, 'What have I got to complain about?'. You?"

Looking around, Carlo couldn't think of any regrets.

"And I think these two gentlemen would have been very proud," Cass said, indicating the picture on the wall behind the bar of the two moustachioed brothers who'd last owned the restaurant from the 1920s until the war. There must have been a third brother once, but no-one seemed to know much about him.

When Carlo had been growing up, people always talked about *I Tre Fratelli* in reverential tones as "the best restaurant in Tuscany" – which really meant "in the world", since most of them hadn't ventured beyond the boundaries, and those that had were convinced the cuisine outside the region wasn't worth risking.

Carlo and Cass had renamed their two most popular pizzas after the brothers: one a fattening mix of mascarpone and walnuts (Pizza Paolo); the other topped with spicy sausage and tomato (Pizza Mario).

The peace was disturbed by a raised voice at the table nearest the fountain.

"I asked for pepperoni on my pizza," a man was saying in an aggrieved tone.

"Here is pepperoni," said the waitress. "Here and here."

"No. That is a pepper." He enunciated clearly, as if speaking to an idiot. "Where is the meat?"

Carlo was tempted to march over and suggest the man learn some Italian before being patronising to his staff, but he took a look round first in case Cass was watching. Sure enough, she was. She placed a hand on his arm.

"I've got this."

A few minutes later, a bark of laughter erupted. Somehow, she must have managed to explain the linguistic confusion in polite terms, and the man stayed to enjoy a *digestivo*.

"Still no regrets?" she murmured, as she turned back to Carlo.

But one ignorant customer wasn't going to ruin this evening.

"None."

A figure crossing the piazza caught Carlo's eye. Sonia stopped by the fountain to talk to someone. For a moment he saw her as she had been, a girl walking with her mother, glancing across at the other children with that wary expression.

It reminded him of the real reason he'd come back to Santa Zita. Yes, it was good to feel that by opening the restaurant he'd helped put some life back into the village, but there was something else. The question had dogged him all these years. Why had she done it? Why had Martina, Sonia's mother, betrayed her neighbours, provoking the appalling incident that ripped the heart out of this tiny village? And perhaps just as importantly, why had other people – including his own mother – been powerless to stop her?

Chapter Three

SONIA

2018

At last, the gates of the villa came into view. There was a board tied to them, but Sonia had to get closer, had to read it for herself. Her heart raced as she climbed up through the honeycomb of cobbled alleys, under stone arches and lines of washing. She'd forgotten how steep these streets were. Somehow that had never occurred to her in all the years she'd spent walking up and down them when she had the cleaning job at the little church below Villa Leonida.

The houses up here were hunched up together as if conspiring; shutters closed, doors shielded by beaded curtains, keeping their secrets inside. At first sight it was hard to tell which of the buildings were still lived in. So many these days were left empty. But another glance revealed glimpses of life: pots of well-tended geraniums stacked on a stone step; a bicycle stashed up on a balcony; a sleepy dog lying across a doorway; canaries in a cage on a window ledge. The occasional cheeping of the birds, a burst of music from a radio, and the smell of cooking were all that disturbed the stillness.

Narrow arches and passageways between the houses revealed slices of brilliant sky and glimpses of the turrets and bell towers of the town below. Steep stone staircases led down to cellars built up against the rock.

The solid front doors displayed tarnished brass knockers, simple rings, lion heads, and human faces – some cherubic, some demonic. The walls were adorned with terracotta suns and moons, and other good luck symbols. After all, this was a village that couldn't afford any more bad luck.

The final lane that led to the villa, along the high walls of the convent, was cloaked in cool, dark shadow for most of the day, regardless of how much sun splashed the piazza below. At the top, up a flight of overgrown steps beyond the little church of Santa Maria del Soccorso, stood the villa.

Villa Leonida stared back at Sonia – coolly defiant, battle-scarred but intact, daring her to come closer. The lemon trees on either side of the door had died in their pots. Grass had sprung up waist-high amid the stone chippings of the forecourt. The shutters were closed, and the skeletons of geraniums were all that remained in the window boxes. The sign tied to the rusted curlicues confirmed the rumours.

Vendesi.

For sale. Which meant only one thing – that the awful business from last year would be dragged up again. A shudder passed through Sonia. Everyone would be talking about the discovery of those bones and the deaths that had followed in this tiny village a year ago. And each time that story resurfaced, the thought twisted inside her – would this be the moment when one discovery led to another and her own secret clawed its way out?

She backed away, turned, and stumbled down the narrow path. Just outside the church of Santa Maria del Soccorso, she faltered at the sound of bells jangling and the familiar shout of the shepherd as he herded his flock of mountain sheep up the path towards the ridge above Villa Leonida. He raised his stick in greeting. She nodded and ducked inside the church to let them pass. The heavy door sighed as it gave way. Her eyes went straight to the wall behind the altar. The space that for so many years had been dominated by the painting of the angry Madonna was bare.

So much had happened here under that Madonna's glare. Good things and terrible things. For a long time, the little church had been a reminder of everything that had been wrong in her life. How could she forget that it was here

13

she'd learned what her mother had done?

She'd been cleaning the church for a year or more before she'd finally plucked up courage to ask the priest. Sitting in front of the painting of the angry Madonna with the candles flickering, he spared her the most distressing details, just gave her the facts in a gentle tone, but she knew anyway how on that day in 1944, more than three hundred people from Santa Zita and the neighbouring villages had been butchered, including an old woman of 90 and a baby of just a few months old. What she hadn't known until that moment was that, for some reason, it had been her mother who'd led the Nazis to their terrible act of revenge.

"But why?" Sonia asked. "Why would she do that?"

The priest couldn't – or wouldn't – give her an answer. "We have to remember it was war," he said. "People make decisions that they wouldn't make under normal circumstances. I doubt your mother realised what it would lead to."

He'd offered to pray with Sonia, but she couldn't hear any more. She'd made excuses and run out of the church, ignoring his pleas for her to come back. She didn't stop until she reached the abandoned villa, desperate for solitude, and found a door that had been forced open. There, in the darkness with the rain dripping in through the roof, and the smell of damp plaster, urine and beer, she'd bumped into Carlo.

They'd frightened the life out of each other. The whites of the boy's eyes gleamed. He screamed. Then, seeing she was crying, he apologised. He didn't laugh, didn't ask what was wrong, just slumped down the wall next to her and sat with her while she cried. After a while, he put his arm around her shoulder. It felt strange but not unpleasant to be touched by another person. When had that little boy got to be taller than her? They sprang apart as they heard a noise. Carlo's mother was standing in the doorway, shouting like a mad woman. Despite being half his size, she clipped him round the head, yanked him to his feet and dragged him away, ignoring his protests and demands for her to calm down.

But how could Sonia forget that it was also here in the church that she'd felt redemption for her mother's sin? It was here that she'd prayed so often for a child, and here, twenty-six years ago, that she'd seen the girl laying the baby in front of the altar. It seemed incredible, thinking about it now, as though the whole thing had been staged. It was hard to believe sometimes what she'd done that night and the lie she'd kept up every day since – quarter of a century of deceit. To take a child even in those circumstances – her legs felt hollow. She sank into a pew.

And yet, as Lorenzo was growing up, Sonia had told herself over and over that taking him had been the right thing to do. Even if she'd done it for the wrong reasons, it was the right thing. He wouldn't have survived. She'd been his only chance. He'd been so small and weak. How could it have been wrong when the outcome had been so right?

If the priest had been in the church now, Sonia would have been tempted to make her confession after all these years. He wasn't. In any case, she couldn't afford the time. As she sat there staring at the blank wall, it became clear what she had to do now that Villa Leonida was for sale again.

She must talk to her son; call him and persuade him not to come home at Easter. Nothing mattered more than that. With all the curiosity about the villa swirling around again, Lorenzo – above all people – must be kept away.

Chapter Four

SONIA

Down in the piazza that smelled of coffee and sweet pastries Sonia could see Carlo wiping down his tables. Please God, he hadn't seen her. But of course he had. He waved and came striding across the cobbles towards her, mopping his forehead with a tissue.

"The villa's for sale again," he said with an anxious smile. "I thought you'd want to know. Cass is handling the sale."

"Thank you. I've just seen."

He sounded apologetic. A splinter of ice entered her. The thought that Carlo might know about the baby belonging to the villa, might have known all these years and had just been biding his time... It was the first thing she'd thought when he came back to the village after all those years away – did he know? He'd always been curious. No wonder he'd been a journalist. He might be running a restaurant now but leopards don't change their spots, do they? A story like hers would be right up his street.

But, of course, that was ridiculous. He must be thinking about the more distant past, about the villa being Sonia's childhood home. Of what had taken place there in the war, the thing her mother had done.

Her stomach knotted tighter. *Bad blood.* That was what they'd say.

"Has your wife had much interest?" she managed to ask. With Cass's agency selling the villa, Carlo would have the perfect excuse to stick his nose in whenever he liked.

He turned his mouth down. "It's early days. She's had a few enquiries, but who knows if they're serious? It won't be easy to sell, that's for sure. There can't be anyone around here who hasn't heard about what happened there last year. Or in the past."

Sonia felt her face colour.

"It'll be foreigners," she said. "They don't care."

To put an end to the conversation, she headed into the bar instead of continuing across the piazza as she'd hoped to do. The door scraped on the floor as she pushed it.

The bar was dark after the dazzle of sunlight in the square, and Sonia stood for a few moments waiting for her eyes to adjust to the change of light. It seemed to take longer these days.

On the counter stood a giant Easter egg wrapped in shiny paper, and the mirrored shelves were lined with smaller eggs, beautifully packaged *colombe*, chocolates, and cuddly lambs and chicks in brightly coloured baskets, but something didn't feel right.

Heads turned towards her and then away again. Voices dropped. Backs spread out to form a solid wall. That old fear was creeping back. It hadn't happened for years, and yet that sense of rejection she'd faced daily in her youth had never entirely left her.

"Hello, Sonia, how are you?" Leo the barman called over the hubbub.

It took a moment to sink in - the faces were friendly, not hostile.

She managed a smile and murmured, "Not bad."

What was the matter with her? Why did she always imagine people could see through to her innermost thoughts? Most of these people were younger than her or had moved to the village recently. They had no idea about her family's past. To them, she was just Sonia, wife of Flavio, mother of Lorenzo. Her stomach squeezed. How would they react to finding out that she'd deceived them all this time?

The cluster of bodies parted to let her through to the

17

marble counter where Leo pressed down her usual cappuccino. She thanked him but declined the pastry from the glass cabinet. Her stomach was too churned up. She picked up the cup and saucer and carried them, with both hands to stop them rattling, over to one of the tables.

She stopped. Someone had got there before her.

It was then, through the murk and shadows in the rear corner of the bar, behind the shaft of sun streaming in from the door, that she saw who it was. Or who it must be. It was the hair she noticed – light brown, drawn tightly into two French plaits. A small, fragile figure sitting quietly with her head down, thumbs tapping away on her phone. Sonia held her breath, waiting for her to look up, certain that when she did she'd see a look of triumph in those glass-grey eyes.

They belonged in a round, pale face that could have been painted by Filippino Lippi. A face that had never left her; one that had haunted her dreams. A child with a bundle in her arms. A child who'd been wearing a shooting star pendant, which she had left with the baby.

If she'd been a decade younger, Sonia would have turned and fled. Instead, mesmerised, she walked towards the girl, feeling everyone's eyes on her. Was this some terrible joke at her expense? Were they all in on it?

As Sonia skirted around the table, the girl lifted her head. Sonia released her breath as she caught sight of the girl's long, angular face, dark eyes, and aquiline nose. She sank into her chair, heart pounding. This time, she looked properly at her, taking in every detail, waiting until her vision had stopped shifting. This girl looked more like a muse for Modigliani than Lippi. She returned Sonia's gaze indifferently before returning to her phone.

Sonia must stop this. It was guilt, of course. Guilt and fear. Over the past year, she'd started to see the girl again in every tourist's face. Because it was always there, that thought that the girl would come back like the avenging Madonna in the church. She'd want what was hers. She'd expose Sonia for what she'd done.

The girl hadn't let herself be forgotten. In dreams, she

was always in that calm, trance-like state. Sonia would open the front door and find her standing there. She never spoke, just held out her arms. So frail-looking and yet so strong.

Sonia would battle against the door, but the girl would push her way through with apparent ease. Or if Sonia succeeded in shutting the door, she'd look up to find the girl coming in from the *loggia*. If she slammed the shutters closed, she'd look round and find the girl had slipped around the back of the house and was standing behind her in the room.

She'd see the girl lifting Lorenzo out of his cot or leading him away by the hand through the olive trees, boarding a bus, or wading into the river, deeper and deeper until the water came over their heads. In those dreams, the girl would always whip round with that startled, light-filled look. But she'd always succeed.

Sonia bit her lip until she could taste blood. She wasn't thinking straight. How could this girl be the same one? She was still young, still a teenager. The one who'd dumped Lorenzo in the church like a bag of shopping all those years ago had been a teenager *then*. She'd be in her thirties now. Probably had children and a husband who had no idea about the existence of another child. Probably guarded her secret as carefully as Sonia had to guard hers.

In the corner of the bar, the TV was on – one of those debating shows with the audience split into different opinion groups, everyone shouting at once. An implausibly blonde female presenter with impossibly white teeth invited their views and recapped every few minutes, alternating between a very grave expression and a radiant smile.

Surely if the girl had wanted to come back she would have done so years ago when Lorenzo was still a child? Sonia sipped her coffee, but it burned her stomach as though it had been laced with poison. Keeping her expression neutral, she made herself focus on the faded pictures on the wall of the bar as it had been in the previous century, waiting for her breathing to be steady again.

Above the general hubbub, one conversation stood out.

"It'll be a relief," Leo was saying to someone. "New owners, new start. As long as it's standing there like a rotting carcass, it'll always be a reminder of what happened. Makes us all feel bad. Someone needs to breathe new life into the place, make some good memories for a change. Then we can all move on."

So, she'd been right. All around Sonia, people were talking about the villa being for sale again. So little happened in this tiny village that the events last year had shocked everyone as much as if an earthquake had ripped through it. Who wouldn't want to sell up and put the wretched business behind them?

"They say the house is cursed. Drives people mad. What happened last year isn't the only bad thing to have happened there, is it?"

"Come on, no-one really believes in curses."

"The new owners will get a bargain, that's all I know. A place that size going for the price of a one-bedroom apartment in town."

"Yes, but would you live there? I wouldn't, not for anything."

Every time Sonia thought the talking had stopped, it started up again. She took another sip of coffee, but it was no good, her stomach was on fire now. She set the cup down.

The TV debate was livening up. It looked as though it might come to blows. A large woman was hurling insults at a young man who stood up now, waving his arms and appealing to those around him to back him up.

It was only recently that she'd finally allowed herself to think the matter was over and done with, but of course it never would be. The acute pain she'd experienced after taking the baby home had receded although it had never left, just turned into a dull ache she'd become used to living with. But if the truth ever got out... She'd forgotten in the intervening years how painful fear was. A churning chaos inside her as though she was being eaten from the inside.

"Sonia?"

She dragged herself out of her thoughts.

"Didn't you used to live there? At Villa Leonida?"

"Only as a small child," she managed to say. "I don't remember it. It was too big for my mother after the war, so she moved to the house in Via della Chiesa – the one where she was born."

And where she'd died. Sonia still felt her presence there sometimes. It was hard to avoid. Martina had been such a strong personality, she couldn't just disappear leaving nothing behind. There were reminders in so many places, from the bed she slept in, to the china she ate from, to the books she read.

Who was she trying to fool? It was impossible to escape the past. There'd always be someone who remembered her mother or who'd been told about how she'd betrayed the village. Sonia would always have a story attached to her, a weight she had to drag around. She'd managed to convince herself that the whispering had stopped years ago, but no, it was still there behind the smiles on these people's faces. Any excuse and it bubbled right back up.

"How's Flavio today?" someone asked.

Sonia closed her eyes. She'd left her husband asleep, oblivious to all this. She should be with him now, but she'd had to see if the villa really was for sale.

"It was a heart attack. He's resting. The doctor says if he watches what he eats and doesn't exert himself, there's no reason why he shouldn't make a full recovery."

The woman squeezed her hand. The warmth and gentleness of human contact brought tears to Sonia's eyes.

"He will. Of course he will. He's strong as old boots."

Not so long ago, that had been true. If only it still was.

A group of tourists came into the bar – young women in their early twenties, with backpacks, dressed in shorts and vests as though it was already summer. Their eyes widened as they spotted the metre-high chocolate egg on the counter. They laughed in disbelief, arguing about whether it was real until Leo confirmed that it was. They took a series of selfies in front of it. One of the girls, in her enthusiasm to embrace

21

the egg, almost knocked it off the counter and Leo had to ask them not to touch. Amid much hilarity, one of them asked if he could pose with them for a picture. Leo gave Sonia a resigned smile.

"Do you mind?" asked the tallest of the girls, handing Sonia her phone and gesturing.

Sonia tried to control the shake in her hands as she took the picture. She took a few to be on the safe side.

"Will Lorenzo be back for the flag-throwing this year?" someone asked.

He would. Of course he would. Lorenzo loved the traditions he'd been part of for so long. Living in Florence had its advantages and its own Easter celebrations, but he missed the mountain air and the tranquillity of this place. No, it was more than that. Santa Zita was his home.

But the full impact of Lorenzo's return sank in like a trickle of icy water down Sonia's neck. What reason could she give to dissuade him from coming back over Easter? That burning in her stomach again. She couldn't waste any more time.

"I need to get home."

She needed air.

As she stepped back out into the piazza, Sonia cast a look back up at the villa, the home she had been born in. It stared back.

All of this is your fault, Mother.

Chapter Five

CARLO

"She's back," said Irena, looking out onto the piazza. "She's got a nerve."

"Who's back?" Carlo asked. He was only half-listening to his mother, while calculating how many tables would be needed at the restaurant that evening and whether extra waitresses would be required.

"Martina. Look. Out there in the piazza."

Carlo joined Irena's small, stout form at the window, half his size these days but no less imperious. He followed her gaze to where Sonia was passing the fountain. "That's not Martina, it's her daughter Sonia. Martina's dead, remember?"

Irena's voice was full of scorn. "Dead? Since when?"

He placed his hand on her arm. The skin was soft and papery, a spider's web of contours. "Must be twenty-five? Thirty years ago?"

The furrows in his mother's heavily-lined face deepened as she thought about this. "No-one told me that. Why didn't anyone tell me?"

There was no sense arguing with Irena when she was like this. At her age, it was hardly surprising she forgot things. Although lately he'd started to worry that it might be something more.

"It was when Cass and I were living in New York. You wrote and told me. You didn't go to the funeral – it was a very small affair, from what you said."

Irena's stare was hard, her small, dark eyes like raisins in her weathered face. "Please don't treat me like an idiot. Of course I know Martina's dead. And not a day too soon either. Good riddance to her."

She looked as though she might spit but checked herself and turned away. Her voice trembled. She turned towards her chair, taking his arm to steady herself.

"What she did wasn't Sonia's fault," Carlo said. "It isn't fair to blame her for what happened. There's been enough of that."

To change the subject, he placed a box on the table in front of his mother.

"I found these. Thought you might like to look through them."

Irena stared at the box but made no move to open it. It wasn't unusual for her hands to shake these days, but Carlo noticed a flicker of panic cross her face, as though she were afraid her memory might let her down.

"Whatever for?"

He could tell her the doctor had recommended it as a way of helping reinforce her memories, but why worry her?

"Remember we were talking about the book I wanted to write for you? The one about the village? I thought these might help jog some memories."

She'd talked so often about writing the book but had never granted herself the time to do it. Always too busy – and then arthritis had made typing impossible for her. Now, with dementia setting in, she had all the time in the world but sometimes couldn't even write her name.

Several guidebooks had been written about the area, but none specifically about the village. And all of them talked about the topology, and the Etruscans, and comfortably-distant historic events, glossing over its more recent past – the things that mattered.

Carlo had never taken the idea that seriously until now, but increasingly he was getting a sense that time was running out. Besides, it might be something he could sell in the restaurant or to his wife's property clients – a bit of local colour. There were so few people left in the village that remembered what it had been like in the last century. He couldn't stand the thought that when his mother died all those people she'd kept alive for him in her stories would die, too.

Some of the stories he'd heard so often that he'd stopped paying proper attention. He'd found himself recounting them to his daughters, and recently his grandchildren, but he'd doubtless embroidered these with a few details of his own so that he was no longer sure he could trust his memory. He felt a little ashamed now that he'd not paid more attention.

Perhaps it was already too late. Occasionally you could still have a lucid conversation with his mother, but so often these days the talk went round in circles. When had she got like this? She'd always seemed indestructible.

While most of their neighbours – those that were left – had packed up and moved away after the war ended, Irena had stayed and watched Santa Zita's slow decline, like a sailor refusing to abandon a sinking ship. Carlo had asked her hundreds of times to move to the States and live with them, as she'd once promised, but she'd always been adamant she couldn't live anywhere but here. She'd no more have left Santa Zita than cartwheel round the piazza.

Irena had known everything about everyone in the village once. And there were still days when she recalled surprisingly small details about people, but others when she didn't know them at all. She'd start a story and then suddenly lose it.

"No, it's gone," she'd say, shaking her head with frustration. As though her mind was a piece of lace with some solid bits strung together by a series of holes.

"I know what's happening to me," she said, fixing him with her dark eyes, the way she always had when seeing straight through an attempted deception. "I know I'm losing my mind. It happens at my age."

She shook her head and looked out across the mountains where a bird of prey was circling.

"Do you know the cruellest thing about it? I forget stupid

things like what I came into the room for, or what I was about to say. Things I actually need to remember. And yet the things I most want to forget are clearer now than ever."

She said this last sentence so quietly he barely heard her. He took her hand, which suddenly seemed very small.

"What do you mean, things you want to forget?"

She shook her head. She wasn't going to talk about them now. She'd always been proud – determined to cope on her own. Before the *alimentari* opened in the piazza, she'd made the arduous walk down the mountain to the market twice a week and back up again with shopping bags – a trip that had taken her most of the day – rather than accept anyone's help. It was only over the last couple of years that her health had shown signs of decline.

Sometimes, and he felt guilty acknowledging it, she was easier to deal with these days. Her sharp tongue had been eroded along with her sharp mind. Her new vulnerability made him feel that he could look after her now, give something back. But at other times she was as shrewd as she had always been, which made him feel young and useless again.

He had a good idea what was going through her mind, but it was useless saying so. Losing most of her family in the war must have had a huge effect on her, but she'd never talk about it. "What's the use in dragging all that up again?" she'd say.

Come to think of it, she'd barely mentioned the war at all as he was growing up. Sometimes, in passing, she'd refer to the scarcity of food, and not having shoes to wear, and the festivals and parades that formed such a large part of her childhood – but never the war itself, or the day that changed so many lives in Santa Zita.

He felt an urgent need to know more before it was too late. How much longer would she be around? And how long would her memory remain sharp enough to recall the details? There were so few people of her generation left. For years he'd shared that sense of shame and defiance about the village's past. Why should Santa Zita be defined by one brutal moment of history? But now he wasn't so sure. Was it right to pretend it hadn't happened?

Reluctantly, Irena took the box and started to rummage through the photographs. At first, he wasn't certain if she really knew who she was looking at, but she recalled most of the names.

"Ah, Michele – he was handsome. Sara – what a beauty! Guglielmo – did I tell you he had nine sons? He used to say he would have his own football team, but the next two were girls."

There was one of Carlo's father and mother when they'd got engaged.

"I didn't look so terrible in those days, did I?" she said in a surprised tone, marvelling at the chubby-faced young woman with wavy hair clipped back at the side. "They say youth's wasted on the young, don't they? I do get annoyed thinking about all the time and energy girls waste worrying about their looks. Most of them have no idea that they look lovely anyway just because they're young. Having smooth skin and bright eyes, a small waist – they take it all for granted. I wish I could go back and tell that to my young self."

The girl in the picture looked too young to get married, Carlo thought. His own daughters were already well into their thirties and showed no interest in tying the knot. But as things turned out, time hadn't been on his mother's side. The young man beside her wasn't especially handsome but had a kind face and smiling eyes. It must have only been taken a few months or even weeks before he died. Irena had rarely mentioned him over the years, although she kept a photograph of him beside her bed.

Carlo and his mother had always felt like a complete unit. It was hard to imagine what life would have been like if his father had survived the war. Perhaps he'd have seemed like an intruder.

He dug around and found a picture of the two remaining brothers that used to run the *I Tre Fratelli* restaurant. Just as she'd described, one was ludicrously tall, the other short and stout, but they sported matching handlebar moustaches and the facial likeness was striking. Irena laughed when she saw it, and recounted some of the stories he already knew so well.

"Paolo and Mario disagreed on everything. They used to scream abuse at each other over the tables. *Madonna,* the language they used! You could hear things smashing in the kitchen, and every so often objects were thrown out of the window. We used to joke we should bring our crash helmets with us when we ate there.

"I've got the clearest picture now of Paolo dragging Mario out into the piazza by his hair for putting too much salt into his sauce. And I'll never forget the time Mario punched Paolo in the face for setting fire to his moustache when flambéing a steak."

"What happened to the brothers?" Carlo asked, studying the photograph.

"That's the interesting thing – we always thought they'd end up killing each other. But in the war, one of them died by throwing himself on top of the other to protect him. The one who survived died a few weeks later, of a broken heart."

As she was talking, Carlo was struck by a photo he hadn't taken much notice of before. "Whose wedding is this?"

His mother's face sagged as she looked at the photograph for a long time. A shadow flickered over her features and her head shook. "No, I don't know those people."

She reached out for the next photograph, but Carlo looked more closely at the wedding picture. Surely that was the road that led up through to the arch into the piazza in Santa Zita? The houses were familiar, too. The street was crowded with people dressed in their best clothes. A child in pigtails and a checked dress and cardigan had climbed up on one of the stone steps outside her house so that she could get a better view.

"None of them? It looks as though the whole village was there."

She reached for her bag and started fumbling in it for one of her mints. He had a sense he was losing her – or was she stalling for time?

"Isn't that Aunty Vittoria? In which case, that must be Stefano? Who's the bride? Surely this is you here, the chief bridesmaid?"

He pointed to the young woman standing next to the bride, her brown hair parted at the side, falling in carefully sculpted waves to her shoulders. She was wearing a 1940s-style floral dress with puffed sleeves, and gloves. Her hands rested on the shoulders of two little girls in front of her, whose sashes and ribbons matched her dress fabric.

His mother's frown deepened. "No, I don't remember."

She stared at the photograph for some time, as though she was seeing more than the picture. Eventually she slapped it down in frustration, knocking the box off the table and spilling prints like confetti around the room.

"It's no good asking me. What's the point? Everyone in these photographs, they're all dead now."

Carlo picked them up as carefully as he could. One or two pictures had stuck together, and he peeled them apart. There was one he hadn't noticed earlier, of two girls sitting on a wall, eating ice cream, swinging their legs and laughing.

"This is a lovely one," he said, hoping to change the mood.

The girls looked about fourteen or fifteen and without a care in the world. So obviously at ease in each other's company and having such a good time. On the back, someone had written a short message: *I'm sorry.*

"Who are these children? Are they relatives?"

She shook her head. Seemed to disappear into her thoughts.

"Isn't this girl on the left you? Whose writing is this on the back?"

She closed her eyes. "I've no idea. It's all in the past, *amore.* Leave it there."

"Do you recognise the handwriting? Why would

someone have written that?"

She shrugged and closed her eyes, making it clear that the conversation was closed. He would have pushed her further, but when she opened her eyes they were glistening. It looked as though her mood had been set for the rest of the day. He had no choice but to pack the photographs away.

Chapter Six

CARLO

When Carlo closed up the restaurant after lunch the following afternoon, he found his mother in the living room. Her face lit up when she saw him, making his heart drop.

"*Amore!* How lovely to see you. They never told me you were coming. I'd have saved you some cake."

Cass had warned him Irena wasn't herself that day. Apparently, she'd been staring at those old photographs for hours and been snappier than usual. He set down a cup of tea and a slice of cake he'd made earlier from one of her old recipes, and passed his mother a small electronic object.

"What's this for?" she asked suspiciously. "Oh, not again. Isn't the restaurant doing very well? You seem to have far too much time on your hands."

"It's a voice recorder. I thought it might be easier for you to tell your stories when I'm not here listening to you. Then, when you're happy with it, you can give it to me."

She didn't look impressed.

"It's easy to use," he persisted. "Look – you press this button with the red dot when you want to talk; this one here when you want to stop. This if you want to erase what you've said and start again."

She waved it away. "You know what I'm like with technical stuff. I've never touched a mobile phone or one of those tablet things and I don't want to. Life's quite complicated enough as it is. I don't need any of that."

"This is simpler to operate than either of those. Really. Why don't I show you how it works?"

"Not now, *amore*. I don't have time."

"Why? What else have you got planned?"

She shook her head and turned away. Her mouth was set firm. Evidently, she didn't think the question deserved an answer.

Looking out of the window, Carlo watched Sonia disappear under the arch that led out of the piazza. He'd felt bad about upsetting her with the news that the villa was for sale again, even though it turned out she already knew. The news had obviously come as a blow to her, but that was hardly surprising. It was never going to be easy listening to the gossip surrounding the house, having your memories of your childhood home sullied.

A memory came back to him of Sonia as a sullen teenager back in the fifties when they were growing up. Walking arm-in-arm with her mother across the piazza, eyes cast down to the stone flags. She hadn't been pretty, not even then. Good skin, but her dark eyes were too deep-set in her bony face, and her hair was always scraped back behind her round ears in an unforgiving style. But mostly, it was because she didn't smile that made her so hard to warm to; although, looking back now, it was clear she hadn't had a lot to smile about. Something about her defensiveness had made him feel guilty and that in turn made him angry, because what had he ever done to her?

With those big hollow eyes and stick-like arms and legs, she reminded Carlo of a marionette in the travelling puppet show that came to entertain the children in the piazza at Christmas and in the summer. It was easy to see who worked her strings.

Everyone knew Sonia was the daughter of Martina the Traitor, although as a boy he hadn't known exactly what Martina had done to deserve the title. He just knew it was connected with the sadness you could feel in the village, the reason old people never talked about the past.

There hadn't been many children growing up in Santa Zita after the war. Carlo and his friends had felt like shadows, keeping out of people's way, knowing their presence was upsetting in some way. They'd hung around together, roaming the countryside, and making dens in abandoned houses left empty since the war. There had been so many to choose from in those days, although his favourite had been the house at the top, Villa Leonida.

More years ago now than he cared to remember, the house had been the perfect teenage den. He'd never thought about what had happened to the owners, why they hadn't come back. What made it all the more enticing was the fact that his mother had banned him from going anywhere near it and it was almost impossible to get secrets past Irena, but he'd succeeded for a long time. Until that day he'd been in Villa Leonida with Sonia after he found her crying. He'd been mortified when his mother appeared in the doorway. Red-faced and breathless after the steep climb, she'd dragged him away, smacking him round the head and shouting at him as though he were still a small child.

"Calm down," he'd told her. "You're embarrassing me."

But she'd given Sonia a filthy look and carried on. "It's an evil place. It's cursed. Don't you ever go in there again."

"What did you mean, the villa was cursed?" he asked her now.

Irena shrugged. "It's what they say. All I know is that once people start living there, they change. They do things you never believed they'd do."

"Like what?"

But however much he pressed her, she refused to give examples.

***

"She's coming!"

"Run."

"Did she see you? She'll put a spell on you if she did."

All the pranks they'd played on Martina when Carlo was a child: knocking on the door of her terraced house and running away; stealing clothes from her washing line; painting words on her shutters. Crouching in the passageway, peering from between the branches of a tree, behind a wall, or through a broken window, he'd felt his heart thumping against his ribs.

It was hardly surprising Martina had taken on bogeyman status. The sombre clothes, closed-in expression, and jagged scar that made it look as though she'd been stitched together like Frankenstein's bride. Although he'd enjoyed the dodging and hiding, the frisson of fear when she approached or looked at you was real.

It wasn't hard to imagine that she was to blame for everything that had gone wrong since the war, as well as during it. A bicycle disappearing, a dog that died, plants that refused to grow – the whispers flew around the children and helped justify their own misbehaviour, and their parents – normally so quick to make sure they behaved – didn't stop them.

None of the children knew what Martina would do to them if she caught them. They only knew that she was somehow responsible for Pilade's mother being the only member of her large family to have survived the war. For Daniele's uncle to have spent two days hiding in a tree, only to return home and find the bodies of his parents and younger sister on the kitchen floor. But why had she done it? Why had she chosen to betray them all?

The children never asked Sonia to join them. Carlo had thought about it, but how could he when half their games involved dodging Martina, her mother? He sometimes caught Sonia looking over her shoulder as she and her mother passed, but if he smiled at her she'd colour and turn away, as though he'd shouted something rude. He had the feeling that some of the older people felt sorry for her, but not enough to want their children to be her friend.

His mother occasionally asked after Sonia, but when he told her she never smiled Irena just shrugged and said "*Beh…*" in her characteristic way that meant that this was no real surprise. They were just strange those two. Everyone knew it.

Perhaps things could have been different. Once, when

Carlo was riding a friend's bicycle through the village – he must have been eight? Nine? - he discovered the brakes didn't work. Hurtling down the winding cobbled lane towards the piazza, he'd felt his teeth rattling. The next thing he knew he was sprawling on the ground tasting blood.

Sonia, who'd been coming through the arch at the other end of the piazza, ran towards him and scooped him up. Speaking soothing words, she soaked a handkerchief in the fountain and bathed his knees and chin, then picked up the things that had fallen out of his pockets and were now strewn about the piazza while he sat on the edge of the fountain dabbing at his injuries. Her face looked quite different that day, lit by a lovely smile rather than the usual defensive scowl.

But then his friends had come through the arch. Seeing Sonia with Carlo, they jeered and made kissing noises. Her face flamed red. She scrambled up and ran away home to her puppeteer.

Carlo hadn't given much thought to how she must feel, growing up as the daughter of the Traitor. It never occurred to him that Sonia and her mother needed or wanted anyone else but, looking back, the loneliness must have been brutal.

It was different now. One of the things that had struck him when he'd first come back to the village was how different Sonia was from the person he remembered – the way she was now an accepted and respected member of the community. Occasional traces of that old wariness remained, but mostly she threw herself into village events with her popular husband and good-looking son all the girls wanted to be around. She was no longer the outsider. He was.

How many people these days knew anything about Martina or what she'd done? Most of those who hadn't died on that day in 1944 or moved away to somewhere with fewer memories, had died since anyway, of old age. Younger ones had left, moving down to the town for a more reliable income and comfortable lifestyle. But now, after years of stagnation, new people were starting to move back into Santa Zita. Most were foreigners who knew nothing about the village's history, and probably didn't want to know. It didn't fit with their image of a Tuscan idyll. And Carlo had been as guilty as anyone else of hiding the truth. After all, he had a business to run.

His guests wanted to believe in the Tuscany they saw on postcards. Wanted to congratulate themselves on discovering this enchanting out-of-the-way village after their stressful drive around the mountain bends. They wanted to sit in a sunny square, sipping cold wine and eating olives, and talking about the magic of the place – the fireflies and folklore and festivals – submerge themselves in an icy pool, or go horse riding through fields of sunflowers. Who was he to spoil it for them? Because all these things were possible. What they saw wasn't a lie – just another truth.

But the thing he found hardest to understand was Martina's decision to stay in the village after the war. Why hadn't she left like the others, and made a new start in a place where nobody knew what she'd done? Why had she been determined to stay here and remind people? That was what they hadn't been able to forgive.

From time to time you heard gossip about Martina having a secret stash of money in that little house she'd moved into after the war, but if she did, no-one ever saw her spend it. Carlo couldn't help wondering: had she ever talked to her daughter about why she'd betrayed her neighbours? What it had felt like when things turned out as they did? She surely couldn't have anticipated the extent of the violence, and yet she must have been aware of things that had happened in other villages. Why had she believed it would be any different for them? Or did she really not care?

There had to be a reason. He didn't want to make excuses for her – he'd grown up without a father because of what Martina did. It was something he'd struggled all his life to understand. Now it was too late to ask Martina, but not too late to ask Sonia.

He'd have to find a way to ask her. They spoke quite often these days, and perhaps Sonia would find it a relief to talk about her mother after so long. He'd stopped asking about it as a child because nobody ever answered. And yet, he'd gone on to make a career out of asking difficult questions. Why should this be the only one left unanswered? He wasn't going to be fobbed off this time. He had to find out the truth before it was swallowed up like so many of Irena's memories.

A beep on his phone hauled him back to the present. A crisis at the restaurant. He'd have to ring the suppliers and sort out the delivery that had gone astray.

"I'll leave this here anyway," he said to his mother before he left, patting the Dictaphone.

"Don't bother," Irena called, turning purposefully away from it.

He pretended not to hear.

IRENA

After Carlo had gone, Irena picked up the tiny machine. The late afternoon sun slanted across the piazza, making the fountain shimmer. An *Ape* van trundled in through the arch, loaded with freshly-cut olive branches in preparation for the priest's Palm Sunday blessing. A group of men was planting geraniums in the beds around the fountain – a nice splash of colour.

She turned the device over in her hand. What was this nonsense? So much money wasted on useless things. Didn't Carlo understand that at her age she was past learning new tricks? Why would she want to talk into a machine? Was this his way of apologising in advance for not being around much now that the tourist season was underway, and the restaurant would be full every night? Did he think it would be some sort of substitute for his company?

That mischievous look he'd given her when she said she was busy. Why should she justify to him how she spent her time? In all the years she'd spent bringing him up, there had hardly been a moment to sit still. So what if she liked to now? Why did he think he had to find things for her to do to relieve her boredom? Hadn't it occurred to him that she was perfectly happy as she was?

Sometimes she wondered about that wife of his. Was Cass trying to put the idea into his head that she was losing her marbles, so they could have the house to themselves? Well, she wasn't going anywhere.

She examined the buttons. They were very small for her arthritic fingers, and they had symbols that meant nothing to her but reminded her of the ones on the remote for the DVD player, which he'd tried to tell her how to use but he'd been wasting his time there too. So much rubbish on the television and the old films were far too sentimental. She was quite happy as she was, sitting here, looking out on the piazza. There was always a drama of some kind She tried one or two of the buttons. A red light came on. Did that mean it was recording? Perhaps, just out of curiosity, she would try to speak. She cleared her throat.

"Well – here I am, my darling. I wish you wouldn't waste your money on these silly things. And that, I'm afraid, is all you're going to get."

She laughed nervously. Not too loudly, in case the people milling outside the window in the piazza might overhear and think she was talking to herself. For a while she experimented, trying to get it to play back to her. Eventually, she found the right button and pressed it.

The voice she heard over and over, she barely recognised. It was the thin, cracked voice of an old woman; frail, tired, and nervous. She snapped the Stop button and put the thing down on the table in disgust. What would he come up with next?

Chapter Seven

2018

"They're selling Villa Leonida."

Flavio's red truck was still parked outside the house where it had stood unused for three weeks, but he was up and dressed by the time Sonia let herself into the house. The plates were piled in the sink and a smell of cigarette smoke lingered. She kissed him, unpacked the bread and oranges, and reached for the moka pot. For a while she thought he hadn't heard what she'd said.

Finally, without looking up from his paper, he said, "Do you want to buy it back?"

She stood halfway to the sink holding the two halves of the coffee pot. Was he serious? Perhaps, after all, it would be the solution – the only chance to keep the truth buried. But living in that house after everything that had happened was unthinkable.

"How could I live there again? I've spent my life trying to escape it."

He put down the paper. "I wasn't serious. But neither can you blame the villa for what happened. I'm not saying your mother didn't have her reasons…"

Sonia turned away, drowning him out with the sound of the tap as she filled the water chamber.

"What my mother did was unforgivable. If it wasn't for Lorenzo, I'd still be paying the price."

She spooned the coffee into the filter, tamping it down with the back of the spoon. Marrying Flavio had changed so many things in her life. Coming from Viareggio, he hadn't grown up knowing about Martina, so he hadn't been as ready as the locals to point fingers about the past. He'd taken Sonia on despite her mother, and she'd always be grateful for that. But it was the birth of Lorenzo that had completed the turnaround, changing her status from daughter of Martina the Traitor to mother of the lovely Lorenzo.

It was only last year when those bodies were found at Villa Leonida that she'd begun to suspect that taking Lorenzo had somehow had fatal consequences. It was no good trying to fool herself these two events taking place on the same night were unconnected. The question that plagued her was, would she still have taken him if she could have known where it would lead? Looking at him now, she felt surer than ever that she would. Flavio put a hand on her arm. "That's too much coffee. Look at the mess." He drew her towards him. "You must have some good memories of being at the villa."

Yes, of course she did. Lately, they'd started to surface, those small flickers of recollection. Dancing with her mother on the moonlit lawn to one of *Nonno's* gramophone records, the notes floating out of the open French doors. Counting fireflies in the velvet night sky. Standing on a chair in the kitchen and helping *Nonna* make a pine nut cake. Sitting on the edge of the waterfall, looking down at her bronzed knees and feeling the damp, mossy rock beneath her legs, blowing bubbles and watching them float off over the roofs and towers below.

Being carried on someone's shoulders through the woods. Whose, she could never remember; just a feeling of being a giant striding through the trees. She'd always thought it was her father, but looking back now with an adult's understanding, she realised that couldn't be right as her father had died so early in the war when he was away. Yet another bit of her childhood that made no sense.

But the only day she remembered in detail was the last one. The day the soldiers came. A small space in solid darkness, the sound of gunfire, the smell of burning. She shut her eyes and shook the memory away.

"I wasn't even five years old when we left," she said, turning her back to fetch the cups down from the cupboard. "How am I supposed to remember that far back?"

Flavio's pills were lined up in different dishes on the counter. She checked he'd taken his dose for the day. It was hard to believe that this man who'd always been her rock was now dependent on so many pills for his survival.

Back in the past when he'd worked at the villa, his days had been made up of hard, physical work: chopping and stacking logs; clearing paths; building stone walls. He was never still. When he wasn't at work in his own wood, he'd be helping others in theirs.

Flavio had thought nothing of carrying Lorenzo on his shoulders for miles in those days. She'd told him not to – it wasn't good for the boy; he needed to build up some strength – but Flavio could never say no to Lorenzo. She'd yet to come across anyone who could.

"Can't blame them for selling the villa, can you?" Flavio said. "Wanting to get rid of the place."

"No, of course not."

Who wouldn't want to sell up and move on after the murders that had taken place there? But then Flavio had no idea where this might lead. How it could shatter his life. No stress, the doctor had said. The truth could kill him.

Sonia bit back a sob. It was so unfair. He was old; she was old. Why now, after all this time? If the truth had come out years ago, it would have seemed like the end of the world, but they'd have had some time to get past it. Now he was old and ill, it would be so much worse.

"I've been thinking about Easter," she said, wincing at the false brightness of her tone. "We should go away this year, so you can recuperate properly."

Flavio's bushy eyebrows shot up. "You always insist on staying here for Easter."

"I'm thinking of your health. We should go somewhere beautiful and peaceful, so you can rest and not worry about this place falling down around our ears. How about Giglio? Or the lakes? If we hired a villa, Lorenzo and Francesca could come, too."

He took her hands and pulled her towards him, kissing her, barely able to conceal his amusement. "Where would we get the money to do that? That's what I love about you. After all these years, I still don't have a clue what you're going to come out with next."

She rested her head against the reassuring warmth of his chest, trying to ignore the churning in her stomach. Could you really say you loved someone if you'd been lying to them for years?

The screech of the coffee pot pulled her back into the present. She broke away.

Chapter Eight

Carlo stood in front of the villa. The forbidden territory of his youth.

The property agency was Cass's business. It would make sense, she'd pointed out at the beginning, for the two ventures to support each other. People staying in the rental properties would eat in the restaurant, and diners who fell in love with their surroundings and dreamed of owning a holiday home would spot the advertisements on the noticeboard in the restaurant for properties for sale.

So, it was normally Cass who showed clients around, but she was out accompanying some other clients to the *notaio's* office in a town further up the coast, and wouldn't be back until late. The English family had called in on spec. Carlo could have asked them to come back another time when Cass was free, but he couldn't resist the opportunity to see inside the place where he'd spent so much time as a teenager.

He accompanied them around the side of the building, through a tunnel of heavily scented magnolias to the terrace at the back. The marble chippings scrunched underfoot, sending up a cloud of dust, which settled on his shoes and the bottoms of his trousers.

He sidestepped the two children who tore past him brandishing porcupine spines in a ferocious sword fight.

"Put those things down – you'll have someone's eye out!" shouted their father, a chunky-legged man in shorts.

The climb up from the piazza had been arduous for the children in the simmering heat. They'd complained about aching legs and bickered over pointless things. But up here they seemed to get a new lease of life and tore off around the gardens.

Last year, from down in the piazza Carlo had become gradually aware of the villa reawakening. For decades it had been hidden in summer by a thick forest, and in the winter by cloud. One morning he'd heard rumours someone had bought the place – foreigners obviously, because what local would live there?

Every so often vans would trundle through the piazza, carrying materials. The air echoed with banging, sawing, and scraping, as roof and floor tiles were restored, chestnut windows repaired, and electricity upgraded. Workmen processed up from the car park with bathroom and kitchen fittings and finally furniture, but the house had remained hidden from view, a slumbering ogre behind the trees and the clouds.

It was only in the weeks leading up to Easter last year that he'd woken to the whine of chainsaws reclaiming the land, and the villa had risen phoenix-like out of the trees in its new guise – a perfect pink palace with gleaming green shutters, almost unrecognizable from the dour grey fortress he'd known. But now it stood empty again.

Carlo shook himself back into the present as the English woman in a white linen dress pushed her sunglasses up on top of her head. "We're so glad you speak English. And so well."

"My wife's American," he explained. "She tells me my accent's terrible."

They protested, but probably out of politeness. They weren't bad people, he thought as he unlocked the door. He'd rather see them own the villa than the previous lot Cass had taken round. She said they'd been full of condescending remarks and questions that seemed designed to catch her out.

Stepping through into the cavernous *salotto,* Carlo felt a curious thrill. He was seized by a sudden vision of the house as he remembered it in the sixties: the smell of damp that had caught in your throat; a thick layer of dust blown in through the broken windows; patches of blown plaster on the walls; cobwebs strewn like paper chains across the room; the floor littered with old bottles and cigarette ends.

Damp stains had smudged the faces of the cherubs painted on the ceiling, turning their expressions sinister. The old dresser had stood against the wall where he paused now – black with powdery mould at the back, but full of glasses and plates, as though the owners had just popped out and the house was still waiting for their return.

All gone now, replaced by a clean, smooth interior, a tasteful mix of old and new, and a smell of fresh paint. But was it really possible to erase the past? Didn't it have a way of imprinting itself in the walls of an old building?

Moving through the *salotto,* the drawing room, he heard laughter, a burst of music, caught a smell of joss sticks. Ghosts from five decades ago shifted at the corner of his vision, old faces turned towards him then melted back into the walls. Shaking the images away, Carlo walked purposefully through.

From the loggia, he pointed out the boundaries of the land. His gaze stalled at the place where the chestnut drying tower used to stand, which had been the focus of the news stories last year. He shifted his gaze and drew the buyers' attention instead to the wisteria-clad pergola, where the couple couldn't possibly guess he'd smoked his first joint, watched for shooting stars, had his first kiss, lost his virginity…

"The sun sets over there, so it's a lovely place to sit in the evenings," he told them.

Below them, two lemon-haired figures flickered in and out of the silvery olive trees in pursuit of a small dark shadow. One of those wild kittens someone kept leaving food out for.

"You'll never catch it," the mother shouted, laughing. "I don't know how they can run about in this heat."

She wandered back to the other side of the loggia, resting her hands on the stone wall. A sudden change came over her. Carlo followed her eyes to the patch of land where the chestnut drying tower had stood, built up against the rock, with a cave where the grisly discovery had been made last year. She pointed to it with a nervous smile.

"That's where they found the bodies, isn't it?"

He wasn't going to deny it. The case was solved, he pointed out. There was no risk of harm to anyone owning the property now. She nodded but drew her arms around herself, and walked off biting her lip. He couldn't help thinking she must have felt it – that cold presence his friends had talked about.

"Shall I show you the other rooms?"

They carried on with the viewing, but it was obvious by now they wouldn't be taking it. They couldn't wait to get away. Carlo sighed. Hopefully the next people would be less sensitive to the atmosphere.

Chapter Nine

"You didn't think I'd get the hang of it, did you? It's actually rather fun."

Carlo grinned as he looked up to the loggia where his mother's face was triumphant. He ran up the steps and sat down next to her. "I knew you could do it."

He pressed the button and heard her familiar voice, tired but clear – a little grander than usual.

"In Napoleonic times, this area was packed with the rich and famous stopping off on the Grand Tour, going to concerts, gambling, swimming across the bay, which accounts for the fine villas and palaces. You can feel their spirits everywhere. They'd come up here to escape the stifling air in the towns – for the views, the peace and tranquillity; writers, artists, musicians, and philosophers, all seeking inspiration for their work. And what work they produced."

She clicked the Off button and looked at him triumphantly. "Well?"

Carlo smiled, struggling to say something that was encouraging but at the same time…

"It's great."

She raised an eyebrow. "But…?"

How was he going to put this? "But it sounds like a guidebook."

She raised her hands. "I thought that was the point. You said you wanted to know about the area."

Perhaps this wasn't going to work after all. "Yes, but I want to know what it was like to live here. For *you* to live here. What it was like to live through the war, how you managed without a car, how it felt when the earthquake erupted. And about the other people who lived here. What they did, things that happened to them. Not all that ancient stuff about poets and philosophers that nobody's heard of. Stories about real-life people – things that readers can relate to."

Her face screwed up in confusion. "I thought you wanted information?"

"I want it to be your story," he said. "Things other people don't know. Like how your cousin saw Puccini chasing the girls down the street. Or how your aunt threw herself off the bridge to see if God would save her, and survived."

His mother looked at him aghast. "That's family business. We don't want everyone knowing about that. What would the villagers say?"

He laughed. "Why not? What harm can it do? These people died decades ago."

"They're still entitled to some respect. Anyway, she didn't survive, *caro*. I made that bit up to give it a happy ending when you were small."

"You did what?" He shook his head at his own gullibility but rather wished she had let him carry on believing after all these years.

Chapter Ten

Irena was asleep in her favourite wicker armchair on the loggia the following day, the voice recorder still in her hands. The air was heavy with rain. Carlo touched the skin on her arm and, finding it cool, fetched a blanket to wrap around her shoulders. Prising the device out of her hands, he was going to put it back on the table but hesitated.

Should he wait for her to give it to him? Surely, she wouldn't mind? That's if she'd used it at all since he'd given his reaction to her last attempt. Perhaps he'd been a bit harsh. He hadn't meant to discourage her, but her recording had sounded a bit pompous and not what he wanted to know at all.

Her hands grabbed for it instinctively, but she settled back into sleep. He waited for a moment, then retreated into the kitchen and pressed Play.

"Ahem – hello? Oh, blast this thing, is it working? Oh yes. Where was I? Well, you asked about the wedding photograph. I may as well tell you, I suppose. You've probably guessed by now anyway. The bride was Martina. And yes, I was the bridesmaid. And the two girls on the wall – Martina and me. We must have been how old – twelve? Thirteen? We were very close back then. I couldn't imagine my life without her. And that will surprise you, I know, because we never spoke to each other after the war. At least, not properly. I don't know why I'm telling you this."

His heart flipped. *Don't stop.* He was surprised by his own sense of desperation.

It was a shock to learn that the girl in the photograph sitting on the wall, laughing and swinging her legs alongside his mother, was Martina. They'd clearly been

49

good friends, relaxed in each other's company, and yet they'd never exchanged a word while he could remember.

He rummaged through the box of photographs until he found the one of the two girls on the wall of the fountain. He was still getting used to the idea that they had been so close.

Yes, Martina had been lovely. Something of a young Vivien Leigh about her. It was so hard to equate this lovely face with the gnarled, dour one he recalled. And on the back, the simple words: *I'm sorry.* It was obviously far from adequate for what Martina had done, but presumably the words had meant enough to his mother to make her hang onto the photograph. How much more did she know?

Carlo poured himself a glass of wine, took it outside, and sat down at the table at the other end of the loggia where he could see his mother but was less likely to wake her.

"You can laugh, but you don't know what it was like to be there," her voice went on. "That's what I want to get you to see. Funny, I remember so clearly saying to her once, 'We'll be sitting here by this fountain in fifty years' time, you and I, and nothing will have changed.'

"How could either of us have guessed that our lives would change by so much?"

His mother had evidently been holding the device too close to her face, and her snort shattered the air with its vehemence. A few moments of silence followed. She must have taken a moment to collect her thoughts.

"Sometimes, I allow myself a little fantasy – an alternative history, if you will – that Martina didn't do what she did. That she and I could really sit here now discussing our children and grandchildren. How could we have had any idea back then how precious and precarious our friendship was?"

Chapter Eleven

SONIA

2018

"Lorenzo, I've been thinking about Easter. Why don't we come to you instead this year? You've always told me what a spectacle it is in Florence, with the fireworks in front of the cathedral. It would be fun."

There was laughter in her son's voice. "But you hate Florence."

"Oh now, I never said that."

Sonia pictured Lorenzo standing in his bathrobe on the roof terrace of his flat in the Oltrarno district. A strong black coffee balanced on the terracotta tiles, and between the plant pots a view of rooftops and cupolas, and the Arno winding its way through like a green ribbon.

"It's chaotic, yes. I couldn't live there, it's true. But it's a splendid city and you always say Easter's spectacular."

"Yes, and you always say you hate crowds."

"Oh, it depends on the reason for the crowd," she replied, although she shuddered at the thought of being hemmed in by so many people, herded about by police with megaphones – not to mention the fear of a terrorist attack.

His voice dropped a little. "But what about Dad? Wouldn't he be better off in Santa Zita where it's quieter?"

Sonia bit her lip. If only she could explain that stressing Flavio was the thing she was so desperate to avoid. It was true the traffic would put up his heart rate, but not as much as finding out that he wasn't Lorenzo's father.

"He doesn't need to come to the cathedral. A rest on your roof terrace would do him the world of good."

Lorenzo sounded reluctant. "I don't know. The flat's so small, and Francesca's really busy at work. I don't think she'd be up to cooking a large meal."

"She needn't do a thing." Confirmation at last that Francesca wasn't much of a cook. "I'll bring the food and cook for us all as usual."

How else to stop him coming, stop him hearing things she didn't want him to hear? As they were talking, Sonia's eyes fell on the photograph on the dresser of Lorenzo at around six years old on the swing in the park, his Wellington boots askew, and his head thrown back as he shouted with laughter.

Even though he was in his twenties now, she still sometimes caught herself thinking of him as that little boy – skinny knees; bright, mischief-filled eyes; thick, looping curls like Flavio; and a smile that would melt any heart. And that smile of his had melted the hearts of her neighbours in Santa Zita, transforming their cold hatred into warmth, removing the shackle of her mother's guilt.

They'd given her the odd courteous nod and polite condolence when her mother died, but it was the baby that changed everything. A new beginning in a village that had lost so many lives. People she'd never spoken to had crossed the square to congratulate her, breaking into smiles, bringing gifts and offering advice. They marvelled at the improbability of a woman her age becoming a mother for the first time – or at all. A miracle, they insisted, as though they were acknowledging that she'd been forgiven for her mother's actions.

Lorenzo was the reason that people talked to Sonia now and asked after her husband's health. It was probably something other people took for granted, but after the cold, isolated childhood she had endured, she never would.

During those first weeks and months after Sonia had brought the baby home from the little church where she'd found him, she'd jumped every time she heard someone at the door or behind her in the street, thinking the girl had turned up to reclaim him.

She'd been terrified that someone would spot he wasn't theirs. As he slept, she used to scrutinise him, running her finger lightly over his silky skin and perfect features, searching for clues that might betray her, waiting for someone to remark that it was curious how his earlobes were attached when theirs weren't, or some other sure giveaway. She'd dreaded hearing someone say, "How odd, he's the image of so-and-so when he was little." And then the whispers starting.

But they'd been lucky. Whoever the father was, he must have shared Sonia and Flavio's dark hair and eyes, and Lorenzo's face was not a replica of anyone else's she knew.

As he got older, Sonia had worried about him falling ill or having an accident, and hospital staff discovering something about his blood group or genes that proved he couldn't be related. But mostly she'd worried that he would just instinctively know he was different, that one day it would become obvious.

Whenever that day came he'd turn on her and demand answers. He'd want to know, among other things, why hadn't she told him, why she'd let him believe these things for so many years. Perhaps that would be the one thing he couldn't forgive.

But month after month and then year after year, it didn't happen. Perhaps she'd misunderstood her neighbours all along. Even those who couldn't bring themselves to acknowledge Lorenzo when he was born had gradually fallen under his spell as he grew up and took the lead in the school plays and the Medieval processions.

It was Lorenzo who'd taught Sonia the meaning of unconditional love. As a tiny child he'd snuggled up to her and promised to protect her from wolves and bears – the worst dangers he could imagine anyone facing. And she'd made that promise to him that all mothers make to their children, and not all are able to keep – that she'd keep him safe no matter what.

As time passed, it was obvious that whatever biological claim the girl might have, she was nothing to Lorenzo, whereas Sonia and Flavio were his world and he was theirs. He was unique, perfect, not like anyone else she'd ever known, and yet also like Flavio and, yes, even like herself.

So much of his appearance turned out to be due to the facial expressions he'd adopted from her and his attitude to life picked up from his father. It made her laugh to hear the way he mimicked his father's groan as he sank into his chair, or the way she turned a yawn into a song.

"Well, I'll speak to Francesca about it anyway," said Lorenzo at last. "I don't much mind either way. Look, I have to go, but I've been wanting to talk to you about something."

Sonia held her breath. "What is it?"

His voice changed. He sounded distracted. "No, it's fine. It can wait. I'd prefer to wait."

Sonia's hand trembled as she replaced the phone. Was there any way he could have found out? She reached for some milk of magnesia and stood at the sink as she swallowed the tablets with a large glass of water. It felt as though she'd swallowed some barbed wire. She turned back to look at Flavio but he was asleep, the newspaper spilling its pages onto the floor. She picked them back up, folded the paper, and put it on the table. His mouth was slack like a child's, the creases in his brow smoothed out in sleep. This was all so wrong.

Chapter Twelve

2018

Irena's voice was stronger now with less hesitation, as though she'd become more comfortable speaking to a machine.

"Where do I start? In 1944, I lost my best friend. It's possible, you know, to lose someone who's still alive, just as though they've died and their body's been taken over by someone else.

"Martina and I were born on the same day, hours apart. Sometimes we were put in the same pram to sleep, and people mistook us for twins. As we grew up, we did everything together. We went to the village school, took our first Holy Communion, talked about our futures. She was always the dominant one – louder, more demanding, dare I say it, more reckless. But life with her was never boring.

"One January, the Befana brought us each a china doll with long hair and a lovely dress. We used to walk for miles pushing them in their prams and chatting to each other just like young mothers. We never ran out of things to say. People would ask us what we found to talk about, but I could never tell them afterwards. On the few occasions Martina wasn't with me – if she was off school ill, for example – I used to feel that half of me was missing.

"Once, a wheel came off my doll's pram. It rolled right off the road, down the bank, and into the river. She insisted we search for it. Wouldn't let me give up until we'd found it. And we did, too. She pulled off her dress, waded in, and fished it out. I still have a picture of her in my mind, standing in her pants with a huge smile on her face, holding the wheel up in triumph, and all the water droplets falling from it glittering like diamonds in the sunshine."

Carlo turned off the device, went over to his mother, and adjusted the cushion behind her head. Her face was blank, lost to sleep. He thought he'd heard all her stories – it would just be a case of getting her to recount them. But now he realised there were probably thousands of other memories stored in her head that he'd never even heard. Or if he had, he hadn't been fully listening.

"…That picture of us on the wall of the fountain brings back so many memories – fond ones mostly. We spent our childhood playing skipping rope games, chalking squares to jump on in the piazza, and catching tiny frogs down at the river. We used to wait on the wall of the fountain every day for Gianni, the boy from Villa Leonida. Then we'd all walk down to school together. Gianni took lots of pictures in those days. He had one of those old box cameras – we thought it was marvellous.

"You can see from the picture how beautiful Martina was. Oh, I know what you're thinking – how she was a dried-up old prune when you knew her, and that scar truly was hideous. But life does that to you. War does that to you. In those days, though, I felt very plain in comparison to her.

"I always had a rather square face and thick eyebrows, and I was heavily built, but now I'm looking at that picture again and I didn't look so bad, did I? And yet, next to Martina I always felt plain and plump, and I suppose because of that it made me want to be good at something, so I studied. She and Gianni called me the Encyclopaedia. They tested me out on facts and dates and they hardly ever managed to catch me out. They used to copy my schoolwork, which made me feel proud."

There were various shuffling sounds as though Irena had got side-tracked by something.

"We all thought Martina would be famous one day. She dreamed of moving on, being someone. This place was too small for her. She should have been a Hollywood star. She had that innate sense of glamour – and the temperament to match. If the war hadn't come, if she'd had different opportunities, maybe it would have happened. So many things would have been different."

That last sentence was barely audible, and he had to play it back a few times.

"I don't know to this day why she married Gianni. I suppose it was because she could. She said she loved him, but I think what attracted her more was the fact that all the other girls wanted him. He was a good catch. His family was the best off in the village. They had the big house with lots of land. If you were being kind, you could say she did it for her parents, to make them proud. No, knowing Martina, I don't believe that.

"Gianni and I were wary of each other for a long time – we both knew we were competing for Martina's attention. But we came to realise that if we both wanted to be with her, we had to learn to rub along with one another. I grew fond of him. God knows, he didn't deserve to die the way he did."

Chapter Thirteen

The restaurant *I Tre Fratelli* was bathed in a warm, golden glow as the sun dipped behind the mountain and the lights came on in the plane trees, throwing the houses and towers into silhouette. While locals still insisted on eating inside this early in the year, holidaymakers preferred to sit in the piazza huddled in their coats so they could enjoy the surroundings and feel they were living *la dolce vita.*

"Any luck with that family you took up to the villa?" Cass asked, as they were setting up the restaurant tables.

Carlo shrugged. "They said it was beautiful, loved the views. Usual sort of thing."

"Do you think they were serious?"

He turned his mouth down. "Doubt it. They had young children of their own. Said it was purely a financial investment, but it's always the same when they get there. They can't wait to get away.

"I took them to Miramonte afterwards, but they said it was too dark with all those trees. They wouldn't even get out of the car at San Giuseppe. But they seemed quite interested in the mill apartments – even though their top criteria was a detached property away from the road."

Cass rolled her eyes with a grin. "People hardly ever know what they want until they've seen what they don't want."

She shook out a white cloth and laid it at an angle over the yellow damask one. "Who are Marisa and Giorgio?" she asked. "I swear I'll never get to know everybody in this place. Do you think they'll be wanting a table for the Easter lunch?"

Carlo laughed. "I doubt that. They died before I was

born."

She looked up, frowning in confusion. "Seriously? Then why does everyone keep talking about them?"

"It's their house. The one by the well? Everyone calls it Marisa and Giorgio's. It's just a landmark."

Sometimes he felt he knew two villages – the Santa Zita he saw around him every day, and the place he had heard older people talking about as he was growing up. Born just after the war, he had watched the village grow smaller with every year he grew older.

But he'd heard so many stories so often that it was sometimes hard to be sure which events had really happened to him, and which had happened to people around him and had somehow become woven into his own memories. That blurred line between past and present. Most of the houses in Santa Zita were known by the names of their former occupants, which is how they were usually referred to.

"Marisa and Giorgio met when Marisa was in mourning for her husband, a local butcher called Salvatore. On the feast of San Silvestro in this restaurant, the owner Paolo had tears in his eyes as he apologised for the meat not being up to its usual standard. Everyone knew the best meat came from Salvatore, but they had done what they could with what they had.

"The diners drank a toast to Salvatore. But Giorgio, who had had too much to drink and was never known for his tact, wiped his moustache on the back of his hand and spat.

"He said, 'Come off it, who are we kidding? The man was a selfish shit who slept with everyone else's wives.'

"A hush fell. All heads turned.

"He looked around for support. 'Well, it had to be said, didn't it?'

"'Perhaps. But not in front of his widow,' hissed a neighbour, grabbing him by the arm and nodding towards Marisa sitting stony-faced and shrouded in black.

"Appalled by his gaffe, Giorgio called round at her house the following day with a bunch of flowers to apologise. He expected her to be angry, call him names, burst into tears – he couldn't believe it when she started laughing.

"'Thank God someone finally said it,' she told him. 'It was all true.'

"She ended up cooking him lunch and they were married a year later," said Carlo.

"It's a good story," said Cass, laughing. "And Alice? Who's she?"

"Not Aliss," he said, tutting at her accent. "*Aleechay*."

The farmhouse just below the piazza was known as the Casa di Alice, even though it had been in the hands of another family for decades.

"Ah, she was a formidable woman by all accounts. Her house sparkled, and her six children were always immaculately turned out. On the day before her fiftieth birthday, she cooked and cleaned for her family as usual. But the next morning, she wasn't up at dawn to light the fire like she usually was. Her family were worried about her. They peeped round the door of the bedroom and found her sitting upright against a cushion."

"She'd died?" asked Cass.

He laughed. "No, she was right as rain. She said to them, 'I'm staying put. I've spent all my life looking after you lot. Now it's your turn to look after me.'

"At first, they had thought she was joking. But no amount of pleading or reasoning had any effect. She stayed there for the next forty years, despite being in rude health, waited on by her disgruntled husband and offspring."

Cass liked that one. She swore if she wasn't given due appreciation for her efforts she would "do an Alice".

"*Aleechay*," he corrected.

Seeing Sonia in the piazza talking to someone outside Bar Fontana, Carlo broke off. He couldn't keep putting off the moment. Sooner or later he'd have to pluck up courage and talk to her about her mother. The book wouldn't be complete without her side of the story. Of course, she wouldn't want those memories raked up. Yet it had happened, and it was part of their common story. Of all the people in Santa Zita, Sonia's story would be the most crucial part of the village's history. It was something he needed to understand.

"No, Carlo, you can't," Cass's voice broke into his thoughts. "I know what you're thinking, and it isn't fair."

"I wasn't going to."

He would, though. As soon he had worked out how.

Chapter Fourteen

Sonia swallowed another tablet, that phone conversation with Lorenzo still running through her mind. The pain in her stomach was worse. How had she got herself into this situation? It wasn't as if she'd ever set out to deceive anyone. The evening she'd found Lorenzo, her only thoughts had been about saving him. How could she have known that people would lose their lives as a result?

1992

She'd never held anything so precious. Sonia wanted to run with the baby to her house, but couldn't risk tripping on the steep, cobbled path, so she'd made herself walk. Each step seemed to take an eternity and it took forever to reach the terraced house in Via della Chiesa. All the time, thoughts raced through her mind. The girl had abandoned the baby. She'd meant to do so. She had no intention of returning. She wanted someone to find it. Otherwise she could have dumped the baby anywhere, couldn't she?

And the necklace was clearly a parting gift. She wouldn't have left it with the baby if she was intending to come back. But what if she'd told someone and they'd come to look for it?

As Sonia closed the door of her house, she leant back against it, her heart thumping, letting the enormity of what she'd done sink in. Any number of people might have seen her cross the piazza. She hugged the baby to her, tears falling on his head. The cries jolted her into action.

She warmed some milk in a pan and fed it to him from an eggcup. It wasn't ideal – it was messy and took ages despite him being so hungry, and the baby was frustrated because he couldn't get it fast enough, but she had to try. She couldn't risk a delay while she went off to buy baby milk. He was already weak.

Sonia was unaccustomed to handling someone so small. It was terrifying, the thought that she might drop him. But afterwards, his crying got worse and panic surged through her. What if she'd done more harm than good? What if he died?

How would she explain that all she'd ever wanted to do was help him? The terror and the shame bit into her. No, she couldn't think like that. Eventually he quietened down, and she lay back on the bed with him across her chest, exhausted, her head whirling with everything that had happened.

She didn't hear Flavio's truck pull up outside. He was on the stairs before she knew it. The room was filled with the smell of acacia wood, petrol from the chainsaw, and rain-soaked foliage. She jolted awake and realised she hadn't thought any of this through.

"What an evening," he said, opening the door into the bedroom and shaking his wet hair out onto the floor. Instinctively, she shielded the baby's head.

He stopped, and for some moments he said nothing. Eventually he whispered, "What's going on?"

His face was etched with shock and confusion. Slowly, he walked towards her, his eyes fixed on the baby. In all the chaos of emotions in trying to keep the baby alive, she hadn't thought about what she'd say to Flavio.

Of course, he'd tell her they couldn't keep the baby. *You can't just help yourself to a human being to satisfy your own selfish needs. This isn't the Middle Ages.* How could he say anything else?

She felt the tears slide down her face as she looked up at him. She swallowed, sorting out her explanation in her head. Of course she realised he wasn't hers. She understood perfectly that he must go back to his real mother or somebody more suitable, whatever the authorities judged.

She was only looking after him, keeping him safe.

Flavio sank to his knees. He pressed the back of his hand to his mouth and then stroked the baby's head with his giant, oil-stained thumb. His breathing was audible. His clothes were covered in bark chips.

"Isn't he beautiful?" she managed to say. At least he should admit that before she had to let the baby go.

She meant to tell Flavio about what she'd seen in the church. About how she'd been praying to the Madonna dell Soccorso just as she had so many times throughout her life when it happened.

Of course he'd need time to get used to the idea. But it was obvious, wasn't it, that the girl had left the baby in the church *for someone to find?* The poor girl, she was so young. A child herself. Imagine the trouble she'd get into if Sonia told anyone about the baby.

"Flavio."

He put his thumb over her lips. "I didn't dare hope." She'd never seen tears in his eyes before. "I noticed you getting larger. I knew you'd stopped buying the tampons and I knew you'd been to the doctor and, of course, I wondered. But it's happened so many times. I thought it would end like all the other times. I mean, who'd have thought after all this time? I didn't dare say anything in case I jinxed it."

The idea started to take shape. He was so happy. Why hurt him with the truth? It could at least wait until morning.

Chapter Fifteen

Carlo poured himself a grappa and sat looking out into the dark piazza. Cass had gone straight up to bed after they'd finally closed-up the restaurant, but he was still buzzing from the success of the evening. Another full house. If it carried on like this over the summer, they might have a profitable business after all.

One thing he was sure of – if Irena hadn't been his mother, he wouldn't now be running a restaurant. It was here in this kitchen that most of his childhood memories had been formed.

Half the size it was now, the tiled room had been full of steam from the range in the huge chimney when he'd been growing up. The cooking smells used to drive him wild. He'd steal a taste of the sauce that was bubbling on the stove, as his mother mixed eggs into a well of flour on the marble table to make *malfatti*. She used to give him his own bit of flour, and he loved stirring it with his finger and feeling its coolness under his flat hand as he patted it into a perfect circle.

The modern units he had installed since they'd moved back from the States were more practical, but the room seemed to have lost part of its soul. His mother had always worn an apron in those days, spotless and crisply ironed at the start of each day. Her hands were rough and smelled of garlic and lemons when she dabbed his face clean, as she did as often as she could catch him.

There was always a sense of urgency about the place. Herbs hung from the beams, strings of tomatoes were tied to the shutters, and vegetables and beans were packed into jars of olive oil.

"Who are we expecting?" he used to ask. "The five thousand?" But it was only ever the two of them.

She always seemed to be preparing for something as she chopped, boiled, and pickled, but the big occasion never came. He teased her about it, but with hindsight that fear she had of running out of food, of not being able to provide enough for him to eat, must have stemmed from the war years.

Although many things had improved after the war, inflation had soared. But the food never did run out, and his mother's larder was more efficient than any modern supermarket. What they didn't have in the house, grew in the garden or in the hills around.

Irena hadn't been a cuddly sort of mother – always too busy to spend much time with him on her lap – but Carlo had grown up with clear boundaries, clean clothes, and a knowledge of how to fix most things. Despite her own distrust of authority, she'd always tried to instil in him good behaviour, and he still found it difficult to be rude to people, even when provoked.

As she worked she talked, explaining what ingredients she was using and why.

"We'll add a bit of milk to soften the dough. And slowly mix in the raisins and aniseed. Now we leave it over here to rise."

He used to think everyone knew these things, but as he grew older he realised many didn't.

"Knowing about food could save your life," she told him as she helped him weigh out ingredients. "If you know what to eat and how to prepare it, you can always survive."

When he'd once ventured to say that someone had told him French cuisine was the most highly prized in the world, she'd given a dismissive snort. The French wouldn't know how to cook if it wasn't for the Italians, she told him.

"It was our Catherine de Medici who taught them. She brought her cooks and ingredients with her to Paris when she became queen…"

Carlo sat and listened to her stories while shelling a huge

66

heap of beans or cracking nuts, dissecting vegetables, and skinning rabbits. By the age of ten he knew most wild herbs and mushrooms and could be reliably sent out with a basket to collect these. He loved leaving the house early, when the air was damp and misty and smelled of the damp earth and foliage. There was constant competition among his friends to find the best and biggest mushrooms.

He had several favourite places that he guarded jealously, sometimes making ludicrous detours to avoid being spotted. Sometimes people tried to follow him into the woods, but he was quick at noticing them and could easily give them the slip, standing still behind the trees or crouching among the ferns. That thrill of evading them and the expression on his mother's face when he returned with a full basket...

He always had something to tell her about his adventures – some deer or a wild boar he had spotted, or some porcupine spines he had found. He used to bring back armfuls of herbs – wild garlic, fennel, coriander, tarragon, camomile, and oregano; Irena used these for medicinal purposes as well as culinary ones. She knew all sorts of remedies, passed down to her by her own mother – basil for nettle stings; coriander for burns; elder for colds; thyme for eczema; sage for indigestion.

Irena's larder was like a medicine cabinet. She had a solution for everything. Her ivy treatment had made Agata's ugly warts disappear, and her bilberry tea had done wonders for Maria's haemorrhoids, while raspberry tea eased Paolina's menstrual pains.

Carlo was banished from the room during these consultations but often crept up to the door, fascinated. He never doubted in those days that his mother knew everything there was to know – although he sometimes wished she didn't. She was impossible to fool. It was no good leaving something unfinished or trying to escape before doing the tasks she'd set him. She'd always know.

His main memories were of taking things apart on the *cotto* floor and putting them back together again to see how they worked. His mother cursed the mess he made, but it sometimes amused her, too.

"You're going to be an inventor when you grow up," she said.

"And you'll be a cook when you grow up," he replied, which for some reason made her laugh.

Taking things apart, creating something wonderful. Yes, he could be an inventor.

Spotting the recording device on the table, he shook himself out of the memory, reached out for it and pressed Play.

IRENA

I hadn't any plans in those days, other than to marry and bring up children – as we girls were encouraged to do back then. It probably sounds dreadfully old-fashioned, but in those days you felt you had a special role. No matter how smart or stupid, rich or poor you were, you had the chance to do this one miraculous thing for Italy that men with all the cleverness and strength weren't able to do.

But I couldn't really see it happening – me getting married. I knew I had to have something to fall back on in case I didn't find someone. My family didn't have much money, and I didn't want to follow my siblings into service or factory work. I wanted to be a teacher.

I had such a thirst for knowledge. Read everything I could get my hands on. People used to give me their books when they'd finished with them, and I devoured them. Every book was like a doorway into a different world. From Petrarch to Proust to Dickens; as soon as I finished one, I'd start another. I don't read much now. I get halfway through and forget what happened at the start.

Pouring himself another glass, he thought about those thousands of words she had crammed into her head. How many were left? It was all such a waste.

At weekends, we'd bring seats out into the piazza and watch a film on a big screen under the stars. They always started off with newsreels of the good work Mussolini had done. Black and white images of men working in fields, digging roads, piling up food. In those days of course, the films were unnaturally fast which made the men seem even more industrious.

I can't remember the days before il Duce was our leader. He was just always there. We knew some of his followers were doing barbaric things, but we didn't blame him personally for that. My mother sometimes muttered about the economy and corruption and money not getting to the people it was meant for, but a look from my father would stop her saying any more. I picked up that you had to be careful what you said.

From time to time, things happened. We children were in the piazza one evening when a van pulled up and a man rolled out of it. Was kicked, I suppose. He lay there, groaning, and we realised he'd soiled himself. We ran away.

"Do you know what they did to him?" Gianni said the next day. 'Forced him to eat live frogs and drink castor oil."

As children, I'm ashamed to say we found it funny. We assumed he'd done something evil and deserved to be punished, whereas he'd probably only expressed an opinion that someone didn't like. It never occurred to us we'd ever be in danger.

***

As Carlo got into bed, Cass turned towards him.

"I'm worried about your mother. She's been muttering to herself most of the day and now she's tossing and turning. I can't think what's upset her. Do you think she might be ill?"

She looked vexed when he explained about the book. "Is now the best time for that? Couldn't you wait until after the summer? If tonight was anything to go by, we're going to be rushed off our feet."

She was right, of course. But Carlo wasn't sure he could

wait. At his mother's age, you never knew, did you? And besides, he had the sense he was on the verge of discovering a side of her he'd never known.

Chapter Sixteen

IRENA

I had very strong ideas about justice even as a child. When I was eight years old, I heard that my younger brother had been given a beating at school for something he didn't deserve. I ran into the classroom, grabbed the ruler off the teacher's desk and hit him with it, shouting that he was a coward for laying into a small child. The rest of the class watched in stunned silence. One by one they started laughing. The teacher was furious.

I took my brother's hand and marched him back home, leaving the teacher too shocked to run after us. I expected my mother to be proud of me, but she was mortified when we told her. She took us back down to apologise, and had to beg to get us taken back into school. Years later, the teacher told me that although he had been enraged by my behaviour at the time, he had also admired me for my courage.

I do have one or two regrets, though. Martina's sense of humour verged on cruelty sometimes, especially when she sensed a weakness in someone and when she had a gallery to play to.

There was a boy in our class called Alvaro – a skinny boy with a squint and thick glasses, who used to mutter to himself and play cards on his own for hours. He knew every fact about insects and engines but could barely write his own name. Mostly, he was very quiet and a bit obsessive, but he had a temper that was easy to provoke and he could be quite frightening when he got angry, although he usually ended up in tears.

Martina played a number of tricks on him: inviting him to fetch something for her that didn't exist; leaving him searching in vain for hours; hiding his glasses when he was changing for sports; or suggesting a game of hide-and-seek but never coming to look for him. Mostly, it was just silly, thoughtless things, but one of the few times she and I fell out was over a trick that really went too far.

Martina knew Alvaro was in love with her. There was nothing unusual in that, of course, but she didn't discourage him. She just let him trail around after her, making a bigger and bigger fool of himself.

On Valentine's Day, he wrote her a love letter, which included a poem that I must say was awful – "The sight of you makes me swoon. I want to taste the sweet sugar of your lips" – that sort of thing.

Martina let everyone read it. I'm afraid we thought it was hilarious. Spurred on by the rest of the class, she wrote him a letter back, everyone chipping in with terms of endearment and appalling rhymes. I don't remember how it went now, but the gist was that the love was mutual, and she wanted to meet him alone in the woods so they could demonstrate their love for each other.

She asked me to deliver the note. I agreed, because I felt sorry for him and I thought it would give me the chance to warn him off. But when I gave it to him and told him not to go, he told me to mind my own business. His face turned purple, the way it did when people riled him, and he became very abusive, swearing at me and choking over his words with rage. Said I was jealous and possessive, and trying to deny my friend happiness by keeping her apart from him. I had to bite my tongue to stop myself telling him what she really thought about him. But in the end, I'm afraid he was so unpleasant I lost my patience and left him to it.

So, that evening Alvaro turned up for their date in his best shirt and a tie he'd probably stolen from his father, stinking of out-of-date cologne.

What he didn't know was that the rest of us were stationed in the bushes for the performance. He tried to kiss

Martina, but she set him a series of dares first, all designed to make a fool out of him. She had him running about singing, then down on his knees declaring his love, reading out his poem. Everyone was in fits.

She ordered him in a sultry, seductive tone to take off his clothes. But when he was standing in front of her naked like a scrawny chicken, she screamed in shock and disgust, picked up his clothes, and threw them in the waterfall. At which point, children started emerging from the trees all around, laughing and jeering, leaving Alvaro scrambling in vain to fish out his sodden clothes and walk home naked and in tears. I stayed behind my tree, not wanting to take part in the jeering, but I wish now I'd had the strength to stop her. Unfortunately, as he walked right passed me, sobbing, he caught my eye, so I'm sure he thought I was complicit in the whole thing. I felt awful.

***

Carlo smiled and shook his head at his mother's confession. He picked up the picture from the floor of her room. She must have knocked it off the bedside table without noticing when she was getting up that morning. He fetched a brush and swept up the broken glass, but would have to warn her about it in case he'd missed any. Meanwhile, he'd look for another frame. She'd be distraught if she found it like this.

It was the only photograph of his father that she had, apart from the engagement one of them both together. It showed him as a young man in military uniform. Carlo would like to have found out more about him, but Irena must have found it too upsetting to talk about and there was no-one else left he could ask. He wasn't aware of any relatives on his father's side of the family. Perhaps they hadn't approved of the relationship, or perhaps they hadn't known about it.

At least his memories of his maternal grandfather were clear. He was a craftsman, making crib figures out of plaster in a workshop several miles away. They were about half a metre high, surprisingly detailed, and meticulously painted. In the run-up to Christmas, large crib scenes were displayed throughout the area, illuminated at night to magical effect. Carlo used to stand for hours on icy winter nights, gazing at the different figures, always certain he could distinguish the ones his grandfather had made.

Nonno had also made other things out of plaster, including cherub head mouldings which could still be seen above the interior doors in larger houses such as Villa Leonida, and he'd made a small white dove for Carlo which he'd loved but had broken by throwing it off the loggia to see if it could fly.

Sometimes Carlo would spend the day in his grandfather's workshop watching him create the figures. He only spoke to him once about his father.

"What did he do in the war? Was he brave?"

Nonno shrugged, pulling down the corners of his mouth. "Yes," he said eventually. "They were all brave in those days."

Carlo sensed he wasn't saying what he really wanted to, but his grandfather became very busy after that and wouldn't talk about it anymore.

Now it was almost certainly too late to find out any more about his father. He couldn't help feeling angry about it sometimes. However Sonia might rationalise it, Martina had taken so much from so many people. Whatever grievance she had or whatever point she'd wanted to make, nothing could justify what she'd done.

Another worry was forming at the back of his mind. If Irena was such a close friend, hadn't she had any idea what Martina might do? Couldn't she have stopped her? For such a strong, independent person, she seemed to have fallen firmly under Martina's spell. She must know more than she was letting on. How was it that Martina still had such a hold over her quarter of a century after she'd died?

Chapter Seventeen

Carlo came hurrying over the piazza as Sonia stood waiting for the bus just outside the arch at the end. She peered anxiously down through the trees. If only the bus would hurry up. There it was lumbering up the road below her, but it had a couple more turns to make before it reached the stop.

"I haven't missed it, have I?" he asked, as he puffed through the arch. "Ah no, good."

A couple of tourists got out, fanning themselves with guidebooks, remarking on the steep climb and dizzying bends. The bus was almost empty. Carlo sat himself next to Sonia, remarked on the heat, and asked after Flavio and Lorenzo before he came out with it.

"I thought you might like to see this," he said, digging the photograph out from his jacket. "I never realised how close our mothers were once."

The picture of the two girls on the fountain took Sonia by surprise. They could have been two film stars. One of them wore shorts, the other a dress, which she was having to hold down as it ballooned out in the wind. Her head was thrown back in laughter. The sun was on their faces, catching the light in their eyes.

"It's a lovely picture," she said at last. "I haven't seen it before."

"I can get you a copy, if you like."

Sonia didn't remember having seen any pictures of her mother as a girl. It was as though Martina had removed all reminders of her younger years, erased that part of her life. Perhaps it was just too painful to look back at a time when life had been easy for her, or perhaps she couldn't look back to those times without having to relive the reprisal and the part she'd played in it. She'd never talked about being friends with Irena, but then presumably she'd had a number of friends before the reprisal. It was hardly surprising they'd stopped talking since.

"Please don't go to any bother."

It seemed only polite to ask after Irena, which led Carlo into talking about the book he was writing from her stories about the village. "I want to give a full picture, and that has to include a chapter on the war." He cleared his throat. "I know this is difficult and the last thing I'd want is to upset you, but I was wondering if I could talk to you about your mother?"

Sonia sighed. It was hardly unexpected. "I'm not upset. I just don't know the answer, I'm afraid. She never spoke about it."

"Never?" He was clearly trying to cover his disappointment.

Sonia closed her eyes. "It wasn't an easy subject."

There had been so many times when she'd been on the verge of asking, and she sometimes regretted not doing so. It wasn't grief alone that floored her when Martina died, but terror and rage at being left to fight on alone in the battle they'd always fought together. Sonia had rarely gone out without her mother. Martina had taken charge of everything, made all the decisions. She'd exercised such control that Sonia hadn't really felt a separate identity. Inside her head, she was someone different – carefree and risqué, the way she was with Flavio. But after all, Flavio was considered a *straniero,* a foreigner, in the village. She had to admit to herself that others probably saw her for what she was – an extension of her mother: defiant, wary, and weary.

For those first few months after her mother died, she'd been so lost. It had taken a long time to gain the confidence to make decisions by herself. Having Lorenzo made her feel her mother's absence most acutely. Martina would have known what the different cries meant, how long he should be allowed to sleep, how many layers he should be wearing.

Instead, Sonia had to rely on instinct, which she hadn't realised until then that she possessed. Gradually muddling through had given her a strength she hadn't experienced before.

Of course, Sonia had sometimes wondered as she was growing up with Martina what it was that had put the glass wall between them and the rest of the world. Very gradually, after one or two things children said and the looks people gave her mother, she'd started to make connections. But it wasn't until she'd badgered the priest to tell her the full story that she finally understood.

***

The bus's brakes squeaked as the driver pulled over to let a car pass on a bend.

"I kept thinking, there had to be a reason why my mother would do something like that," Sonia said to Carlo. "She was strict, yes, humourless perhaps – but not evil. She really wasn't. Something very powerful must have driven her to do what she did."

"Like what?"

"I don't know. Love? Greed? Revenge? At any rate, it made sense at last why people in the village shunned her, and why they couldn't bring themselves to look at me – the child who'd been able to grow up when theirs hadn't. I must have been a constant reminder as I crossed each of the milestones that their children would never see."

The bus stopped outside the school and a crowd of children piled in.

"How could she have kept it from me? Allowing me to believe that I was just unlikeable?"

Carlo gave a sympathetic shrug, but she felt a pang of shame, remembering the secret she'd kept from Lorenzo.

"The strange thing is, when I got home after the priest had told me what happened, I didn't tell my mother I knew. That was my chance, and looking back now, I wish I'd taken it. If only I could believe there was some justification

77

for what she did, however small – some kernel of hope that she wasn't simply evil or mad."

"I'm sure she wasn't evil. Perhaps she gave the Nazis the information they wanted by mistake," suggested Carlo. "Isn't it possible she was overheard talking to someone? Or perhaps she was threatened. Tortured. Or she might have done it for a good reason, even if it was a misguided one – accepting a bribe for the village, believing it would help others. What was it that stopped you from asking?"

Sonia frowned, holding the back of the seat in front as the bus lurched round another hairpin. "Oh, I wanted to. But I'd thought up so many reasons – not ones that could justify it but that could explain it. I couldn't bear the thought that I might be wrong, and the truth was as ugly as everyone thought it was. I don't think I could have carried on living with her if I'd known for sure."

"I'm sorry," said Carlo. "I don't think any of us thought about what it must be like for you."

Sonia shook her head. The anger had gone a long time ago. There'd been a time when it had eaten her up. Perhaps it was unfair, but although finding out what her mother had done made it easier to understand why people shunned her, it hadn't stopped her resenting them for it. They probably felt they couldn't help it, but how was it fair to extend their feelings about what Martina had done, to her? It wasn't as if she could put the clock back. And even if she could, how could she, a tiny child, have done anything to stop her mother?

"I didn't mean you, of course," she said. "Your mother was one of the few people who used to acknowledge me."

Carlo looked surprised.

"When Lorenzo was born, I worried for him, of course. I don't think I would have been able to stand it if he'd been punished for it as well. But your mother was kind, and then everyone else was too."

She'd always protected Lorenzo from the truth about his grandmother so that he could grow up free of her inherited guilt. And yet, the fear was always there that he'd find out anyway from another source.

"I used to watch him so carefully to make sure he wasn't taunted or disliked or even just whispered about by the other children, the way I was, but I never saw any evidence of it. By the 1990s when he was born, it wasn't fashionable to talk about the war. Not good for tourism.

"But after the ethnic cleansing in Bosnia, the atrocities in the world wars were talked about again. They said children needed to know about this side of human nature, in the hope they could grow up in a better world. But as far as I could see the children in Lorenzo's school didn't make the connection between the reprisal in Santa Zita and his grandmother. After all, she was dead by then, and there weren't many people left who knew her name.

"All I could do as he was growing up was hope that by the time his peers found out about the connection, as they inevitably would, their friendships would be secure enough to withstand the blow."

The bus pulled into the arcaded piazza in town and they got up.

"If my mother had had any idea what her actions would result in, I'm sure she wouldn't have done it," she said. "You must understand why I don't want it brought back up after all this time."

But something was coming back to her – a box of diaries and letters she'd found after her mother's death, which she'd never allowed herself to look through. It had been too soon after the death and her feelings were too raw. Besides, she'd been thrown into the role of a new mother, and there hadn't been a moment to spare. But perhaps after all, now was the time to discover the truth for herself.

Chapter Eighteen

IRENA

1940

Martina and Gianni's wedding took place on such a beautiful day. Despite the scrabbling, panicking, fretting, and bickering I'd witnessed in her cramped little house that morning as she got ready, she came down the stairs looking like a graceful swan.

She looked glorious in her grandmother's old ivory silk dress. It had been cleverly adapted by her seamstress mother to fit her much slimmer figure and incorporate the fashionable V-neck and beaded waist panel. Her hair had been styled in large rolls, like a film star. It wasn't too difficult to stand out in a tiny place like Santa Zita, but Martina, with her glossy dark hair, fine nose, and long-tailed, bright eyes, would have stood out anywhere.

It wasn't always easy being her best friend, but I didn't begrudge her having everything her way on that particular day. Nobody could. As the couple cut the ribbon across the front door that afternoon and started their walk up to the 12th century church, most of the village spilled out of their doorways to join the procession.

She and Gianni stepped out of the church of Santa Zita into a cloud of rose petals thrown by the crowd, and I remember thinking to myself if only I could hang onto this moment. We were all afraid of the future, you see.

The petals hung in the breeze for a moment in the perfect blue sky, before cascading down over the happy couple, settling on their hair and clothes. Martina threw back her head, laughing as she shook some of the petals away from the long, scalloped veil, lifting one of her slender arms to clutch her headpiece and stop it from sliding back.

It didn't seem any time since we were dressing up in grown-ups' clothes. I can see her now staggering around in shoes that were much too large, a streak of smudged lipstick across her mouth, pretending to be a bride, throwing flowers behind her for me to catch. Now her time had really come.

But I knew from that moment that nothing would be the same again. Life would change for me, Martina, and Gianni, whether we wanted it to or not. Still, it was hard not to get caught up in the excitement, and we all needed something to celebrate.

Martina threw her arms around me and whispered, "Promise me we'll stay friends for ever?" I was happy to promise, but I was praying at the same time that it was a promise I'd be able to keep.

I was laughing and brushing away tears. I teased her that she wouldn't want to know me any more now that she would be living at Villa Leonida, but she said that was nonsense.

"Look this way, Martina."

She turned this way and that for the photographer. But beneath the laughter and shouts of Vivi gli sposi! (long live the married couple) you could feel a tiny current of apprehension and anticipation. With war having just been declared, none of us knew what was going to happen, but I think we all sensed it wasn't going to be as speedy and straightforward as il Duce would have us believe.

The reception took place at the Tre Fratelli restaurant. Tables had been set out in three long lines across the square, just as they were at the end of olive-gathering in the autumn, with lines of brightly coloured bunting suspended above. Candle lanterns were lined up along the windowsills and strung around the trees.

As we took our places at the table, the guests raised a

toast and there were cries of 'Per cent'anni!' wishing the couple a hundred years of happy married life together. Wine flowed and the food kept coming – antipasti, soup, pasta, meat, and fruits. Each plate of food was arranged like a work of art by the two brothers who owned the restaurant. I don't know how they managed to produce it; we weren't used to eating so well.

Every so often someone would chink their glass and call out, "A kiss for the bride!" Gianni would kiss Martina and another burst of applause would break out. The meal was followed by dancing until the early morning.

Towards the end of the evening, Gianni and Martina smashed the vase. At least, they tried to. But it stayed intact despite several attempts to break it – a bad omen. I held my breath. Nervous laughter was followed by wild applause as Gianni picked it up and hurled it across the square. It slammed into the church door, and this time it splintered into tiny fragments, symbolising the many happy years they could expect together in the future.

Martina tossed her bouquet into the air. There was a scramble among the young women, each hoping to be the village's next bride. Despite those years of practice, I didn't catch it. I don't remember who did.

After the dancing, the newlyweds followed the line of lanterns up the steep path towards the house where Martina would be joining Gianni's family to live. I watched them until they disappeared.

Turning back, I spotted her father Vincente sitting at the table nearest the fountain, and sat down next to him.

"It's been wonderful, hasn't it?" I said.

"One down, three to go," he replied gruffly, but his eyes glistened as he smiled. No wonder he was proud. Whatever happened in the next few years, he'd at least not have to worry about Martina.

But despite the warmth of the evening and the wine I'd drunk, a shiver crept through me. I felt abandoned by the two people I cared most about in the world.

Chapter Nineteen

MARTINA

1940

Martina had dreamed for most of her life of living in Villa Leonida. After the noise and clutter of her old terraced home, the space and solitude at the villa had thrilled her when she first moved in. The frescoed walls, the gilded cherub heads above the doors, and the kaleidoscope pattern on the ceiling created by the electric light reflected off the crystal droplets of the chandelier, were still wonders to her. It was amazing to be able to wander from one end of the house to another without bumping into anyone.

Her own home in Via della Chiesa had been crowded – everyone talking at once, voices raising in turn, nobody listening, always some drama erupting. One sister singing, another in tears. The two boys fighting over everything, racing around the place, tearing lumps out of each other. And the youngest sister slyly helping herself to things that didn't belong to her then putting them back broken. The house was built on four floors, so they were always on top of each other.

In the warmer months, it wasn't so bad. They could mostly live outside on the small terraces, only needing to use the interior for sleeping, but in the winter, they were forced to endure each other's company at close quarters.

How different things were at the villa. Martina could throw open the enormous French doors onto the balcony and look down over the family's splendid estate, the rooftops and bell tower of the village of Santa Zita, the town below, and the glitter of sea in the distance. And yet, living here was nothing like she'd imagined it would be.

Today, as she pinned back the shutters, there was nothing to see. A dense wall of fog hung over everything, heavy and oppressive, brushing against her face like a gloved hand. It had been there for days, closing around the villa like prison walls, gradually sucking up everything in its path – people, houses, and mountains.

It muffled sound, too, so that it was possible to believe as she stood there on the balcony that nothing existed beyond it, and the house was islanded in a silent, grey sea. The air smelled of damp, ice, and wood smoke. Standing out here in the cloud was as close as she could get to escaping.

Although her old home was only a short walk away, she may as well have moved miles into another world. As a child, she'd first visited the villa when accompanying her mother with dress samples for Elena. For weeks she used to watch a piece of clothing taking shape on the kitchen table in their small home, awed by the transformation from a piece of fabric to a thing of beauty.

She'd helped her mother package the dress, and between them they'd carried it up the steep cobbled path, right up above the roofs, until their own house below the piazza looked like a doll's house.

They'd had to stop several times to shake out their arms and wipe the sweat from their hands, so they didn't drop the package.

"*Madonna*, I just hope she likes it," her mother said.

At the villa, they followed the housekeeper through miles and miles of echoing marble-floored rooms. Elena greeted them coolly, as though their presence was a disturbance.

Martina stood by her mother, gazing up at the cherubs on the painted ceiling as Elena examined the stitching under a lamp, frowning.

"It's good," she said at last.

They discussed the design for a jacket. She showed

Martina's mother some pictures from a magazine and they talked about colours and cloth. Martina stood gazing around her, awed by the grandeur of the place and by Elena's tall, commanding presence and fine clothes. But after a while listening to the grown-ups, her legs started to ache, and her gaze wandered. She saw a beautiful blue and white glazed urn on the dresser, and when the women's backs were turned she reached out to touch it. It was perfectly smooth and cool beneath her fingers.

I want to live here. I want to own things like this.

A stinging slap brought her to her senses and she whipped her hand back, nursing it under her arm.

"Don't touch."

She bit back tears and looked to her mother for support, but her mother's face was red. On the way back down the steep path, she told Martina she'd let her down, and she should have known better, and did she have any idea how much that vase was worth? But it didn't stop Martina wanting to live at the villa.

***

Now, after all these years, she really did but none of this was what she'd imagined. She could feel Elena's eyes on her, following her every move. Both of Gianni's parents kept a watch on her but Elena was the worst. She was always the one in command, her strident tones resounding through the house. Martina was expected to fall in like everybody else. With just a lift of the eyebrows, Elena had a way of conveying surprise at someone's lack of good sense or taste if they didn't do as she wanted, and Martina hadn't yet worked out a way of countering this without being openly rude.

She rested her forearms on the cold iron rail of the balcony. She thought about running out into the mist and losing herself, but there was no escape from Elena. If only the old bat would leave her alone.

"Who left those doors open?" Her mother-in-law's voice

rang through the house. "Whoever it was, you're letting in the draught and making the fire smoke."

Martina took a last breath and pulled them closed. She twisted the handle to drive the bolt down and pressed her head against the glass for a moment before turning with an acquiescent smile.

She tried to make herself look busy tidying the room, although it didn't need tidying. No doubt Elena was thinking of a dozen other things that Martina could more usefully be doing, but she didn't say anything.

She lifted each of the framed photographs on top of the piano in turn and dusted them, reminding herself that she was now part of this handsome and distinguished family. Elena herself had been a beauty in her day, with her aristocratic neck, high forehead, and hooded eyes. The skin around her eyes and mouth now creped when she smiled, but she was still strikingly elegant – tall and straight-backed for her age.

Cesare was quiet and taciturn, with simian features worn by time and the weather, like the house. He was more difficult to read. They had both viewed Martina with suspicion since the engagement. It had been easy to charm them until that point, but they clearly felt they had made a great concession in allowing her to become part of their lives. Martina knew they had tried their best to dissuade their son and that he had enjoyed defying them.

It would be nice to think that Gianni had won them over by telling them he'd no interest in any of those insipid girls they had lined up for him. Perhaps he'd fought for Martina, pointed out her intelligence and strength of character. Or perhaps it had all been a game to him.

There must have been some reason for them relenting. Probably they'd drawn the conclusion she'd bear them healthy, good-looking grandchildren. And they knew she'd carry off her new role as successfully as anyone who was born into it. She wouldn't let them down.

In her childhood games, Martina had always played the role of queen or empress. It seemed natural to her that she would marry into the wealthiest family in the village, whatever anyone else might have thought.

No, it was more than that. Martina knew, even if she wasn't supposed to, that Gianni's parents couldn't afford to be so picky these days. The family's fortune was a mere shadow of what it had been.

The blue and gold paintwork, the gilt mirrors and Napoleonic style furniture in the drawing room at Villa Leonida, gave the impression of a successful, established family whose wealth and status was assured as far into the future as it stretched back into the past. But the rest of the rooms, which looked as though they had had the life knocked out of them, gave a far truer picture.

For most of Martina's life, the villa had held a mythical status – it had been a storybook palace, into which she'd never expected to be invited. When she was growing up, all the talk in the piazza was about the glittering parties held up at the villa – glamorous women in silk dresses and gentlemen in dinner suits silhouetted on the balcony, music and ripples of laughter floating through an open window on still summer nights. Resting her elbows on the stone sill of her home below the piazza, Martina would gaze up at the villa, whose lights were aglow long after the rest of the village had retired.

But after a series of bad investments, the finances had dwindled. Last year, a forest fire ripped through the chestnut trees, destroying many of them. The exceptionally harsh winter that followed killed off most of the olives.

After Italy joined the war in the summer, most of the labourers had been called up, leaving Cesare to do the bulk of the work on the estate himself. As the economy worsened, he couldn't afford to keep house staff. Soon after the wedding, the cook and then the housekeeper were let go. Had it been part of their plan that Martina would replace these with free labour? It was hard sometimes to think otherwise.

She'd soon come to understand that there were disadvantages to living in Villa Leonida. Although the fire damage had been repaired, most of the heirlooms and treasures had been lost. The high ceilings made it difficult to heat, the windows rattled, and during storms rain crept in under the frames, running down the walls in unsightly grey trails. Damp seeped in everywhere, up through the floor and into her bones. It formed black mould on walls and behind the skirting boards, and created fluffy breeding grounds for scorpions and centipedes, with whom she battled daily.

But there was something else – a whisper, a restlessness that worked its way through the house. It made her want to break out and run. She would have, if there had been somewhere to go. Gianni said it was just the wind in the chimneys, but it seemed to have a life of its own.

She sometimes had a longing to go back home, despite the chaos and bickering. No, her pride would never let her to do that. On her wedding day she'd felt triumphant. But she was starting to suspect that this trophy was made from fool's gold. She couldn't help feeling that she had been duped. The glittering prize she'd dreamed of throughout her childhood had turned out to be a poisoned chalice.

Perhaps Gianni felt the same way. But it was all right for him, wasn't it? He'd found a way to escape.

Chapter Twenty

Driving away from Santa Zita the morning after the wedding, Martina had felt a new person. A *signora* rather than a *signorina*. The bride who lived in Villa Leonida. She felt she was on the cusp of something brilliant. There should be music to accompany a moment like this. As the gleaming motor car slid through the arch at the end of the piazza and made each turn down through the olive groves, apple orchards, and vines, Irena's madly waving figure, like those of the rest of the cheering crowd, grew smaller and smaller until they had left Santa Zita behind.

The drive over the mountains and through a series of coastal towns to their hotel in Liguria was beautiful. Through pine branches and bougainvillea, they glimpsed colour-splashed houses, churches with rounded bell towers, craggy cliffs, and the sea.

They found the hotel at last, perched above a picturesque harbour. For the first day or two, it was idyllic. They played hide and seek in the hotel gardens, took a boat trip, spotted dolphins in the bay, and explored the village. At the market he bought her an orange tree in a pot. She laughed at his impracticality – how were they going to get it home? But gradually over the next few days she felt Gianni withdrawing.

One evening, they ate dinner in the main piazza with its pebbled floor, orange trees, and view of gleaming yachts. The autumnal sun drenched the narrow, multi-coloured houses with their *trompe l'oeil* shutters, pediments, garlands, and balconies. As the sun dipped, the darkening sea looked as though someone had poured a pot of gold paint across it.

Perhaps it was the wine or the long walk in the heat, but Gianni seemed to tell her about the money without thinking.

"I didn't mean to mislead you," he said.

"It doesn't matter. Really." Everyone knew that money wasn't everything. But inside, Martina couldn't help feeling cheated. It wasn't the money as such, more the fact that he'd deceived her. It confirmed her growing suspicion that she didn't know Gianni half as well as she had thought she did.

"So, if that's what you married me for, I'm afraid you're going to be disappointed," he said, watching her as though challenging her. "To be quite honest, we're barely managing, so you'll have to pull your weight."

"Of course it wasn't why I married you." But it was hard to keep the indignation out of her voice. Admittedly, the lifestyle had been part of the attraction, and what was wrong with that? Why shouldn't she take the chance of a better future if it was offered to her? And why had he waited until now to tell her? He could have put her in the picture months earlier but had deliberately withheld the information until after she'd married him.

As though he'd read her thoughts, he said, "I would have told you before, but I was afraid I'd lose you if I did."

So, it had been calculated. Something in his mischievous smile was triumphant, as if they were back at school competing in some pointless game and he'd been holding onto the winning card under the table.

She tried not to mind, or at least not to show that she minded. As the lights came on in the harbour, they finished the wine and talked about other things, but the deception brooded there between them like an unwelcome guest. Until they came away, her worries had all been about the wedding night, which had turned out to be unfounded because he didn't seem that interested in consummating the marriage anyway. But lying next to him in the darkness now, she had new things to worry about.

Over the next couple of days, she tried to push it to the back of her mind but he, perhaps out of guilt, had become defensive. After breakfast, as they sat on the palm-shaded terrace of the hotel reading the papers, it was becoming obvious they had nothing to say to each other.

"It's *nice* here. Is that all you can say?"

She rolled her eyes. "All right – it's wonderful. Exquisite. Is that good enough?"

Looking down over the ancient port and the castle across the bay, she had to admit the surroundings really were beautiful. But in this atmosphere they might as well have been at one of the courtyards in Santa Zita.

"That's the point though, isn't it? Nothing's ever good enough for you."

They struggled on, but most of their conversation had become forced and punctuated by awkward pauses. Why had it never been like this before? Perhaps because they'd never really been alone before and never really talked, not in the way adults talked to each other. It had all been teasing and one-upmanship and sharing centre stage to an admiring audience. Now they were playing at being grown-ups and it wasn't working. Anger and disappointment crept through her.

"You've changed," she said.

He held up the paper, which was full of stories about ruthless and ineffective air raids on Italian cities and the invasion of Egypt. "Yes, well in case you hadn't noticed, the world's changed. Everything's changing."

"I know that," she said at last. "I just don't see why we have to change because of it."

"You're disappointed in me, aren't you?" he said a few moments later.

"I never said that."

"You didn't have to. It's the money thing, isn't it?"

"Of course not. I keep telling you – it doesn't matter."

He laughed. "Don't lie. Everything's fake with you. You say all the right things and do all the right things, but do you actually feel anything? Well, I'm sorry – again – about the money. You've got me; I'm all there is."

"And I've said it's enough."

It was maddening. And yet when she looked around her,

everything was almost perfect. The air was scented with thyme and laurel and the last of the honeysuckle. The bay was beautiful. Some tiny adjustment must be all that was necessary to set them back on course, if only she could think what it was.

But over the next couple of days, Gianni became even more dismissive and agitated, as though he was holding something back from her. He took long walks on his own, coming in late at night or leaving early in the morning smelling of drink when he thought she was still asleep. Was that normal on a honeymoon?

She was forced to spend the days in the company of an older couple who had evidently taken pity on her, which was so humiliating, and a tedious mouse of a woman, whose bald husband Gianni seemed to find fascinating company. They talked in intense low voices for what seemed like hours. Anyone would think they were the honeymooners.

"I'll talk to whom I like when I like," he shouted like a sulky schoolboy when she asked where he'd been that night. She could smell the brandy on his breath.

"All right, you do that. I've had enough." She swept out of the room into the night with no idea where she was going and not caring. The air was balmy, and she felt a sense of release being outside. She walked through the moonlit rose gardens, barely aware of their beauty. She heard his footsteps behind her and quickened her pace.

"Martina, please. I'm sorry. You know I love you."

"I don't believe you."

He caught her up and they walked wordlessly down through the steep terraces of pine trees, past lichened statues of emperors and goddesses, to where a grotto overlooked the sea. They stood side by side at the stone balustrade and watched the moon dancing on the water. There was only a short distance between them, but they may as well have been miles apart.

There was so much that needed saying. She watched him staring out towards the horizon, the ink blue of the sky reflected in his eyes. The sky and sea were indistinguishable now, as nebulous as the thing that was destroying their relationship. It was too dark to see the waves, but they could hear them crashing on the rocks and the boats in the harbour creaking. What was going through his mind? There was no point in asking. She'd done so enough times and his responses had been sharp and belittling.

"It's all so fucking beautiful," he muttered, and kicked the parapet with a force that startled her

She had no idea what he meant, but seeing he had tears in his eyes she reached up and ran her hand down his face.

"I'm sorry," he said, catching her hand and kissing it, and for a moment he had a look of the old Gianni about him, the boy she had grown up with. "I don't know what's happening to me."

She took his face in her hands and kissed him. He led her into a grotto. How did they end up making love? She wasn't sure. Perhaps to avoid saying anything more. But they did anyway, under the blind stare of mythical creatures made of shells and pebbles. All that anger and hurt seemed curiously to make it easier on that occasion. Lying there in his arms afterwards, it was as though the clouds had lifted and things would be fine from then on.

"I don't want to lose you," he whispered.

"You won't."

But the next morning, she woke up alone again.

***

Thinking about it now on the balcony of Villa Leonida, perhaps Gianni had already been looking for a way out – from her, from his parents, from life in Santa Zita. If so, his prayers had been answered. Within weeks of being back at the villa, he'd joined up to fight in Albania.

So, now he was out there fighting the Greeks. Why, she had no idea. Building a new empire, he'd said. She pictured him strolling through ancient ruins, the proud conqueror of a backward nation grateful for the civilisation bestowed upon them by the second Roman Empire.

If only they'd parted on better terms. She worried for his safety, but she couldn't really say she was sorry to see him go. Perhaps the separation was what they needed. It would give them both a chance to think about things, and start again when he came back and everything was restored to normal.

After all, it would be over in a week, Cesare told her. The Greeks were undisciplined, woefully ill-equipped, and had no real idea how to fight. They needed bringing to order.

"It's their own doing. *Il Duce*'s ultimatum was perfectly clear. They refused to abide by it. How could we let them go on pretending to be neutral when all the time they've been letting the British use their ports to attack our country? All they had to do was allow our troops in."

But progress seemed to be slower than expected. It was snowing now, and why had the army retreated to Albania?

There must be a reason for the delay, he insisted, banging his palm down on the table with uncharacteristic force. "They know what they're doing. It won't be long now."

But a shiver of guilt ran through Martina as she allowed herself the hope that it wouldn't so straightforward as he believed, and that Gianni would need to stay away for longer.

Chapter Twenty-One

Walking down Via della Chiesa below the piazza, towards the house where she'd grown up, Martina was struck by how dark and narrow the street was. The houses seemed smaller, shabbier even than she remembered, the washing that hung across the street looked like rags, and the children sitting on the mossy steps outside the houses looked like urchins. She knocked on the door. It seemed somehow wrong to open it herself although it was never locked. There was the usual kerfuffle inside, everyone pushing and shoving to get to the door. But once they'd opened it, her siblings stood there staring at her, suddenly shy.

Her sisters asked after Gianni, admired her hair and clothes, and wanted to know about life in the villa. Their questions were polite but sounded as though they were being addressed to an acquaintance. Back at the wedding, Martina had enjoyed the envious looks Rebecca and Alessandra had given her, but now they seemed relieved that she belonged to a different family. They seemed annoyingly cheerful without her, and eyed her quizzically, as though wondering what she was doing here.

Inside the house, everything was smaller, flimsier, dingier than she'd remembered. Her mother put on a good show of being pleased to see her, but her face was strained and puffy.

"Have you been crying?" Martina asked. "What's wrong?"

"The factory's been burned down. Your father's out of a job."

Looking down at the valley out of the window, Martina could see that the framing factory had been reduced to a

95

blackened shell.

"What happened?"

"No-one knows."

The owner hadn't been seen since, and no-one expected to see him either. Her father would have to find work elsewhere, but he wouldn't be able to mention his employer's name. Couldn't risk the association.

"Perhaps Gianni's father could find him some work on the estate?" said Martina's mother. "After all, we're all family now."

Her heart leapt at the thought of having him closer to her, but remembering Gianni's family's financial situation she realised it was unfair to offer false hope.

"I don't know if they'll have anything suitable. Is there nowhere else you could try?"

Her father shrugged. "Of course. It was just a thought. There's a new factory about thirty kilometres up the coast taking people on. We'd have to move, but I've a cousin who lives out that way. He might be able to squeeze us in."

"Can I come with you?" she found herself asking. The words were out before she could stop them.

Vincente evidently thought she was joking. "What are you talking about?" His expression changed from puzzlement to vexation as he rounded on her. "Martina, you're the only one who's got a future in this village now. You make the most of it. For God's sake, can't you for once in your life be happy with what you have? You've made your bed, girl – lie in it."

He was right, of course. She had to stop pretending, she told herself on the climb back to the villa. Things could never go back to the way they'd been before the wedding. How proud her parents had been that she'd married into a good family. They'd never forgive her if she threw it away. The last thing they needed was another mouth to feed. Villa Leonida was her home now. She'd just have to get used to it.

Chapter Twenty-Two

"Italy wants peace and quiet, work and calm.
I will give these things with love if possible
and with force if necessary."
Mussolini

1941

In the town, an old man just ahead of Martina stopped in front of a poster of Mussolini. He spat. The gobbet hit *il Duce*'s bald head and ran down over his eye. It shocked her, but not nearly as much as what happened next. From seemingly nowhere, two uniformed young men fell on the perpetrator.

They weren't more than boys; perhaps sixteen years old. She thought they were going to arrest the man or merely give him a warning. She froze as one of them punched the man in the stomach. As he doubled over, the other one kneed him in the face.

The man curled into a foetal position as they rained kicks on him – a series of thuds followed by howls of pain. When they stopped, he lay there. One of them shouted at him to get up. He tried, but staggered and fell back. As though outraged at his disobedience, the men set about him with their clubs. Ridiculously, Martina had a vision of the painting in the little church below the villa in Santa Zita, of Mary brandishing a similar-looking club – but they weren't beating off the devil, just an old man.

His head hit the ground with a crack. Blood seeped out

onto the collar of his coat and ran in rivulets across the paving stones. Martina jumped back in horror as some of it splattered her shoes and stockings.

His face twisted towards her as he writhed, his eyes pleading directly into hers. A boot stamped on his head. She looked away, shaking, trying to control her breathing. What could she do? If she walked off, it would show that she disapproved of what they were doing. There was no choice but to stand there and endure his cries.

People around her watched in silence. They came out of shops, leaned out of windows. Male passers-by shielded their female companions from the sight. Some were visibly shocked, embarrassed to be witnessing the event. Others seemed to be enjoying it. More disturbing still was that some seemed unperturbed, chatting and lighting cigarettes. As though it was easier to pretend nothing was happening.

Still trembling, Martina drew her coat around herself. She tried to concentrate all her energy on the dried golden leaves that skittered across the piazza and the slanting gold light cast on the walls of the buildings by the late autumn sun, but she could still hear the blows and the old man's moans. She felt her face jump with each groan. When they stopped, the silence was worse. She glanced up. She couldn't help herself. The body was twitching. Then it was still.

The youths, their faces alight with adrenalin, thrust out an arm straight in front of them in the Roman salute. Someone stepped forward out of the crowd to help the man, but they shouted out a warning. Some people returned the salute. The boys looked her way. Martina felt nausea rising and a tingling sensation in her face. The sounds faded out around her. She retreated to the wall for support but didn't reach it in time. Her legs were hollow. The next thing she felt was someone catching her as she slumped, and a sea of faces peering at her full of curiosity and concern.

She looked up into the eyes of a man she didn't know. A pair of caramel coloured eyes. Everything else was a blur. She had to wait for it all to make sense. Where was she?

Whose eyes were these?

After a few moments, she saw that they belonged to a man. Young, a kind smile, his hair ruffled. He helped her to her feet. Holding her by the arm, he helped her gently across the piazza into the café, where he brought her a coffee and offered her a cigarette. She couldn't face either, so he ordered a glass of water instead.

Someone brought her a napkin to wipe the blood spots off her shoes, but she couldn't remove the ones on her stockings. They'd have to be thrown away. A waste, but she knew she could never wear them again or she'd be reminded every time she put them on of what she'd seen, and she couldn't bear that. She sat and stared out of the window for a long time, seeing the assault take place over and over.

She'd been getting easily upset about lots of things recently, but they seemed so insignificant now. It was unsettling in the house without Gianni, knowing that he was in danger a long way away but not hearing anything from him, although letters were clearly getting through because plenty of other soldiers had got in touch with their families. But now this thing had happened which was truly terrible, it put everything else into perspective.

"You've been very kind. I'm sorry to be so silly."

"Not at all," the man said. "You've had a shock."

He picked up the blood-stained tissues and threw them away, then sat down across the table from her, looking at her with concern. "Don't try to get up too quickly. You should stay until you feel better."

Her legs still felt empty. His sympathetic words touched her, and she felt tears slide down her cheeks too quickly to catch. She hid her wobbly mouth with her hand. He fetched some more napkins, and she felt his hand close on hers for a second as he passed them to her. The unexpected contact sent a shockwave through her, and she snatched hers away.

He sat back in his chair, contemplating her. He had fine lines around his eyes that stayed when he smiled. He was handsome in an understated way – dark hair, a good jawline. Or perhaps she had been starved of company for so long she would see beauty in anyone who showed her kindness.

"I'm sorry," he said. "I didn't mean to offend you."

She closed her eyes. "You didn't. This thing's made me jumpy."

She had an impulse to reach out and touch him again, to feel the warmth of another human being after feeling alone for so long. She suddenly wanted to tell him everything.

I dread my husband coming home. I should never have married him. I feel a stranger every day in his home.

Instead, trying to make sense of it all, she asked, "Was he Jewish, the man they killed?"

He shook his head.

"A Communist?"

He cleared his throat. "I don't think his politics were that thought-out. He's been in and out of prison so that they could 'redirect' him. Obviously, they didn't succeed in breaking his spirit, so I suppose they thought they'd shut him up for good this time. Make an example of him in case others should choose to follow suit."

She shuddered. "It was horrible."

"Yes, it was."

The body had been covered with one of the tablecloths from the café. It was still out there – a lumpen shape under the bizarrely cheery red and white checks, a dark patch of sticky blood on the cobbles just visible when a corner of the cloth was lifted by the breeze. The spectators had melted away by now, leaving the grotesque thing alone in the piazza. A dog scampered up and sniffed at it, but his owner roared a threat at him and he darted off again.

She put her head in her hands. "What's happening to this country? I just don't understand." She almost hadn't realised that she had been speaking aloud. She looked up startled and could tell that she had.

"I know what you mean," he said quietly, almost in her ear. "None of us saw it coming. Not like this."

And I didn't see that Gianni would be taken away so

quickly, before we'd had a chance to put things right. Leaving me with this life I no longer recognise, living with people I don't like and who don't want me there. It's all such a bloody mess.

But she carried on talking about other things, things that didn't matter – the weather, the surroundings, the history of the place. They stopped abruptly as the café door swung open. A middle-aged man came in, issuing a general greeting to which they both replied.

"I haven't seen you here before," said the man she was with.

"I live in Santa Zita. I came down to pick up some things for my father-in-law."

He nodded. "I have some relations up there. It's a pretty place."

All the time, her mind kept flitting back to how she'd seen the old man die right there in the piazza and she had his blood on her stockings.

The door opened again, and a pair of young militiamen came in, different from the ones she'd seen earlier. They looked around them, then sat at the bar where they were served immediately. There were other people waiting but no-one objected.

"I must go," she said at last. "I hadn't realised the time."

"Are you sure you'll be all right?" he asked, getting up and walking with her to the door.

"I'm fine now, really. Thank you."

He held the door open for her. Outside, she turned down a small street to avoid walking past the patch where the body had been. It had finally been taken away, and the stained paving stones were being scrubbed. If she'd come into town tomorrow rather than today, she'd have had no idea it had happened. If someone had told her, would she have believed them?

She caught her breath as she felt rather than heard someone come up close behind her.

"I'm sorry. I couldn't just let you go without asking your name."

As she swung round, she was struck by the nakedness of his expression – a half smile of surrender that revealed desire, hope, and a small amount of something that looked like fear.

"It's Martina." Despite everything, she felt herself smile.

She held his gaze for some moments, then began to turn away again. He caught her by the shoulders and swung her back round. She should stop him. She thought about screaming. But as he drew her towards him, she forgot about everything else in her small life and allowed herself to believe she was someone else, the kind of woman that did things like this.

Chapter Twenty-Three

"Who's the steak for?" asked Carlo.

"The um, large lady," said the waitress, suppressing a grin. "Australian, I think. Or South African"

Looking out through the dark restaurant into the bright piazza, he saw the woman fanning her ample reddened bosom with her menu. It must be uncomfortable for her in this heat.

"*Bistecca alla fiorentina,*" he said, setting it down.

The woman grabbed it from him and started attacking it before he'd even let go of the plate. Feeling sorry for her, he wished her a good appetite and left her to it. But he'd barely reached the kitchen when there was a clatter and a shout.

"He took it – that bloody animal. Thieving bastard stole my steak right off my plate. I'd hardly started it."

Carlo hurried out to see the broken plate on the floor and Bruno, a Labrador cross, tucking into something. He shouted at the dog and he scampered off. Carlo stared after him, bewildered.

"I'm so sorry. He's never done that before."

The dog was well known in the village. While not quite a stray, his owner took a very relaxed attitude to his wandering, and the dog would sometimes hang around the piazza in the hope of getting a titbit from someone. But he was also quite timid, and a raised voice or extended foot would soon send him off.

"We'll cook you another one."

The waitress came up, hands on hips, glaring. "It wasn't Bruno. The dog didn't take it. I saw what happened."

"Are you calling me a liar?" the woman demanded in English.

"She dropped the plate – I saw her. She'd nearly finished anyway."

There was a short silence and then a murmur went around the other diners. Carlo wasn't sure what to do. He believed Anita, but didn't want the situation to turn ugly. He agreed to cook another steak for the woman, but Anita refused to carry it out to her.

"She ate it herself. No wonder she's so fat."

"For God's sake, be quiet," he snapped. The shocked silence around him told him it was too late.

"I heard that." Heads lifted as the woman's voice carried through the restaurant. "Don't think I don't know what *grossa* means." She began to cry loudly and desperately, balling her fists against her eyes like a huge, chubby child. One of the diners leaned over and handed her some tissues, and she started recounting her version of the story to anyone who'd listen, between great choking sobs.

When the second steak was ready, Carlo gave it to the waitress.

"I'm not going," she said, folding her arms.

"Take it and apologise," said Carlo.

"No. She's the liar."

"Anita, go."

"No."

He closed his eyes. "Just do it if you want to keep your job."

He hadn't meant to snap. All this worry about his mother's memory problems was getting to him. Anita looked as if she wanted to kill him, but she went anyway, and he heard her murmur an apology.

A slap rang out.

Carlo whirled round and saw Anita clutching her face. The deathly hush was followed by a collective intake of breath. He strode over, horribly aware that everyone was watching, took back what was left of the second steak, and asked the woman to leave. She did so, shouting expletives all the way and threatening to let everyone know about it in a review.

One or two of the other diners caught his eye and gave him sympathetic looks. Others buried their faces behind their menus, convulsed in silent laughter, or just looked down at their plates, shocked.

Cass was appalled to hear he had cooked her a second steak.

"But you're the one who keeps saying 'the customer's always right'," he protested.

"Yes, but *she* clearly wasn't."

Merda. Could this day get any worse? The Dutch couple in their thirties who'd just sat down were prospective buyers who'd popped into the restaurant earlier and asked to view Villa Leonida that afternoon. He hoped to God they hadn't witnessed that little scene. And wasn't that the English schoolteacher sitting next to them? Much as he liked her, she'd be sure to start rabbiting on about curses, and bang would go another chance of a sale.

He took a deep breath and emerged into the square, greeting the couple warmly.

"You may be more comfortable inside," he said, indicating the clouds that were gathering over Villa Leonida. "It looks like it's going to rain."

"We'll take the chance," said the woman, nodding over to two small boys who were chasing each other around the fountain, giggling and screaming in delight. "They've been in the car all morning. It's nice for them to let off steam."

Carlo ran through the day's dishes with them. Later, when their father called across to the children, they raced each other back to their seats, almost cannoning into Sonia as she crossed the piazza.

"That was lovely – as always," said the English schoolteacher as Carlo handed her the bill. She turned to the couple next to her. "I couldn't help overhearing. You're interested in the villa up there?" She motioned towards the house. "It has quite a colourful history that place. It's supposed to be cursed, you know."

The couple glanced at each other.

"Oh, I don't know about that," Carlo said with a forced

laugh.

"It's well documented," she insisted.

"What kind of curse?" the woman wanted to know.

"A young English poet – Thomas Winterton – was in love with the girl who lived in the villa. I started researching him when writing a paper for my local literary society, and I got quite hooked.

"He was a very colourful character. Ideas of grandeur; passed himself off as a lord. He was a hanger-on in the circles of Byron and Shelley. A second son, you see, inherited nothing. I suppose he came over to Italy seduced by the faded glory and art treasures. He had a lucky streak here – won a lot of money gambling. But he lost a lot, too."

She handed over a credit card to pay for the meal, and Carlo quickly put it in the machine. If only the damned thing wasn't so slow.

"Hmm, but didn't they find he'd stolen his poems from someone else?" he said, trying to dredge up something he'd read, and head her off from talking about the curse.

"Ah yes, that's what they say. But then there's no such thing as an original idea, is there?"

He laughed. "I didn't know you were such a cynic."

"It comes of being a teacher for thirty years. Anyway, the plagiarism they could probably have accepted. It was the social deception they couldn't forgive."

She punched her PIN into the machine.

"His poems are actually beautiful – a vast improvement on the ones he's supposed to have copied. His later ones are entirely his own, as far as anyone can tell, and have much more feeling – desperate, savage, very eloquent. Especially the ones about Antonella, the girl who lived in the villa."

"Sounds like he was well and truly smitten," Carlo said.

"He was. Madly in love. But her parents wouldn't hear of her marrying a foreigner, especially a poor one. So they set her up with a local man.

"The story goes that Thomas marched up to the house after a night drinking and gambling, and challenged the lover to a duel. The other man laughed in his face. Thomas pointed the gun at him, but the girl ran in front of her lover and begged him not to shoot."

She paused to allow other diners to picture the scene.

"Thomas gave her an ultimatum – to come back to him, or watch him die.

"And she chose the latter?" Carlo said, handing her back her card.

She nodded. "He shot himself. Through the head. Right there in front of her."

The young couple winced, imagining.

"But not before laying a curse on the house?" the man prompted. Carlo couldn't quite tell if he was laughing at her.

"That's right. I don't know the exact wording, but it brings misery to the families who live there and an untimely death to the daughters."

She dug out a generous tip which Carlo refused, but as usual, she insisted.

"The sad irony was that Antonella was pregnant with his child. The shock of watching him blow his brains out caused her to miscarry. It was a girl, of course."

He threw up his hands. "So, they must have thought the curse was working already."

"Exactly. She didn't have any more children, and I've heard that quite a few baby girls have died there since. Not that that was particularly unusual in those days. And then, of course, there was that ghastly business with the English family whose bodies they found last year…"

Carlo remarked that the curse made a good story if most unlikely to be true, and warned her that the fine weather was forecast to break that afternoon. He turned back to the couple but, noting the woman's hands placed protectively over her swollen stomach, was hardly surprised they were reluctant now to go ahead with the viewing. How were they ever going to sell this wretched villa? It seemed to be cursed in more ways than one.

Chapter Twenty-Four

1940

Martina had suspected she was pregnant for some time. Perhaps it helped explain her feelings about that kiss with the stranger in the town. Because it was just that, a simple pressing of lips on lips. It shouldn't have happened – it wasn't like her – although these days she wasn't sure any longer what 'being her' meant. Two strangers in a quiet street, the world turning inside out around them. It hadn't even lasted that long. How long? Five minutes? Half an hour? She had no idea.

He'd have forgotten it by now, of course. He probably kissed women like that every day. Maybe several times. So, why couldn't she forget it, too? She couldn't keep lying to herself, pushing it to the back of her mind. But it shouldn't be so important.

She'd only just begun to understand on the morning of that day that she might be pregnant. That must be it – some chemical imbalance was to blame for the way she'd behaved. Of course, she shouldn't have kissed him back, but she hadn't been thinking straight. And she'd hardly encouraged him, had she? He'd taken her by surprise. And she hadn't wanted to make a scene.

She hadn't expected the pregnancy to make her feel so unwell. Elena, who'd been watching like a hawk for the symptoms ever since Gianni had left, recognised them at once and was delighted, as though a part of Gianni would be re-born. Martina hoped it would be a girl.

The frost that normally surrounded Elena fell away, to be replaced by an oppressive concern for Martina's welfare.

Suddenly, she was fussing over her, cooking her special meals, and encouraging her to eat more than her fair share. Martina was allowed to lie in late in the mornings and take a rest in the afternoon, with Elena continuing to see to the running of the house. She brought Martina ginger tea, and assured her cheerfully each time she vomited that this was her body's way of protecting the baby from anything that could harm him.

But it turned out there was almost nothing Martina could safely eat. She began to worry she might have a more sinister condition. Elena was convinced that the cause of the sickness was not eating properly.

"There's nothing of you. People will think we're not feeding you."

Martina felt as though she was being fattened up like a pig. She looked at her growing stomach with distaste. She'd never taken much interest in food before and took no enjoyment from it now, but discovered that if she didn't eat regularly she was sick. Smells were more acute and preparing food invariably made her ill, so she was excused this duty, and retired to the bedroom when family meals were served.

Alone in her room, she had time to dwell. Sitting up against the monogrammed pillows, feeling the cool, silk bedspread under her and the breeze from the open window rippling across her swollen body, watching the clouds march over the mountains, she thought about all the things that had happened to her in the last year.

She sometimes thought of the incident with the old man spitting on the poster. The way his eyeball had rolled when he was lying on the ground. The way he twitched, and all the blood. Perhaps because it was the first time she'd seen violence up close, it made everything about that day seem unnaturally sharp in her memory. That was the first time she'd felt truly frightened. Now she was afraid most of the time.

She kept seeing herself back in the café with the man she'd kissed. She remembered the outline of his face so well she thought she could draw it: the fine tracing of lines under his eyes; those twinkling, toffee-coloured eyes; the roughness of his jaw; the warm lips. The whole encounter had lasted only moments, but it seemed to take on a significance that was out of all proportion.

She'd fainted a few times since, but for no reason at all. "If you must go out in the heat with an empty stomach..." Elena used to say. On coming round, she half expected to find his intense eyes searching her face and hear his reassuring voice. She imagined him lifting her up and carrying her away. Thank God she didn't know his name. She didn't trust herself not to use it in those incoherent moments; couldn't even allow herself to make one up.

Sometimes in her imagination she didn't leave him in the street after that kiss, but walked away with him arm-in-arm and disappeared through a door into a house she'd never been to. After making love, they'd lie in bed and talk about how their lives had got confused. They'd each climbed aboard the wrong train, but now they had a chance to jump off together.

If only she could have met him at a different time, under different circumstances. Sometimes she imagined bumping into him again. If she went back to that same café, would he be there? No, she mustn't go back. It would only end in disappointment and she couldn't bear that.

Even so, she occasionally thought she saw him, just a glimpse of his head in a crowded street, the outline of him on a bridge, or the shape of his shoulders several rows in front at a concert. She saw him everywhere. Places he might have been and places he could not have known existed. Caught his reflection in a shop window, noticed his hand on a rail in front of her. The smell of his cigarettes, his footsteps in the street behind her. Every man reminded her of him – his smile, his gestures, his voice. She never had the urge to call out or confront him. That would spoil everything. It was enough to think she'd seen him.

It wasn't that she was unused to men falling for her. Quite the reverse. It was just that it never happened the other way round. She was never the one to fall for them. Once she even thought she saw him in Santa Zita, standing in the middle of the piazza, looking into the fountain. But that would be impossible. What reason would he have for coming all the way up here?

It was just a kiss. A stupid, unthinking kiss, so why couldn't she get it out of her mind?

Her stomach felt big and hard and uncomfortable as she changed position. She sometimes caught herself wishing the baby was his instead of her husband's; he didn't feel like a husband. Gianni was little more than a name now – a shadow that cast itself over her life. Yes, that was it. That was why the encounter with the stranger meant so much. She could have carried on fooling herself all her life if she hadn't met him. But she had to admit the truth to herself if nobody else. She'd made a mistake in marrying Gianni, and she didn't want his baby.

Marrying him had been a practical decision. He was a good catch, the best in Santa Zita. How was she to know how much the war would shake things up and present other possibilities when it was too late to take them?

She bit her lip. What was wrong with her? Having these fantasies, falling in love with an idea, an impression, nothing more? She was married. She'd be a mother soon.

And what about him, whoever he was? Who did he think he was? Why had he taken advantage of her like that, knowing she was frightened and confused after what she'd just witnessed? Hadn't he stopped to consider what might be at stake for her? Elena had persuaded her to surrender her wedding ring for the war effort, but he must have noticed the steel band she was wearing and understood what it meant.

He seemed to take it for granted she'd want to kiss him there in the street like some common tart. He didn't deserve to occupy her thoughts.

One moment she felt angry and embarrassed, the next she felt trapped like a caged bird above the village below, desperate that she'd let the moment pass. How many opportunities did you get in your life? She'd thrown away the chance of something more. But how much more? Probably not much, probably nothing. Surely these confused feelings would disappear with the passing of time? But as the weeks slipped by, she found she was thinking of him more rather than less.

Chapter Twenty-Five

Once the sickness had passed, Martina felt a rush of energy and optimism returning. The pregnancy was at first cherished as a family secret, but once confirmed by the doctor it became a cause for general celebration, and she basked in the attention. Although she felt much better, Elena still insisted that she do nothing around the house. It wouldn't do to take any chances with Gianni's baby.

But although she enjoyed being looked after, there were still times when she felt trapped. It seemed there was nothing she could do these days without it being commented on. It made her want to do something reckless to annoy Elena. Sometimes the whispering in the chimneys upset her so much she had to burst open those French doors and get some air.

The one thing that remained constant in her life was Irena. She, of all people, could be trusted not to change, and Martina looked forward almost childishly to seeing her on the occasions she could think of a pretext to escape. They could walk together and discuss things that were happening, and things they'd heard on the radio and in the bar. Only when she was with Irena did the annoying things seem funny and the awful things seem not quite so hopeless.

"What's the old dragon been saying now?" Irena would ask, and Martina would pour out her latest grievance about Elena.

She could ask Irena for hints and tips on how to do household things – ordinary things which practical people like Irena had picked up as children, but which had passed Martina by. Somehow, they hadn't seemed important.

"For God's sake, Martina," her mother used to say, "it's a

good job you're pretty because you can't cook, you can't clean, and you certainly can't sew."

Irena also kept her up to date with things that were happening down in the village.

"The Gramscis have left," she told her as they sat on the wall of the fountain. "The professor's been away on business for some time – now his wife and the children have gone to join him. The housekeeper says they left in the middle of the night. No note or anything. I don't suppose we'll see them again."

They were getting used to people disappearing. There one day, gone the next. Sometimes they came back after a spell in a correction centre. Other times they didn't.

"There'll be no-one left at this rate," said Martina, looking around the quiet piazza. "I expect even you'll leave one day. Be swept off your feet by some rich, handsome man."

Irena shook her head and laughed. "That's never going to happen – there's nobody left for me. The only eligible men have joined up. We'll be sitting here by this fountain in fifty years' time, you and I, and nothing will have changed."

She didn't mean to tell Irena about kissing the man in town; it just came out.

"You don't think, do you? You never think." Irena's eyes were wide, and her nostrils flared the way they always did when she was angry. "You had the pick of all the men round here. You could have had anyone. You *chose* Gianni. You made it happen. And now you're wishing you could trade him in for a stranger who didn't even have the manners to introduce himself before he kissed you? Gianni's out there risking his life for you and the baby. And what will happen if it gets back to Elena and Cesare?"

Martina stopped. "It won't."

"No? How can you be so sure no-one saw you? It's not just about you any more – you'll have a child to think of soon."

She was right, of course. Anyone might have been there. Anyone might have seen her kissing that man. If word got back to Elena and Cesare, what would they do? Just because they hadn't said anything yet didn't mean they never would. Villa Leonida was Martina's home now – and since her family had moved to be nearer the factory where her father now worked, she had nowhere else to go. She tried to explain to Irena that the pregnancy made her especially vulnerable, but Irena didn't look convinced.

"Promise me you won't look for him."

"I said I wouldn't."

Anything to stop her nagging. She should have known Irena would react like this, and not just because she had principles. Wasn't that a spark of jealousy? But her friend was right, of course. She couldn't jeopardise her child's future by doing stupid, impulsive things. It must never happen again.

Chapter Twenty-Six

Irena pressed the record button again. It was funny how she'd been afraid of the machine at first. Now it was starting to become a friend. The best sort – one that listens without interrupting, and then forgets when you've told them on command.

People judged Martina because of her manner. And yes, she could be selfish, stubborn, condescending. But she was different with me. I always felt confident she wouldn't let me down. I thought that somehow, whatever happened, she'd be true to me. She'd never given me any reason to doubt her. She promised me she'd never do anything to jeopardise our friendship, and I believed her.

When she married, I felt bereaved. It was as though I'd had an arm ripped off. I knew she wasn't going far, but I saw it as the end of our childhood. Everyone was entering a new life just then. Factories stopped making one thing and started making others. People I'd grown up with, who had no ambition except to work someone else's land, were suddenly busy, at the factory, joining the Army, even going into politics.

People who'd struggled in class were commanding respect as members of the militia. I seemed to be the only person who didn't have a new life to go to. I was afraid Martina wouldn't want to know me any more.

Something puzzled him. It was the voice. It wasn't so different from her normal voice, but it was the one she used for other people, not the one she used for him, her son.

"She's forgotten," he murmured to himself. "Forgotten I'd be listening."

I needn't have worried. Martina wasn't happy. I'd never

seen her so wretched, sitting there in those beautiful surroundings, all alone. She told me how it felt being under Elena's eye all day, as though she was an intruder in their home. She couldn't understand why Gianni never wrote. Everyone else had heard from their husbands and sons, but at Villa Leonida they heard nothing.

She tortured herself half the time, wondering if he'd been killed or captured. The rest of the time, she imagined him having the time of his life in brothels or setting up home with a local girl.

I felt guilty then and sorry for her. But I must admit a tiny part of me rejoiced, because it meant that she must be missing her old life. I had a little fantasy she might turn up on our step one night with a suitcase and say she'd chucked it all in.

Some of the other girls were livid when she bagged Gianni. They'd always been jealous of her. They said things behind her back but never to her face. They didn't believe she really loved him.

As for me, my chances of getting married shrank even further as the war went on. The pool of eligible men was small enough in Santa Zita before the fighting broke out, and even smaller after, so I buried myself in my studies. Martina teased me that I was married to my books, which annoyed me rather because what else could I have done? But looking back now, I suspect she was envious that I had the chance to learn things instead of playing the rich lady of the villa.

I wish now I'd made more of an effort to understand her. If I had, who knows if things might have turned out differently?

Chapter Twenty-Seven

MARTINA

A few of the houses in Santa Zita had orange trees but the one at Villa Leonida was magnificent. Martina had even received praise for it when visiting an aunt in the village of Santo Stefano in Alto, that lay directly across the valley from Santa Zita.

It was the one Gianni had bought her on the first day of their honeymoon, when everything seemed simple and he was still trying to impress her. It was the last real connection she had with him. Somehow, it felt as though by caring for the tree she was keeping hope alive. As long as the tree stayed alive, so would he, and perhaps the Gianni that came back would be the old Gianni

Despite the prodigious rainfall that battered the village in autumn, and the harshness of the winter, the plant managed to flourish, and bore plump, sweet oranges.

It stood in a loam compost in a large blue glazed pot on the long, wrought iron balcony at the back of the house, displaying fruits like giant Christmas baubles, and filling the living room with its fragrance when the French doors were open.

The pot stood on a little stand with wheels that Cesare had made especially for the plant, and at different times of the day it was wheeled along the balcony to take full advantage of the sun.

Martina fed the tree weekly with a fertiliser that she made to Cesare's secret recipe. She watered it sparingly in winter and just enough in summer, inspecting the soil and leaves on a daily basis to look for any signs of scorching or yellowing, and pinching out the branches to encourage a bushy growth at the centre of the plant.

"You give that plant a lot of love," Elena said.

Her words felt like a rebuke. *What about my son? Why couldn't you have fussed over him in the way you do that damned weed? Then he might not have been in such a hurry to go.*

Martina bit her lip to stop herself saying, *I do it out of guilt. It's all I have left of the old Gianni. The boy I loved before I married him.*

Sometimes she imagined seeing him walking up to the villa from the town below. As he looked up to the house from the road, the orange tree would be the first thing he'd notice. But sometimes the fantasy would go wrong. When he lifted his face, it wasn't Gianni at all. Despite seeing his photograph every day on the piano, she found to her shame that it was harder and harder to recall his features. Over time they were fading like an old photograph. But the face in her imagination was clear, and it clearly wasn't Gianni's.

It was a man she'd met only once, in town, the day the old man was killed. The one she'd kissed outside a café. That perfect jawline, the calm, steady eyes. The look of hope and surrender – that kind smile. But if she couldn't remember Gianni's face properly, how on earth could she recall with such precision the face of a man she'd seen so briefly? The answer, of course, was that in her head she'd probably tweaked and perfected his features over time. He was no longer real, either – just an image. But there were days when she ached to feel his hands and lips exploring her body. Some days it was all she could think of. It was ridiculous, but it got her through the day.

Chapter Twenty-Eight

MARTINA

"The bump's lower today. The baby's on its way."

Martina felt a surge of annoyance. She hadn't perceived any difference. Sometimes it felt as though her body belonged to Elena. As the birth date drew nearer, she found herself under even sharper scrutiny. The staring, the prodding, being followed everywhere – it was intolerable. Elena's greedy eyes were constantly on the lookout for signs.

"Are you needing the bathroom more often? Has the indigestion eased? Do you feel you have more energy suddenly? Let me see your feet – are they swollen?"

The questions were endless. Martina couldn't think straight any more. She was feeling more and more detached from her own body. But now she came to examine her stomach, the bump was lower and the heartburn had eased. Elena flew into action making the arrangements.

"You can't have the baby here," she announced at breakfast under the pergola. "It's too much of a risk, too isolated. If anything should go wrong…"

She let the awful possibilities hang in the air. It was obvious what was at the back of her mind. That wretched curse. How could such a smart, practical person, who had no truck with superstition, be taken in?

"I don't believe in curses," Martina said. "They have no power over people who don't believe in them."

Elena took hold of her hands. "I can see you think it's all nonsense, but please don't be like me, Martina. I was stubborn and opinionated, just like you."

The change in tone took Martina by surprise. Elena's voice was soft and seemed on the verge of breaking.

"When you're young, you think you know everything and nothing can hurt you. I ignored the curse and my first child, a girl, was stillborn. I was very ill myself. I nearly didn't survive." She drew in a long breath. "At the time, I wished I hadn't."

Her face, usually so haughty, had such a vulnerable expression Martina had to look away.

"I never even saw my baby. They said it was better not to, but I sometimes wonder about that. The birth took too long. She was in an awkward position – starved of oxygen."

Her voice had dropped to a whisper. Her skirt rustled as she stood up and walked over to the edge of the terrace and examined the plants.

"Look, I'm not saying I believe the curse had anything to do with it. I don't. But what I do know is that it would make things easier for you if anything does go wrong. You won't have to deal with the guilt. I couldn't get it out of my head that there was just a possibility it was my fault. That all that terrible grief could have been avoided, if only I had moved out of the house and stayed with a relative as Cesare had begged me to do."

She smiled at Martina, but she seemed to be fighting to control the emotion in her voice.

"Now I have the chance to make sure it doesn't happen to someone else, however silly it sounds. I couldn't bear to lose my grandchild."

It still seemed unnecessary but Elena's expression, the softening of her voice and the tears in her eyes, made it hard to argue. But Martina had to bite her lip to stop herself saying what was really on her mind. If she left the house, would she ever be allowed back? She couldn't help the thought that this might be a trick to get her away. Why should that bother her when she hated the house anyway? But this was her home now. She had nowhere else to go. Dislike each other as they did, she, Elena, and Cesare needed each other.

Chapter Twenty-Nine

MARTINA

Nuns in their immaculate white habits floated like doves through the marbled corridors of the maternity hospital in the convent below the villa, with an air of reverence that lent the anticipation of the birth an almost religious significance.

"Get back to bed. Eat it up. No more reading until morning."

They were calm but strict. Even Martina, accustomed to getting her own way, and Elena, who always gave the orders, had no sway when it came to extending visitor hours or varying the routine. The Sisters knew best what was right for mother and baby.

Being in the convent was restful, but Martina couldn't help thinking about the young women that must have been incarcerated in these walls in the past against their will. "Difficult" girls, whose fathers or husbands wanted rid of them. Girls with forbidden lovers or inconvenient pregnancies, and obstinate girls who refused to marry the man chosen for them.

The view over the patchwork of rooftops and the piazza with its fountain was the same as the one from Villa Leonida, although from a little further down. She kept picturing Elena and Cesare up at the villa, adjusting back to their old lives, just the two of them, laying two places at the table instead of three. What if they told her she couldn't come back? What if they wanted the baby but not her? What if they heard rumours about her kissing another man?

Perhaps it was due to nerves about giving birth and being a mother, but she couldn't stop the creeping suspicion that she'd also been put away for good.

Sonia was born in April 1941, a few days before Athens capitulated to the Germans, after a seventeen-hour labour in which the Sisters had feared for both of their lives.

"She's perfect," said Irena, gazing at the baby through the viewing window. "Perfect in every detail."

But through her exhaustion, Martina sensed other people's disappointment. A girl. Somehow she'd failed to produce the grandson Elena was expecting. Elena behaved as though someone had died rather than been born, and kept consoling her.

"She's a pretty girl. She'll have plenty of brothers after the war when Gianni comes back."

Everything would be better when Gianni was back, according to Elena. Surely now that Athens had been captured he'd be allowed to come back, or at least write?

Despite her annoyance, Martina was forced to play the part of the dutiful daughter-in-law as Elena showed off her new grandchild to an endless stream of visitors. Even if she always prefaced each visit with a wistful, "We had hoped for a grandson but…" and a delicate shrug of the shoulders as if to say, "We all have our crosses to bear." Still, it was a relief to be welcomed back to Villa Leonida. She'd had no idea until that day how strong a hold it had on her.

When the three of them walked to church with the new baby on a mild spring day, pear blossom falling on the pram like confetti, they were showered with compliments and gifts. No doubt they looked like a perfect family, but Martina felt an overwhelming sense of loneliness – as though she'd passed through the final doorway to a new world, from which there could be no return.

Chapter Thirty

"She's too cold. You mustn't let her sleep too long. You haven't winded her properly."

Elena's constant fussing drove Martina to little acts of rebellion – failing to wake Sonia at the appointed hour, picking her up when she was still sleeping, or letting her feed for longer than her mother-in-law deemed essential.

During those early months, she'd been encouraged to eat well – or as well as the rations and their own food stock permitted – and rest as much as she liked. But now that Sonia was ready for weaning, she sensed a change in Elena's attitude. It wasn't anything she said so much as an air of impatience. The implication that Martina must pull her weight and make herself useful now that her job was done. She couldn't be lazy any more. Perhaps she shouldn't have been surprised, but it wasn't a nice feeling knowing that she'd only been cared for as a vessel.

"Signor Marconi from the school has asked me if I'd like to be a teacher," Irena told her as they pushed the pram around the village. "He said I was his best student."

"That's no surprise," Martina said. "And it's what you've always wanted to do, isn't it?"

"It is, and they're short of staff after the last teacher joined up. As soon as I get my Party membership card, I can start training. After all, it's the closest I'll probably ever get to having children of my own."

"Don't be silly. This war isn't going to last forever."

After all, the radio broadcasts, always preceded by martial music, sounded so victorious. It was surely only a matter of time. Although Martina couldn't help the thought that whispered through her head: *And then what?*

It was becoming harder and harder to imagine what life would be like after the war. As the weeks passed with still no word from Gianni, a numbness settled inside her. She'd thought he'd have at least replied to the letter she'd written telling him she was expecting his child, and the one she'd sent after Sonia was born. She'd asked if he had any preferences for names, but apparently he hadn't. Elena had had several suggestions, but Martina had stuck to her guns about choosing Sonia, her own mother's name. She thought even that might provoke Gianni into writing, but it hadn't. He must surely have asked about the possibility of leave so that he could come back for the birth? What father wouldn't want to see their first child? Which made her wonder if he was unable to reply. But if something bad had happened to him, they'd have heard, wouldn't they? The tension in the house had soared during the spring offensive. Elena kept insisting that no news was good news and Gianni would get in touch when he wasn't tied up saving lives and building Italy's future. Yet even after the victory in June, they heard nothing.

In her positive moods, Martina still pictured his return. Not as the Gianni who'd been so agitated before he left, but as the old Gianni, the boy she'd grown up with, who could make her laugh, understood her need for excitement and adventure, who could match her in speed and agility – at least some of the time. Then everything would be fine. But in lower periods, it seemed obvious they were all fooling themselves. Gianni was dead. If he wasn't, he'd have written.

She wrote to him frequently, mostly out of guilt, telling him about the minutiae of her day, but she read back through what she'd written with loathing – how banal these things must sound to someone who'd been on the battlefield.

"Your daughter's growing every day. She's smiling now, and I know it sounds silly, but I'm sure she's nearly able to talk. She's very noisy, chattering away, practising her sounds all day long. I show her your picture each night so

that she'll recognise you when she sees you. I think she knows it already. We all see different bits of you in her. It would be lovely if you could write her a few lines so that we can keep them and show them to her when she's older."

Martina hesitated as she sealed the letter. It really wasn't fair to use Sonia to blackmail Gianni into writing. But in any case, she needn't have worried. It got no response. Sonia diverted her attention, but Elena was fiercely capable of managing the baby, leaving Martina the mundane tasks of boiling nappies and pressing clothes in between feeds.

Sonia was a hungry baby. She was underweight and desperate for her own survival. Exhausted as she was, Martina admired her daughter's spirit; despite everything, she felt a bond growing. She cherished her time with the baby, uncurling the little fingers, stroking her soft cheek. At last there was one thing that nobody could take away from her.

Chapter Thirty-One

Martina timed her visits to the park to coincide with the end of lessons, so she could catch Irena. Peering through the open door of the school building, she saw the children in their clean pinnies bowing their heads in prayer for *il Duce* before being dismissed, each politely wishing Irena a good day.

Irena gathered up her books and took Martina's arm as they walked through the park. "You seem to have them under control," Martina said. "How do you remember all their names?"

Irena laughed. "Some days are better than others. Massimino – he's a terror! Alessia – such a dreamer. Claudia – a dreadful show-off." As they walked, she regaled Martina with stories. "They're not bad children. It's so funny to see them there sometimes and think we used to sit in those same chairs – you, me, and Gianni. Any news from him?"

Martina quickened her pace. "None."

People stopped them to compliment Martina on the baby. So like her grandmother, what a wonderful lady. Martina forced a smile and agreed.

"And before we know it, this little one will be sitting there," Irena continued, looking into the pram and giving the baby an affectionate pat. "Everyone says the time goes so quickly."

Back at the villa, Elena played the piano effortlessly, her fingers sweeping over the notes as though they were dancing. She lost herself in the music, oblivious to any interruptions, her straight back inclining and receding with the tempo. Perhaps this had been her means of escape once, Martina thought, but it had since become habit. Elena had been moulded into the house, just as she was being.

Martina loved to hear her play. For one thing, it gave her the freedom to move around without being watched, away from the clipped comments and sharp looks. It also meant that as long as she could hear the music, she knew where Elena was.

But Elena's playing also did wonders for Sonia's crying. Even when the baby had worked herself up to a crescendo, Elena only had to start playing and that angry, squalling little demon would stop, her expression startled. You could see the calmness washing over her.

As the months passed, Sonia started exploring the piano as she sat on her grandmother's lap, delighted by the different notes her doll-like hand produced when planted on them. When Elena played songs and they all sang along, Sonia would clap her hands and bounce up and down in delight, and during those moments it almost seemed possible for them all to forget their differences.

The piano had been Elena's mother's. On it stood the treasured photographs, dusted daily. Martina found it hard to look at the one of Gianni in his military uniform – dignified, but with his mouth parted as if about to break into a smile. But she made sure she showed it to Sonia each day. Sonia seemed to take for granted that her father lived in a small frame on the piano. How would she really react to seeing him? It was getting harder to imagine Gianni being part of the household again.

"Play that one again," said Cesare. His breath was short, as though he'd been running.

Martina had noticed his health deteriorating since she'd moved into the house. When she'd first known him, he'd rarely sat still, but now he was doing so more and more often under the pretext of listening to Elena play. He didn't say much but Martina had noticed him grimace as he sat down. The problem seemed to be that he could no longer get his usual medicine.

A couple of years ago, Gianni's brother Sebastiano had been killed in Abyssinia. Elena's dark hair had turned grey in a matter of weeks, but she'd carried on with life. Now she held resolutely to the belief that, unlike his brother, Gianni was fine and would return safely. Expressing a contrary belief was not an option.

Even if, as was supposed, Gianni had been taken prisoner by the Greeks, Elena was certain he'd find his way back to them now that the victory had been secured with a little help from the Germans. Martina tried not to think about the conditions in which he must have been held.

"Gianni's different," Elena kept saying. "He's the lucky one, he's always been a survivor. He should have died when he had TB as a child. Should have died when he fell out of that tree and right down the terraces. And he should have died when he got run over in town by that fool of a bank manager. But he's lucky. He'll survive."

Yes, but luck can run out, thought Martina.

She no longer knew what she thought about Gianni. If only he'd write just once so that they knew he was okay. If he could only explain to her how he really felt about her, and what in his view had gone so wrong on their honeymoon. Then she'd know what to do with her feelings. Because at that moment, she didn't know whether to love or hate him.

Things had improved for a few weeks after the honeymoon, but he'd still been distant and incapable of communicating his thoughts. It was as if he couldn't wait to get away. But if he'd decided the whole thing was a mistake, why didn't he just say so? She'd welcome it. Then she wouldn't have to feel guilty all the time.

Chapter Thirty-Two

There was nothing remarkable about the morning that led up to the arrival of the news. Looking back, she'd always think there should have been some sign to warn them that things weren't right – a storm, or an earthquake, or a plague of insects. But it was an ordinary day, and one that most people would forget in an instant.

Seeing the boy come up to the house, she already knew. She'd stood in front of the door, not able to open it, knowing that when she did her life would change. But Elena had moved her to one side and taken the telegram.

She watched Elena read and re-read the message as though the words didn't make sense. Her eyes darted back and forth across the page, her mouth repeating the words as though they were in a foreign language. As if by staring at them she could rearrange them and make them say something different. She kept whispering the words like an incantation until Cesare shouted at her to stop, and she crumpled into his arms.

Killed in action.

Erased. As though he'd never existed.

Martina felt numb. She sat with her face in her hands, stunned, appalled, and ashamed of the fact that there were no tears. As though nothing could reach her. She was aware of Sonia growing restless for a feed, but the cries seemed to be coming from miles away.

At last, she came to her senses enough to lift the baby, check her nappy, and bring her to her breast, glad of the excuse to sit and stare into nothingness for half an hour as the facts began to sink in. What was the future now? Could she stay here in this gilded prison with people who were to all intents and purposes strangers, now that Gianni had gone? Would they let her? But Sonia, of course, belonged here, and she belonged to Elena and Cesare, too.

Over the next few days, other questions crowded her head. Had Gianni received any of her letters before he died? Why hadn't he replied? Did he think of her at all when he was out there? Did he think of her at the end? She checked herself. What did it matter what he thought? And why couldn't she *feel?*

But gradually over the next few days, the numbness wore off and the anger started to creep in. Killed in action. What action? What for? What had he seen? What had he felt? It couldn't have been so clean, so simple as that bald message suggested. You couldn't just dismiss someone's life in those few words, but no-one seemed willing or able to give her more information.

For weeks, Elena seemed unable to digest the news. "It's a mistake," she kept saying. "They do make mistakes. It happens all the time." There'd been that fellow in the village opposite who'd later been found alive, hadn't there?

It was agonising to watch her tearing open letters, convinced each time that this would be the one that explained there'd been a mix-up. Every time there was a knock on the door, Elena leapt up expecting to see Gianni or at least hear some better news.

But confirmation came several weeks later, when one of Gianni's regiment returned to the village.

"It's Alvaro Paschi," Cesare said. "He's come to tell us about Gianni. He was there when it happened."

"No." Elena's face was white.

"*Amore*, we have to accept it. He's gone."

His wife closed her eyes, gave a long shuddering sigh, took a deep breath and nodded.

Martina found herself staring at Alvaro, the school misfit, as he stood awkwardly in the doorway. The boy she'd made a fool of so many times. She felt a stab of shame remembering. But then, he was one of those people to whom bad things always happened, wasn't he? The things she'd done surely wouldn't stand out when he looked back over his school days. He probably had no recollection of them.

And yet, how ironic that of all people to have survived the fighting it should be Alvaro. That he should have been lucky when it really counted, and Gianni who'd always been lucky until then had not.

Alvaro's eyes grew wide when he saw Martina, and his face filled with colour.

"How are you?' she managed to ask.

He looked at her warily. His eyes were underlined with purple shadows. He'd lost his hearing when a shell exploded close to him, so his voice was unnaturally loud and hoarse. He was taller and broader than she remembered, but his clothes still hung off him. She had the feeling they were being addressed by a ghost.

She could see Alvaro was nervous – the way he fiddled with a loose thread on his shirt. His eyes flicked towards her as he spoke, but his words were addressed to Elena. He told her all the usual things people tell the mothers of dead soldiers.

"He was brave, you should be proud of him. He wouldn't have felt a thing."

"How did it happen?" Martina asked.

Alvaro stammered when he answered. She bit back her impatience and softened her tone. Surely he could see she was a different person now? How could someone who'd fought in a war be scared of her?

"He stopped to help another soldier. He was killed instantly."

He was lying. She could tell. Or at the very least, he was giving her a sanitised version of the truth. For the first time since they'd received the letter with the news of Gianni's death, emotion ripped through her.

Alvaro said his piece and made his escape as quickly as he could. She went with him to the door and stood watching him walk down the path. Seized by a sudden impulse, she slipped out after him and followed him back to his house.

She called out several times on the way down the steep lanes, but he didn't hear her, leaving her voice to reverberate around the stone walls. When eventually she caught up with him outside his house, he shook her off with surprising force for his feeble frame. She tried to speak to him, but he slammed the front door. Incensed by his rudeness, she kept bashing it with her fists until he opened it.

"What do you want?" He looked even paler and more hollow-eyed in the natural light than he had back at the house. He was shaking, too. "Look, I can't bring him back. I'm sorry. What else do you want me to say?" He sounded as though he were going to cry.

"I just want to know what really happened," said Martina. "Not some version you've been given to make mothers and widows feel better. I want to understand what he went through. And there are things I want to ask you."

He shoved the door shut but she kept calling, making a nuisance of herself.

"I know it can't be easy," she said. "I'm sure you don't want to revisit whatever's in your head. But please, I have no-one else to ask. Did he know about the baby? Did he mention her to you?"

At last, he let her in. They stood awkwardly in the tiny room that smelled of damp clothes drying out. He looked at the floor. His voice was barely audible. She felt like a bully again.

Alvaro turned away. "He went to inspect a building. There were two others close behind him. Inside, there was a pile of blankets. As they approached it, the whole thing blew up. They were there one minute, gone the next."

She digested this. "Is there no chance at all he might have survived?"

His change of manner took her by surprise. His voice shook as he shouted, his face right up next to hers, "Didn't you hear what I said? What else do you want to know? Do you want me to tell you what he looked like? Do you? Can't you use your imagination?"

Before she knew what was happening, he was lunging at her with his fist raised. "Leave me alone."

She jumped back. He was mad. He was going to punch her in the face. She screamed as she brought up her own hands to cover her head.

A bout of coughing saved her. Alvaro doubled up. He sank to his knees, struggling for breath, spitting on the floor.

"I'm sorry," she said, backing away. She ran.

***

"At least it was quick. He didn't suffer," people said, when they heard what Alvaro had told Elena about Gianni.

"Are you saying we should be grateful?" Elena's voice was ice cold.

"He wouldn't have known anything about it," Cesare said. He put his arm round his wife, but she didn't seem to feel it. She sat for hours at the piano, monstrous and fragile, staring into space.

For the first time, Martina went to pieces. All the feelings she'd kept in check until now crushed her like a tidal wave. Memories swept in, ones she'd stifled for months, of Gianni as a boy, before she'd married him, before they'd fallen out – his face aglow with pride as he revealed the toy gun the Befana had brought him at Christmas, the pictures he'd taken with his camera, or climbed out of the very best hiding place in the area, a cave hidden at the back of the chestnut tower. The way he'd looked on their wedding day, in his best suit and his hair slicked back. If only they'd known what lay ahead, perhaps things would have been different. Maybe they'd have both made more of an effort on the honeymoon, given each other a chance to adjust. Now they'd never have the chance to put things right.

Elena played the piano for three days with hardly a pause. The notes resonated through every room, drowning out the whispering in the chimneys. Her eyes were fixed ahead of her and Martina wondered what she was seeing. Perhaps a photo album, turning over the pages of Gianni's life. But mixed up with Martina's grief was a shame to which she hardly dared admit.

"It's almost as if I willed this to happen," she whispered to Irena, her tears soaking into her friend's shoulder as they sat under the fig trees, watching the mountain opposite catch fire as the sun sank.

"What are you talking about?"

"It's the second time I've been granted my wish. First to marry Gianni, and then for him not to come back."

Even saying the words, she hated herself. She wanted to grieve for the boy she'd grown up with, but memories of the honeymoon still tortured her.

"Do you know what I think he was seeing that night he was so agitated looking into the sea?" she said. "I think he was having a premonition of his own death."

Irena put her arm around her. "Come on, you can't know that."

But Martina clung to her until she had no more tears. "This house is cursed. Everyone says so. I feel that I... I don't know... there's some evil presence here, and it's rubbing off on me."

"That's ridiculous," Irena said. "You know it isn't possible."

If only Martina could find these words a comfort. But if this darkness wasn't coming from the house, seeping through its walls into her soul, then the truth was worse. Because that meant it must be coming from inside *her*.

Chapter Thirty-Three

MARTINA

Winter 1941

Martina could sense Elena standing behind her as usual as she fed the orange tree. She knew what she was thinking.

It's not enough, this demonstration of love. You never loved him, my son.

Her mother-in-law made a show of being extra attentive to Sonia at these moments, singing to her as she brushed her hair with a soft brush. It was as though she were saying, *You're neglecting this little girl; my son's daughter. You failed as a wife and you're failing as a mother.*

The winter was the coldest anyone could remember. The ice made the roads treacherous, cutting the village off from the rest of the world. Fuel supplies were low, partly because so many trees had been cut down so the land could be used for growing food, and the log piles were raided almost as soon as they were left.

Sometimes it was hard to think about anything other than being cold and hungry. Sugar had been rationed before war broke out, but over the last year rice and pasta had been restricted, and meat was only available on certain days. Even if you had enough ration points, food was hard to find. The influx of evacuees who'd come to Santa Zita to escape the bombs in their cities were straining resources even further, and fights broke out between native and evacuee children. They kept Irena busy, leaving little time for their old chats.

Meanwhile, the price of non-rationed food had shot up. Most things were available on the black market, but at a price few could afford. Martina had to take long bicycle trips into town to barter their oil and chestnuts for essentials.

Still, she had to remind herself that it must be so much worse for the troops in some places, freezing to death in their trenches. Despite the relentlessly positive news reports, there were rumours about lack of kit and scarcity of food. She tried not to think about what Gianni must have gone through before he died. And for what? Although lately, she'd heard things about Gianni that surely couldn't be true?

Chapter Thirty-Four

IRENA

"I thought only Jesus could come back from the dead."
"Well, Gianni too, apparently.'
I first heard them talking about it down at the bar. Nothing was said directly, at least not in front of me. It was just whispers - half finished conversations left hanging in the air, questions left unanswered, looks exchanged. Gianni's death was a lie, a piece of trickery. But how was that possible? Had Alvaro made a mistake? Or was he the one who'd been lying?

The problem, you see, was that during the war there were so many rumours. You didn't know who or what to believe. Alvaro might have seen someone blown to bits and thought it was Gianni. Or he may have said so to cover for a man he'd always been in awe of – perhaps in love with, although none of us realised it at the time - who didn't want to be there any more, seeing heads blown off and limbs exploding.

It would have been easy in the confusion. Three men had gone into that building and been blown apart – or it could have been only two. Either way the stories began to circulate that Gianni had survived, although nobody knew where he was.

When we first had the news that he'd died, I overheard the other girls saying how Martina was enjoying playing the part of the grieving young widow. I told them what I thought of them for criticising her at a time like that, and I hoped for their sakes they never got to know how it felt. They looked a bit chastened, but I'm sure the whispering went on when I wasn't around. Now, it had all started again.

"I didn't know if I should tell you," I said to Martina. "Sometimes it's dangerous to believe."

But she'd already heard the rumours. "I don't suppose it can be true," she said.

I went with her to speak to Alvaro. It was our only chance of getting to the truth. But his house was shut up. No-one had seen him in a while.

"Why would he lie?" Martina kept asking. "Did he hate me that much? And Gianni – he can't be alive. If he is, why hasn't he got in touch with me?"

We agreed not to tell Elena or Cesare. It would be monstrously unfair to offer this slender thread of hope, and confusing for Sonia. Besides, there was Cesare's health to consider. The idea that Gianni had deserted would destroy his father, who took such a pride in his country.

It made me so angry that people had nothing better to do than put about these stories. If the wrong person got to hear of them and believed there was any truth in them, it could put all our lives in danger.

But as weeks and then months passed, the idea began to seem more like a fairy tale. If Gianni were alive, we'd have heard from him. He'd have found a way to get a message to Martina, even if he couldn't face his parents. Villa Leonida was his home after all, and he had a daughter he'd never seen. Elena and Cesare would have been ashamed of him deserting, especially if he was helping the other side, but he must have known Martina wouldn't judge him for that. Her own instinct was to do anything necessary to survive. She wouldn't blame anyone else for doing the same.

But she carried on looking after that orange tree with almost as much care as she gave to Sonia.

News from the battlefront was far from positive and public opinion was turning against il Duce, *but you had to be very careful who you were talking to. Still, we had no idea what was coming.*

Chapter Thirty-Five

Cass found Carlo in the empty restaurant, listening to the voice recorder long after the staff had left. "Here are the menus for the Easter lunch. They look pretty good, don't you think?"

He took one and ran his eyes over the dishes. Stuffed quails' eggs, asparagus lasagne, roast lamb, raspberry parfait, colomba, and prosecco.

"Perfect," he said, handing it back. "Except you've put basilica instead of basilico."

"What?" She snatched it back. "Why didn't you point that out this morning when I showed you a rough version?"

"I'm sorry. I'm telling you now, okay? A basilica's a church. It's a funny thing to find in your pasta."

"Yes, I know what it means," she snapped.

She turned to go but paused at the door, as if weighing up whether now was a good time to speak her mind. "By the way, your mother's being especially difficult at the moment. She seems quite worked up. Do you think you perhaps ought to lay off the memories for a bit?"

"What do you mean?"

She blew out her cheeks. "Just that it seems to be stressing her out, trying to recall these things."

He sighed. "If I don't, all those memories will be lost. I mean, it's our memories that make us what we are, isn't it?"

Cass frowned. "I'm not sure that's right. Isn't it our choices that make us who we are? And to be honest, I don't think it's doing you much good either. We're really busy and you're distracted. It's your restaurant, remember."

"Mmm?"

She banged the door in disgust.

Chapter Thirty-Six

MARTINA

From the summer of 1943, things got really got confusing. Resentment soared among the families in Santa Zita over the appalling losses in Russia and North Africa, which might have been avoided if troops hadn't been tied up in occupying Greece. Turning on the radio with shaking hands, Martina heard about city after city being bombed. It seemed Mussolini's forces weren't so indestructible after all.

Down in the piazza, people were muttering grievances. Why had they been dragged into this war when they didn't have the resources to defend their cities? Where were the anti-aircraft guns and air raid shelters they'd been promised? Why hadn't they been better prepared? And soldiers returning on leave or being sent back wounded told them the war wasn't going nearly as well as they'd been led by the press to believe. Families were furious their sons were being sent off to fight without a proper kit. One neighbour's son wasn't even given a uniform.

There'd been whispers for months of a growing movement to overthrow Mussolini, but then so many things were talked about and never happened.

On 19th July, shortly after the Italian troops had surrendered in North Africa, the Allies landed in Sicily. Bombs pounded Rome. Cesare shook his head as he laid down the newspaper showing scenes of Sicilian locals kissing the soldiers and giving them a rapturous welcome, and Roman buildings in ruins.

"Liberators? Is that what they call themselves? Assassins,

more like."

But Martina couldn't help feeling a flicker of hope. A few days later, she opened the French doors onto the balcony and was hit by a barrage of noise coming from the village below. Shutters were banging open, people were running into the piazza shouting, whooping, embracing each other. A crowd was spilling out of Bernardo's bar, punching the air and chanting.

Ignoring Elena's demand to close the shutters before the mosquitoes got in, she ran down the path to the piazza where the crowd had swelled. People were dancing, some with children on their shoulders. Someone threw a picture of Mussolini out of a window and others stamped on it.

"What's going on?" Martina asked the doctor's wife.

The woman's face was pink with excitement. "Haven't you heard? *Il Duce*'s gone."

"Gone? Gone where? You mean he's resigned?"

"He had to. The Fascist Grand Council voted him out."

"Can they do that?"

"They've done it. His son-in-law among them. The King's dismissed *Il Duce*, and he's been arrested and taken somewhere. See how he likes it."

"Where've they taken him?"

"God knows. Who cares? This country's in bits because of him."

The atmosphere was jubilant, people unleashing their pent-up anger at the state of the country and the way the war was going. Bernardo couldn't serve the drinks fast enough.

"But what will happen now?" Martina asked anyone who would listen. "Are we still at war?"

The noise dropped around them as though someone had turned down the music at a party.

"The King's put Marshal Badoglio in charge," said Bernardo. "But the war's as good as over."

Whatever Badoglio was saying about continuing the war, most people felt the pact with Germany was finished. Italy would make peace with the Allies, chase out the Germans, and get rid of the Fascist scum. They'd had enough of the fighting. They wanted their sons and husbands back – those that were left.

Just audible over the din, a middle-aged woman said, "The English killed my two sons in Africa. How am I supposed to make friends with the people who did that?"

Another woman dragged her daughter away, shouting, "It's not over yet. The Germans aren't going anywhere, and they're not going to like seeing you behaving like this." Another was in tears, shaking her head. But it was hard not to get caught up in the elation. Martina hardly dared hope. An end to all this; an end to Fascism.

Despite the newspaper headlines insisting that "La Guerra Continua", Mussolini's arrest was taken as confirmation that Fascism was finished and the war would stop. Overnight, red flags appeared out of windows and Fascist emblems were torn down.

All through August, they were expecting to hear that Italy had reached an agreement with the Allies. But following the fall of Mussolini, the Axis troops evacuated from Sicily to the mainland. Meanwhile, strikes broke out all over the country, and in the town there were demonstrations with people holding banners saying "bread, peace and freedom".

On September 3rd, the Allies crossed to the mainland from Sicily, with more following at Salerno. Surely now it would only be a matter of time?

Five days later, huddled around the radio in Bar *La Fontana*, Martina and most of the Santa Zita residents listened to Badoglio's announcement: the Italian troops would cease all acts of hostility towards the Allied forces, but would oppose other forces.

"*Other forces?* Does that mean we're at war with Germany now?" Martina asked.

No-one seemed to have an answer. The man next to her shrugged. "If the Allies can help us get the Germans out of this country, it's fine by me."

But a veteran in the corner spat on the ground. "How can it be fine? We'll become the battlefield for them to fight it out on."

143

Martina felt a chill pass through her despite the heat. She pulled Sonia onto her lap. Bernardo gave the child a home-baked *cantuccio*. A woman chucked her under the chin. "Bambolina!"

Yes, at two years old, she was like a little doll. Her soft hair had grown just long enough to tie into bunches, and her arms and legs had turned a deep brown in the sun. She'd outgrown the dress Martina made for her out of some curtains, but Elena had tacked a ribbon around the bottom to make it last a bit longer.

She sat there sucking on the almond biscuit – it was a luxury she wasn't used to – following the animated speakers with her huge, dark eyes. If only the fighting would stop and Sonia could grow up in a peaceful country that wasn't torn apart by war and politics. Surely now there was a chance?

Chapter Thirty-Seven

"What did I tell you?" Cesare was sitting under the pergola, newspaper spread out before him.

Martina felt her stomach twist as she read. Hitler was incensed by what he saw as Badoglio's act of treason in signing the armistice. Although the Allied invasion took the Germans by surprise, they'd already been getting their troops in place and had had no difficulty seizing control of the Italian forces in Italy, south of France, and the Balkans. Within a few days, most of Italy except the far south found itself under German occupation. Their job was made easier by the fact that most of the Italian forces hadn't yet been told of the armistice, and had no clear orders about whether they were to resist their former allies.

Prisoner of war camps were abandoned by their Italian guards. The Nazis took over, sending the Allied inmates to German camps. POWs who escaped joined the growing resistance movement in the mountains, and either fought with the partisans or were helped out of the country despite warnings from the Germans that families caught sheltering a POW would be punished by death.

"Check the door to the chestnut tower's locked," Elena said. "We can't take the risk of someone sleeping in there."

The day after the armistice, to avoid capture by the Germans, Badoglio and the royal family moved to the coast where a government was set up under the protection of the Allies, leaving Rome to its fate.

And the following day – 10th September – the Germans took Rome. Seeing the tanks roll into the cities was a chilling sight, but things were about to get much worse.

A few days later, Cesare slapped the newspaper down with a flourish. "I told you he wasn't finished."

Martina caught her breath as she read the headline. Mussolini was free again. In a dramatic air mission, the Germans had rescued him from the mountain hotel in the Abruzzo mountains where he'd been held prisoner.

Silence fell as they contemplated what this might mean. Had it all been for nothing? If his Fascist government was reinstated, what would happen to the people who'd been celebrating its demise?

Eventually they heard that the new Italian Social Republic government had been set up in Salò, a place she'd never heard of up on Lake Garda.

"So, we've got two governments now?" Elena asked, frowning.

Martina bit her lip. She had to be careful what she said, even in Villa Leonida. Cesare still believed in Fascism, maintaining that the awful things that happened were due to men who'd "gone bad" and not the fault of the system. If she dared voice a different opinion, he'd explode.

As if he read her thoughts, he said, "My two sons died for this country. Your husband died for this country. How dare anyone say their sacrifice was for nothing?"

It must be happening in houses all over Italy – people within the same village or even the same family supporting different sides. Every Italian now had to make a choice, and that sometimes meant turning against the people closest to you, perhaps even killing them.

Chapter Thirty-Eight

1943

As the weeks passed and Italy officially declared war on Germany, fear dug in its claws. Thousands of Italian soldiers were drifting home, having abandoned their regiments. Would Gianni be among them? Now that Rome was under German control, those that weren't picked up and sent to labour camps in Germany had to choose between fighting for the Italian Fascist army or laying low and joining the partisans. Either way, they'd be fighting their own people.

After occupying Rome, the Nazis demanded a ransom from the Jewish people to be allowed to remain in the city, but in the end the money made no difference. They rounded up more than a thousand Jewish men, women, and children, and sent them away on trains. No-one expected to see them again.

"Surely the Pope could have done something to stop it?" Irena whispered.

"He must have tried," said Martina, but she couldn't feel sure of anything any more.

Week after week passed with little sign that the Allies were making any progress since they'd taken Naples in October. Nothing had changed much during the winter except that the cold and hunger had become unbearable.

"What's taking them so long?" Irena said in the bar one morning.

"The Allies should have stopped those German troops in Sicily before they evacuated to the mainland," said

Bernardo. "Now they're having a hard time fighting them off. They won't be able to do any more in this weather. My guess is they'll wait until spring."

The winter was wet and cold. Rain washed the earth down the mountain, turning the roads into rivers and waterlogging the crops. The land fell away now that the trees, which would have held it, had been chopped down. A renewed military offensive after Christmas didn't seem to make much progress and resulted in more stalemate. Those months seemed like an eternity, but with the terrible stories coming from the south Martina was starting to fear the liberators, too. The Allies' bombs had flattened towns, leaving those who survived homeless and starving.

Villages were evacuated as they were turned into battlegrounds. When they returned, people found only rubble where their homes had been. Many were starving but daren't risk going into their fields to get to their crops because of the mines the Germans had laid as they retreated. The thought that these things could be repeated around Santa Zita was too awful to contemplate.

The only solution was to focus on everyday things. Growing vegetables, feeding and slaughtering animals, and keeping the trails to the chestnut tower clear of the tenacious brambles and acacias that seemed to thrive despite the weather. Martina made clothes for Sonia out of scraps and used the remnants to patch her own clothes.

Apart from the emotional pain, there were the practical worries. Gianni's father was too weak to manage much of the work, and there were no young men left that could offer their help. After another fruitless shopping trip, Martina walked home hungry and slumped at the table, resting her head on her forearms.

"What did you get?" Elena asked.

She tried to keep her voice level. "Nothing. I got nothing."

Elena clutched the sides of her head. "It can't go on like this. What use is a ration card if there's nothing to buy with it? If we can't produce enough food of our own, we'll have nothing to exchange."

Although the fighting was still a long way off, the hills around Santa Zita reverberated with the sound of gunfire, with people shooting anything that they might be able to eat. Cesare's health deteriorated further due to the cold weather and the poor supply of medicines he needed for his condition.

Despite this, he'd impressed Martina with his resourcefulness over the past year. He could identify every type of mushroom and berry, and he shot and trapped all kinds of animals and birds for her to cook. Frogs, snails, squirrels all went in the pot. She often didn't know what she was eating, and didn't dare ask.

She hadn't really any idea how to cook these things, but they always ate them anyway, the four of them sitting in the lofty dining room whose grandeur seemed to make a mockery of their circumstances.

A knocking interrupted their meal.

"Who is it this time?" Elena moaned.

"I'll go."

Martina steeled herself before opening the door. You never knew these days who to expect.

"I'm sorry. We can't help you."

"Please," asked the elderly man. He was rake thin and wheezing from the climb up the hill. "I have money."

"We don't need money, we need food. I'm sorry."

She tried not to notice the tears in his eyes as she shut the door with a polite smile. What food they had, they couldn't store because getting hold of salt to preserve it was impossible. And anyway, they had to eat it before someone stole it or demanded it off them. If it wasn't the soldiers, it was the partisans hiding in the hills who helped themselves to chickens from the yard or the potatoes in the cantina. There'd been an endless trail of them coming to the house to ask for food, but even if she'd been able to help it was questionable whether she should.

"You never know who you're dealing with," Elena warned.

The men weren't all local. Half the time she didn't recognise them. They wore a variety of uniforms with the badges torn off. And the way they spoke made her both frightened and indignant. They had no ration cards, so had no choice but to beg, and she understood that. But if they didn't get what they wanted, their behaviour could soon turn threatening. They talked of duty, but she didn't have any sisterly feelings for them.

"Everyone seems to think they have more right to our own food than us," she fumed, clearing away the dishes.

"Don't be taken in," Elena said. "A family in Santo Stefano opened the door to some partisans asking for a meal and a bed for the night. They were found the next day in blood-soaked sheets. The robbers had slashed their throats and taken everything."

Chapter Thirty-Nine

Because the balcony at Villa Leonida was so high and the ground below fell away to almost a sheer drop, the oranges were not stolen from the tree at night, unlike the fruit and vegetables in the orchard below and the animals in the yard. So, despite the scarcity of food, Martina was able to give Sonia oranges to eat most of the year, which must surely be the reason for her daughter's lovely skin and clear eyes. At least in that regard she could feel proud.

She hugged the little girl close, feeling Sonia's ribs as she wound her bony arms around her waist. Her own ribs were visible, too, and she was walking more slowly these days, like an old woman. She tried not to look in the mirror. It was always a shock to see the face that stared back – the limp hair and the hollow cheekbones. She'd passed the stage when she could get away with having a fashionably small waist. Scrawny was a more accurate description. She covered her chest with a sense of self-loathing.

If Gianni was really out there somewhere, it was no surprise he hadn't come back to her. He'd hardly find her attractive these days, would he? Nonetheless, she continued to care religiously for the orange tree.

From the balcony, Martina could see the whole of the valley, as the river meandered its way through the town, and she could count no less than seven tiny villages perched on top of the surrounding mountains, clinging precariously to the side of the hill. They looked as though they might topple down at any moment.

But at night, when the curfew was imposed and the villages under blackout, all she could see was stars. She could hear the planes, though, and the occasional thud of bombs as the fighting began to intensify between the Allied troops and the Germans. It was surely only a matter of time now before things reached a climax.

Chapter Forty

IRENA

Everyone knew, or thought they knew, people who belonged with the partisans up in the hills around Santa Zita. From time to time someone was arrested for their views. They were usually found later, dumped on their doorstep in soiled clothes, caked in blood. Afterwards, they either went into hiding or joined the Fascists, although whether they'd really changed sides was anyone's guess.

There were Fascists who joined the partisans and passed on secrets, too. There were so many double and triple agents, the confusion was terrible. You didn't know who to trust. And it wasn't just the men – women and schoolchildren were involved, too, smuggling weapons in prams and delivering food parcels by bicycle. Or telling on their neighbours.

Someone told me Gianni was with the partisans. I had no idea how they knew, or if it was just gossip that had got out of hand, or if it might be true. I said nothing to Martina about it. It seemed a strange thing that he could be living so close to the villa and in such primitive conditions, but I was starting to think that anything was possible.

We were coming through the arch into the piazza when we saw the trucks.

"What's going on?" Martina asked one of the brothers from the I Tre Fratelli *restaurant.*

"The Germans have arrived. They're helping themselves to food, so you'd better hide your animals," he said.

"That's not a good idea," muttered Bernardo, wiping

down his bar tables. "You'll only anger them. Refusing them anything is taken as an act of disloyalty."

But over the next few weeks we got used to seeing them in town and sometimes even up in the village, sitting in the restaurant or propping up Bernardo's bar. They played cards with locals, sang songs, and passed round photographs of their families. Unlike us, they could afford to buy meals and drink good wine.

Once as we were passing, we saw them handing out sweets to children. Sonia put out her hand but Martina yanked it away. She burst into tears.

"Let's see what's going on over there," I said to distract her.

A little knot was gathered around the door of Santa Zita church on the other side of the piazza. As we got closer, we saw it was a list of crimes punishable by public hanging: being caught out after curfew, tearing down posters, helping partisans. We tried not to show much emotion because Sonia was with us.

"They wouldn't really kill someone for things like this," whispered Marisa, wife of the outspoken Giorgio. "It's just their way of getting us to comply."

Her companion agreed, "They need us on their side. They can't afford to turn us against them."

"I wouldn't bet on it," said the blacksmith's daughter.

As we turned away, a German soldier, flint-eyed, pink cheeked, and beardless, offered us cigarettes. It was disconcerting to see how young he looked.

"No thanks," said Martina.

But she said it less sharply than she normally would have done. Despite my feelings about the Germans, his accent made me smile. I had the feeling he didn't want to be there any more than we wanted him there.

"What's your name?" he asked Martina.

She studied him for a moment, then told him, eyeing him coolly before adding, "What's yours?"

"It's Dieter."

"Short for Dietrich, I suppose?"

"That's right." His cheeks turned even pinker. *"I just wanted to tell you that I find you devastatingly beautiful and I would be honoured if you'd show me around the town."*

He was so young – a boy really. Martina burst out laughing. "I'm afraid I'm busy."

But he could tell she wasn't, and she didn't move away. He laughed, too, a little disconcerted but not apparently offended.

"Come on, I'm sure you'd like one of these."

"No thanks."

But on our way back to the villa, we found that he'd slipped some cigarettes into her bag anyway. I was furious with her afterwards. That list of crimes and punishments was still going around my head.

"What were you doing back there, flirting with that boy? You saw the notice on the church. You shouldn't get too close."

She just tossed her head the way she used to. "And you shouldn't take everything so seriously."

It made me think I didn't know her as well as I used to. Living at Villa Leonida had changed her. After that, the young German often called out to her, and she'd reply rudely but with a smile that implied she wasn't entirely serious. I'm pretty sure I caught her turning her head sometimes as she walked off, to check that he was still watching her, and I noticed that from time to time she had new stockings and lipstick and other luxuries.

Although I didn't believe like the others that she looked down on us, I think living in Villa Leonida she felt a bit removed sometimes from things that were happening. Even though she was my oldest friend, I sometimes felt I should be careful what I said to her.

I had a sinking feeling that she would get us into trouble one day.

Chapter Forty-One

MARTINA

Looking up from the piazza, Martina saw men in uniform standing on the balcony of Villa Leonida.

"They're looking for somewhere to accommodate some of their men," Bernardo told her, following her gaze. Looks like they've have chosen your place. You'll have to find somewhere else to live."

"What? They can't do that."

He smiled grimly. "No? How are you going to stop them?"

Her heart thumping, she raced up the path. With its commanding position and views from either side of the ridge, Villa Leonida was the obvious choice. The men passed her on their way out. They greeted her courteously, but one of them made what she guessed was a suggestive remark because the others laughed.

She found Elena alone in the drawing room. They'd been polite and respectful, she said. But the idea of being turned out or squeezed into a couple of rooms while foreign soldiers had the run of the rest of their family home, was unbearable.

"The strange thing is, they decided they didn't want it."

Eventually, and much to Martina's surprise, they chose a house across the valley which had a similar view of the main town, and a bit more of the road that led north. After the initial relief, Cesare seemed quite affronted by what he took to be a snub, and for days went around muttering, "This house is in much better condition," and, "That house has always been damp. It's full of mould spores."

"I hope it is," Elena said.

He saw the funny side then, but it didn't stop him saying, "Of course, it doesn't get the amount of sun that ours gets. It's no surprise that they've never been able to grow much over there."

"Well, you can't expect Germans to notice something like that," she replied. "They get food whenever they want it. The two brothers in the restaurant don't even bring them a bill. I don't expect they'll pass up on the opportunity next time, though.".

In any case, they had to plan for the possibility of the house being requisitioned. Cesare and Elena insisted they would stay. "Not you, though," she said. "You couldn't possibly, with the baby. I couldn't let Sonia grow up in a house full of foreign soldiers. You'll have to take her away from here."

But where could they go? Martina's family was living in a flat that was much too small for them already since they had moved to be closer to her father's work at the munitions factory. The little terraced house in Via della Chiesa in which she'd grown up stood empty and in a very poor state. It wouldn't do Sonia's breathing any good to live there in that damp atmosphere. But Elena started talking about sending Sonia to stay with some of her relatives until after the war. Martina was at least able to put her foot down about that – wherever Sonia went, she would go, too. But it was getting harder to imagine a future in which they could all be happy.

Chapter Forty-Two

When Carlo got back from the restaurant, his mother denied any knowledge of the recording device.

"I don't know what you're talking about. I've never seen anything like that."

The strange thing was that when he looked under the chair for her reading glasses which she'd dropped, he saw it. At first, he'd thought it was just another example of her forgetfulness, but the suspicion crept in – she'd done it deliberately. He slipped it into his pocket, so he could listen to it later.

Martina was playing a dangerous game stringing this young German along. If you want to know the truth, it reminded me of how she used to be with Gianni before she married him. His hopefulness – and the hopelessness of the situation. She'd got her fingers burned last time, but this was so much worse.

We saw less of each other those days. Our lives had diverged, and it was harder to find things in common. I had my job, she had the villa. But I was happy at school. I loved being able to teach, seeing that magical moment when it all made sense to a child – the light coming on in their eyes. I told myself that should be enough. I didn't need to fall in love to be happy.

But then, just when I thought my life wasn't going to change, it was turned upside down. It's a terrible thing to say, but I thanked my Great Aunt Lucia over and over for dying when she did. If she hadn't, it would never have happened. My mother said we must go to her funeral, and that would mean staying with my grandmother for a few days in a town several miles away, although she wasn't in the best of health herself. Oh, the palaver of packing up to go there! My mother acted as though we were going for a month, but we hardly ever went anywhere in those days. And with the lack of public transport, it took forever – and a few favours – to get us there.

I don't remember much about the funeral – when you get to my age, you've been to so many they tend to get mixed up – but afterwards we all crammed into my grandmother's dark little flat in a cramped street off the marketplace. It was an old person's flat, stuffed with ornaments and heavy furniture, and a smell of polish and cheap tobacco. A clock ticked away somewhere, chiming every quarter hour. We crowded around the table in the dingy living room – it was so highly polished you could see our reflections. It was strange to see so many faces from my childhood - the same and yet different.

Don't you think it's funny the way people behave after funerals? There's a false jollity I find hard to muster. I never feel like eating or drinking – it seems disrespectful. But my aunts had pooled their ration books and laid on a feast, and it looked quite grand. Although to tell the truth, the food was quite meagre.

It was the last place you'd imagine falling in love.

It was obvious by now that Irena no longer considered the Dictaphone to be Carlo's property. He felt like a boy again, sneaking biscuits when her back was turned. It wasn't what she was saying that intrigued him so much as the way she talked. It was as if she had forgotten what he'd left her the machine for. As though she were talking to the machine and not to him. She'd established a relationship with the Dictaphone that he could never hope to penetrate.

He laughed at himself. Was he really jealous of a machine?

My mother's cousin, whom I called Aunty Aurelia, had her son Roberto with her. He was a doctor and had been wounded himself out on the Russian Front. He looked unharmed to me, but I imagined the wound must be on the

159

inside and was given strict orders not to talk to him about it.

I'd met him before at other family events, probably other funerals, when I was much younger. I hadn't paid much attention to him. He was one of three boys, and I remembered his brothers as being bolder, funnier, louder. Looking at him now, I wondered how that could have been.

We had soup – one of those robust Tuscan soups, with cabbage and beans and pasta, that could be stretched to suit any number of people. We ate in silence, except for a clinking of spoons in china bowls and the guttural sound of my Aunty Vittoria blowing over hers to cool it down. Then gradually everyone started talking at once, the way they always had.

Roberto was quieter, more thoughtful than I remembered. A little older than me, very well-educated. He was good-looking but not in the way that would turn heads. He wouldn't be the first person you noticed in a room. But he'd be the one you'd remember afterwards. Little things would come back to you over time – a twitch of the eyebrow; a remark that hadn't registered; just a recognition somehow, of a space that he'd filled and that wasn't there any longer.

I wish I could describe him for you. I want you to be able to see him as I did. I was an avid reader back then, as you know, but I've never been a writer. Never spent time building a picture out of words. And even if I could, I doubt I could do him justice. But anyway, I'll try.

There was something about him, a quiet kind of intensity. An understated beauty that revealed itself slowly and imperceptibly. It may have had something to do with his features being so symmetrical. Or the subtlety of his expressions or the light that flickered in his eyes, as though he were harbouring some private joke.

You had to ask yourself, was his hair brown or blond? Were his eyes green or brown? The answer, of course, was something in between. That was the thing about him – nothing was obvious. Perhaps that's what made him so interesting to me – he was a blank canvas onto which I could project all my dreams. Perhaps that's how it was for *everyone.*

I watched him sitting squeezed between my elderly aunts, listening to their banal chatter, politely fielding their enquiries, and responding to their endless list of ailments with patience and courtesy when he must have had many better things to do and more interesting people to spend time with.

And that's when I fell in love.

Carlo had the uneasy feeling that he was intruding now. Should he switch off and leave his mother to his memories? Probably. But he wasn't going to.

Chapter Forty-Three

The more I looked, the more I realised how attractive he was. It dawned on me slowly over the evening, the little things about him that made him handsome. When he smiled at you, you had that sudden sensation of being bathed in warmth and light.

With his colouring, if he'd lived in the north he probably would have been pasty, but as it was he was gold, from his skin to his hair to his eyes. If I'd been able to see beneath his clothes, I guessed his whole body would be golden.

"Irena!" My mother's voice burst through my thoughts. "Are you even listening to Giovanna's story?"

Giovanna's story was long and tedious, but I forced myself to listen.

"Gangrene it was," she repeated for my benefit. "His toes completely black. Terrible. He had to cut them off himself. It was the only way to survive."

I looked at my aunt as she talked. Her face was scrunched up like an old paper bag, the lines channelled into her skin, bearing witness to her careless attitude to the sun. She was the cautionary tale in our family, the most rebellious of the sisters, the one least willing to accept convention and inherited wisdom. The one I was accused of being like.

She was always held up as an example of the ill that can befall a person who doesn't stick to the proper path. Next to her, he looked like a god. He could have had any number of women hanging round him, but instead he let this old crone bend his ear.

My mother, like the rest of them, insisted on running through every illness and near-death experience she had ever had. He listened, the occasional twitch at the corners of his mouth the only sign of amusement – or was it exasperation?

Why did he put up with it? I had the idea it was for my sake, but perhaps I saw what I wanted to see. I wished they'd stop. From time to time his eyes flicked towards me, a ghost of a smile playing around his lips. I gave him what I hoped was a sympathetic smile in return, but in all honesty, it was probably more of a simper.

I had the sense my mother and Aunty Aurelia might have been trying to set me up with him, but dismissed it as nonsense. They were as resigned as I was to my staying single. Every family needed a daughter who stayed. I couldn't say I relished the idea of dedicating my later years to caring for elderly relatives, but it seemed a long way off, and in those days it was hard to see beyond the war anyway.

As the evening went on, it became clear that he was as passionate about literature as I was. I'd never met anyone who loved books in the way I did. It was fantastic to be able to talk about something in a story, and for him to get it straight away and quote something back at me.

Nobody understood what we were talking about. The others gradually lost interest and carried on their conversations around us. It was as though a spell had been cast and they were outside the invisible dome that encased us. I felt them all melting away in a blur of background colour.

I loved his constrained enthusiasm, the way he chose his words carefully. It made me feel I was only seeing a glimpse of what he really was, and there was much more to learn. The only time I saw a chink in that restraint was when someone suggested that God had saved him from his injuries for a purpose.

"I don't believe that," he said.

"Well, if it wasn't God, it was fate," Aunt Vittoria told him.

His face tightened. He rounded on her a little too sharply. "Do you really think it's all pre-ordained? I'm

163

afraid that's nonsense."

He must have felt the need to explain, because he said in a kinder tone, "The only fate I believe in is the choices people make."

He caught my eye as he said it and I felt a thrill run through me. It was as though he realised that I alone in the room would understand.

The talk turned back to my poor dead aunt until my mother eventually pointed out that my grandmother was tired, and we must leave her in peace. There was a scrape of chairs as everyone stood up to leave. I thought I caught a look of disappointment as he said goodbye.

Chapter Forty-Four

The next afternoon, he called round. I think it was on some pretext of checking on my grandmother.

"I'm glad I caught you," he said. "I was wondering if you'd like to come for a walk? I could show you the fresco I was telling you about last night."

I tried to make it look as though I had other possibilities to consider, but I didn't want to leave it too long in case he changed his mind, so I grabbed my hat and we went.

Sitting in his car after visiting the hypermarket, Carlo switched off the machine. He wondered why his mother had tried to hide the device from him that afternoon. It was obvious now she distrusted his motives. Was she right to? Perhaps, in a way. How much right does anyone have to someone else's thoughts? But surely a son should be able to learn from his mother, even if that son is old enough to be retired?

Perhaps she felt embarrassed by something she had done or said back then. He had often suspected, now he came to think of it, that she was holding something back despite instilling in him the need to always be truthful. It wasn't really a surprise. She was his mother, and adults kept a lot of things to themselves. But now he had the sense that he was close to finding it.

As he let himself in, Cass came out of the kitchen looking flustered. "Where've you been?"

"Sorry, I got held up." Carlo kissed her cheek. How could he admit that he'd been sitting in the car park listening to the Dictaphone?

She wasn't fooled. She bit her lip and then decided to say

what was on her mind. "Carlo, I know your mother's past life is interesting, but you have to remember we live in the present, even if she doesn't. I mean, come on – we've got a restaurant to run."

"I'm sorry. I'm here now."

She gave him a resigned smile and handed him a plate of bruschetta to take out.

**

IRENA

It started with that first walk the day after my grandmother's funeral. We wandered down the streets to the main piazza. It was quiet. There must have been other people – children playing, mothers pushing prams, old men playing cards under the trees – but I didn't notice any of them. It was such a release to be away from the clucking of my grandmother and the smell of cabbage in that dingy flat.

I noticed for the first time how tall he was. I was aware of my heels clicking on the cobbles, the rustling of his coat as we walked. We brushed against each other as we walked, as though a magnetic force was pulling us together however hard we tried to correct it.

What did we talk about? Everything, I suppose - books, art, history, the war, after the war. Although, there were moments when he seemed to retreat into his own thoughts and I wondered what scenes he was revisiting. It came to me gradually that beneath his calm exterior was a tortured soul that only I could reach. Perhaps that's how he made all women feel.

He took me to see the frescoes he'd told me about the evening before. They were as lovely as he'd described. The faces, the hands, so real the centuries seemed to fall away. It was as if they'd been painted yesterday. Their beauty was almost frightening in the dim light of the church. But something he said took me by surprise.

"It's a tragedy, all these works of art being left to rot. Some of them won't survive this bloody war. That painting in your village of the Santa Maria del Soccorso is in a shocking state these days."

"How do you know that?" I asked. "I thought you hadn't been to Santa Zita since you were a child?"

He looked thrown and I felt bad about challenging him, but he was spared an explanation as the door opened and a party of school children filed in to escape the cold weather. Later, when I asked him about it, he just shrugged and said, "I must have heard about it from someone."

Afterwards, we crossed the river and climbed up the steps to marvel at the view. It was as though it had been put there for us. We sat in some gardens that had been turned into allotments until the air grew cold. He noticed the goose bumps on my arms and put his coat around my shoulders as we walked back.

When we first kissed, I felt weightless, as if I'd been lifted off the ground. I don't know how I managed to stay upright. I've no idea how long we stood there in each other's arms. But afterwards, when I looked up at him, his eyes were searching mine with that strange, intense expression that he had, as if he was searching for something. I suppose he thought he'd found it.

And so that's how I found myself falling head over heels in love at an age when several of my friends were already widows. It was amazing to be so happy. So giddily, violently in love. Every time I looked at him, I felt a surge of joy.

That night after the walk, I lay awake for hours going over everything that had happened and things that I hoped would happen. It was wonderful that this man loved me. Unthinkable that I should feel so happy. I couldn't sleep, I had such energy. Every nerve in my body seemed alive. I wanted to tell everyone, wanted to shout it from the top of the clock tower. And I wanted it to be my secret.

I questioned if it was right to feel this way, to be embarking on this adventure when friends of mine had lost the loves of their lives. What had I done to deserve such

167

happiness? But then I told myself, this was my chance. I'd waited long enough. I grabbed it with both hands.

Chapter Forty-Five

MARTINA

Christmas came and went. It wasn't the festival Martina remembered as a child. There'd never been much money, but she remembered the thrill of anticipation as the Befana's visit drew near, and the small gifts she'd found in her stocking on Epiphany had never been disappointing. That year she'd been given the doll, she couldn't believe how lucky she was. She rushed out into the piazza to show Irena and found her hugging an identical one. It seemed miraculous that the Befana should know they'd want the same thing.

This year she'd made Sonia a little doll out of scraps of fabric and put in an orange from the tree and felt full of shame. Sonia was delighted, but it wasn't right. She'd make it up to her after the war.

One morning she was woken by the rumbling of an engine in the piazza below Villa Leonida. It was unusual to hear a truck so early in the morning. Looking out of the window, she saw a family being brought from their house and herded onto the covered vehicle.

At the last moment the woman looked up in Martina's direction as though she'd sensed she was being watched. Martina inhaled sharply as she recognized Luisa, with whom she'd been at school. She hadn't even realised Luisa was Jewish. Perhaps it went back further, to her grandparents. Under the old system, perhaps that hadn't counted, or perhaps the authorities had turned a blind eye to it.

She froze in horror. She wanted to throw open the window and shout at the soldiers, ask what the hell they thought they were doing, demand they at least let the children stay. But what was the use? It wouldn't do any good. She stepped back from the window, turned away and closed the shutters and slumped to the floor, hating herself.

It was at times like this she missed Irena most. Irena was one of the few people to whom she knew she could always talk freely, and they'd have been able to speak about what she'd seen. It was so hard to know who else to trust these days. Irena had been away a few weeks now, and she missed her so badly. Surely they weren't still dealing with her aunt's affairs? Whatever was keeping her, she wished it would go away. There were so many things she wanted to tell her about, and writing a letter wasn't the same. But she did write them nonetheless, although she had to be careful how she worded things just in case the letter was intercepted.

For one thing, she'd heard more rumours about Gianni.

***

IRENA

We met a few times after that first walk to do the passeggiata around town, and then it became a daily event. My grandmother had a bad turn so my mother suggested we stay on for a few weeks until she was better. I wasn't complaining.

One day, he turned up with theatre tickets. "There's a performance of Turandot *this evening. I was hoping you might like to go?"*

It was the most wonderful evening, although to be quite honest I don't remember much about the opera. The theatre was a spectacle in itself, all red and gold, and the costumes were extraordinary and the music sublime. For those few hours it was even possible to forget the war. I kept gazing

170

around and thinking I couldn't believe my luck being there with him, as though I now belonged to the glamorous set. But what I remember most from that evening is what it felt like to be part of a couple. I felt invincible.

I don't remember how we spent all those days and weeks that followed. I only know that my feelings for him grew stronger each time I saw him. I'd have done anything for those eyes, that smile.

I was lying to myself for most of that time. I realise that now. Perhaps I already knew it was hopeless, but I'd fallen madly in love. And when you love like that, you'll believe anything you want to.

It could never have worked. I loved him too much.

Chapter Forty-Six

IRENA

I think I knew even from that first kiss that he wasn't being honest with me, but I chose to ignore it, that little worm of doubt that tried to drag me back down to reality. I think he loved me as much as he said he did. He said so many lovely things.

But there were times when he seemed dislocated and was hard to reach. I supposed he was being driven mad by horrific memories from the conflict, ones he couldn't share with me or anyone. I believed, though, that in time I'd be able to help him get over them.

Looking back now, I wonder if the truth was that he was with me because, like me, he was scared of ending up alone. After all the misery he'd seen in the war, lives cut short and others irreparably damaged, perhaps he wanted to secure some happiness, some normality for afterwards when it was all over. And I was as normal as you could hope to find. I was so proud of him. I couldn't wait to get back to Santa Zita so I could tell Martina about him, and for him to come and visit so that I could show him off. It was nice to be back in the village, but I knew I'd miss him dreadfully. Martina knew something was up as soon as she saw me.

"What is it?" she asked me. "There's something, I can tell. You're hopeless at keeping secrets."

"It's nothing."

"It isn't. It's someone, isn't it? Come on, you must tell me."

"Not until you promise that you won't work your charms

on him."

She rolled her eyes and said of course she wouldn't and then turned quite serious, and I saw the hurt in her eyes. "I'd never take anyone from you, not even if they looked like Rudolf Valentino."

I told myself I was being unfair. Things were different anyway now. She had Sonia to think of, and Gianni's parents.

And I was stupid enough to believe it.

Cass's voice broke into Carlo's thoughts. "Carlo, can I remind you again this is your restaurant? Could you *please* give me a hand out here?"

"Of course, I'm on my way." He barely heard her as he pressed the button again.

After a few weeks of being apart, he asked me to marry him. Said he knew it was sudden but he didn't believe in hanging around once he'd made a decision that he was certain was the right one. As a doctor, he'd been trained to think clearly and make up his mind quickly.

He said he'd spent too much time too close to death in Russia. Patching up wounded soldiers and then getting wounded himself. But he was alive, and he wanted to get on with living.

I asked him about his past. There'd been other women, of course, but they'd been a certain type. "I know what I want now," he said. "I want what's real."

The truth is I misread what he said because I wanted to. I thought 'real' implied something wonderful and pure that other lovers only aspired to. That day when he asked me to marry him, I wanted to throw my arms around him and shout 'Yes!' But I didn't want him to know how desperate I'd become, so I made him wait two days before giving him my answer.

The recording broke off. Perhaps his mother had grown tired or was overcome by emotion. Perhaps a simple call of nature or the need to sleep. Carlo had no way of knowing how much time had elapsed before she added the next words.

There were signs. There were always signs, if I'm honest. He so often gave the impression he was holding something back, but I thought in time I could draw it out of him. That I was the only one who could. And that would make us stronger.

How could I have seen that it would tear us apart?

***

"Carlo, this is ridiculous. It isn't healthy."

Cass was standing in the doorway, bleary-eyed, her hair wild. He almost laughed.

"It can't be doing your mother any good, and it certainly isn't doing you any good. You need to come to bed, not sit down here listening to that thing for hours on end. How do you know these memories are even real?"

"All right, all right. I'll just be a few minutes."

She was right, of course. But he couldn't stop now.

174

Chapter Forty-Seven

MARTINA

Irena led Martina through the crowded room, which smelled of cigarette smoke and was full of laughter and the clinking of glasses rising above the music from the gramophone. A flurry of colour, a flash of pearls, a swish of hair – she hadn't been to a party in such a long time, but here for this short time it was almost possible to forget there was a war on.

He was standing with his back to her, talking with a group of people. She barely noticed Irena putting her hand on his shoulder, but she saw his profile as he turned to put his arm attentively around her. Martina's breath stalled as she recognised him.

The last time she'd seen him she'd felt his lips on hers in the street outside the café in town, the day she saw the old man beaten to death. Just a kiss, and yet it had lasted all these years – the memory and the thought of what could have been.

"Darling, this is Martina. I've been dying for you two to meet."

Martina didn't remember Irena's flushed face and shining eyes and the breathless tone in her voice until after. She felt the ground give way just as she had the last time she saw him. Yet she was still standing there, staring in dumb incredulity. Recovering herself, she took the hand he was offering, and shook it as though they'd never met before. Did he squeeze hers a little too firmly? She thought she saw a jolt of recognition in his eyes, as she felt her own face catch fire. As they exchanged niceties, she didn't dare look into those familiar toffee-coloured eyes.

This isn't happening. It can't be him. Here. With her instead of me.

It was clear from the looks her best friend gave him that Irena was in love. She seemed different that evening – softer, lighter. She'd done something different with her hair – twisted it into a chignon. She laughed more. Why hadn't Martina noticed before how attractive she'd become?

Roberto. So, he had a name. She thought she caught him looking at her once or twice as the conversation went on, a slight twist of the head, weighing her up, trying to work out where he'd seen her before. All the time she was wondering if he'd really reacted in the way she thought he had.

Do you remember?

He was the same and yet not the same. Perhaps the nose was a little longer, the eyes a little greener than she remembered. But in essence, he was the person she'd pictured in her mind over the years and felt she knew so well. She'd spent more time with him than with her husband, but only in her head. In reality they'd only ever exchanged a few words; she when she was so fragile and stupid. The absurdity of it struck her. There was no reason why he should remember her from the poster-spitting incident. Why should it have made any impression on him?

There were one or two moments in the whole evening when they could have talked, but it was hardly the right time to begin a conversation they'd not be able to finish, so they continued to make small talk, as though they were strangers. She caught him looking at her once or twice, perhaps trying to work out where he'd seen her before. All the time she was wondering if he really had reacted the way she thought he had.

She watched Irena lead him away to dance, her hand on his back, his arm draped protectively around her broad shoulders. He kissed the top of her head absently.

Martina had a sudden vision of being in his arms as he helped her across the piazza. Of feeling enveloped in those arms as he kissed her, feeling his sweet breath on her face. She needed air.

Excusing herself, she pushed through the bodies pressing against her until she half fell through the doors onto the loggia.

"Well?" Irena asked eventually, appearing next to her, a Martini in her hand. "What do you think?"

The garden below them was bathed in moonlight. A couple sat on the bench by the pond. The tip of their cigarettes flickered like fireflies.

"Yes. A lovely man. Lucky you!" Martina managed to say with a smile, and drew on her own cigarette. Irena's eyes were shining. Her own reflection in them was pale and sunken.

"I'm so glad you like him," Irena said. "He's asked me to marry him."

Chapter Forty-Eight

The words struck Martina like an artillery shell. This couldn't be happening. Around her everyone carried on chatting, dancing, laughing. Oblivious. They had no idea they were part of this bizarre scene.

"Congratulations," she said later, when she found Roberto next to her. She'd intended the greeting to sound cool and breezy, but as she spoke, it sounded like an accusation.

He looked startled but recovered quickly. "Yes. Thank you."

After an unbearable pause, he added, "Irena tells me you lost your husband in the fighting. I'm sorry."

Martina looked away. So, he knew she was a widow. What else had Irena told him about her? He must think her insensitive, disrespectful, living it up at parties while her husband was in his grave. *If he really was, and not in the arms of some whore.*

"It was a long time ago."

"That doesn't make it easier." It felt like an admonishment.

"But you have a daughter – a lovely little girl, from what I hear. I suppose it helps."

Yes, she had Sonia. She could never wish Sonia away. But was this who she was now? A widow and a mother; no longer a young woman in her own right, with needs, desires, ambition? Was that how he saw her? She had to say something. Had to see if he had made the connection.

"You realise we've met before?" Her voice sounded too bright in her ears. She twisted the wine glass round in her hands.

It tumbled out, the story of the old man spitting at the poster and the way the younger men had kicked him to death right in front of her, just a metre or so away from where she was standing. How she'd fainted and he'd helped her. She made light of it, tried to make it an entertaining story – except, of course, it wasn't funny. Someone had died. She didn't mention the kiss.

He looked as though he were only half listening. He was probably searching the crowd for someone more interesting – or less deluded – to talk to.

"Don't you remember?" she found herself asking, trying hard to keep the note of annoyance out of her voice.

His golden eyes met hers for a moment. "Now you mention it, I think I do. Well, I'm glad to have been of some help anyway. How extraordinary you should remember."

"Not at all," she said, feeling the colour rise in her cheeks. "I have a good memory. I remember most things."

He smiled. "That's quite a gift. I'll have to be careful what I say to you."

Another silence. She'd obviously made him feel uncomfortable. She'd wanted to. So why didn't it bring her any satisfaction? Anger she knew she wasn't entitled to swelled in her chest. It clearly meant nothing at all to him. Over the years when she'd imagined meeting him again, the conversation had taken so many different turns but never this one of unbearable politeness and indifference.

She wanted to shout at him, ask him how it had felt to take advantage of a pregnant woman whose husband was fighting for his life, for all their lives. She ought to let Irena know what sort of person he was. Instead, she turned and walked away.

She felt his eyes on her back. If she turned now, what would she see? Would he be staring at her as intently as he had in the street that day? But when she allowed herself to look, he'd fallen into conversation with someone else.

Over the next few weeks she saw him several times with Irena. Now that Irena had moved back to Santa Zita, he would become a regular visitor. It was hardly Irena's fault.

179

Oblivious to the whole thing, she was gloriously tactless, coming out with gauche remarks, placing a proprietorial hand on his arm, or fondling the back of his neck while they were talking. She made it clear she wanted them all to be friends, while having no idea she was making that impossible.

"Oh, but Martina loved that film, too. That's just what Martina says. How funny – Roberto had a similar experience when he was a child, didn't you?"

It should have been easy to form a friendship, to put that one silly incident out of her mind and get past the awkwardness to a stage where they could laugh, even invite Irena to laugh with them at the ridiculousness of it all. But somehow, he made that impossible. Roberto fell comfortably into conversation with most people he met. He was friendly in his quiet way, and people spoke well of him after he'd left.

Yet with Martina, he remained aloof, almost rude – but never actually rude. That would have made things easier, because then she'd have felt entitled to hate him. She wanted to shake him, break through his maddening restraint, smash down the wall he'd built around himself. What was he hiding anyway?

But what did they have to talk about? They were opposites. All they had in common was the fact that she had once fainted, and he'd helped her – which, being a doctor, he would naturally do. And then he'd kissed her – which, being a doctor, he should not have done.

He must be embarrassed by the incident now. It was painful for her, too, thinking about her overblown reaction, how it had formed her thinking over the years, how she'd constructed this ridiculous fantasy. How could it have had such impact? Of all the things that had happened to her in her life, why should it stand out?

Because, for God's sake, she told herself as she watched Roberto and Irena saunter down the lane hand-in-hand, it was never what it seemed. It had never been about him, not really. It had been about her feelings for Gianni, but it had somehow taken on a life of its own. She began to dread seeing him, feeling the chill of his polite indifference.

Chapter Forty-Nine

MARTINA

In January, the Allies made a renewed offensive but seemed to hit another stalemate. The weather improved slightly, but for much of the time an icy mist hung around the village of Santa Zita.

"We were saying it reminds us of that poem we studied at school. You know the one?" Irena said, when she joined them on a walk.

Martina had to admit she didn't. Irena was at her most irritating when she was like this, trying to shut Martina out with her superior memory of things she'd learned. Perhaps she and Roberto were better suited, with all their talk about art and books. But the thought only lasted for a moment.

Irena carried on, "About the valley submerged in a vast grey sea, no waves, no beaches…"

Roberto stopped, his hands dug into his coat pockets. "Oh yes, and something about the eternal, echoing footsteps…"

And, laughing, they both said at the same time, "Down I stared but I saw nothing, no-one looking back…"

Martina curled her hands into fists inside the sleeves of her coat. Was he blind? How could he not see? Just because someone remembered something that someone else had written didn't make them an interesting person.

She watched them go on ahead, not even registering that was she no longer with them. It was happening more and more these days – making her feel like an intruder. They walked swinging hands, Irena's broad calves planted heavily on the ground, her wide hips swaying. That girlish laugh she'd developed. What did he see in her? This was a new Irena, and Martina didn't much like her.

**

Anxiety about the future of the country soared as the Germans, under threat, showed resistors no mercy. In March 1944, a partisan bomb in Rome hit a column of SS policemen who were marching and singing through the city. The Germans retaliated by rounding up at random three hundred and thirty-five men and boys and taking them away to be executed.

The Nazis made it plain that similar reprisals would be carried out on any town that showed disloyalty, and at the ratio of ten civilians for every soldier killed. Looking around her at people in the piazza – a grandmother sitting on a chair outside her door, a mother hanging washing out from her window, three small children playing a skipping rope game – it was impossible to imagine something like that happening in Santa Zita, and too awful to contemplate.

2018

"What are you doing? Leave that alone," said Irena. "I lost it earlier. Someone's been moving my things about."

She looked suspiciously in Cass's direction. Carlo had sensed her mood as soon as he walked in. She had that closed look, sitting bent over in her chair as though she were withdrawing into herself, gazing at a point on the floor, not really acknowledging him.

He made several stabs at conversation, but she waved him away like an annoying insect.

"Are you too hot in here?" he asked. "I can open the window."

She shook her head. "I'm fine. I can't stand being cold, you know that."

"I was wondering if you'd like to come out for a drive?"

Her face furrowed. "Whatever for?"

He sighed. "Because it's a beautiful day, and we're going to be run off our feet in the restaurant over the weekend because of Easter. I was going to the azalea festival. Thought you might like to come along?"

His mother turned away. "Not today. I'm too busy."

He tried to conceal the smile in his voice. "Doing what?"

She huffed and waved her arm as though she wouldn't know where to start.

He handed her a couple of books. "Cass thought you might like these detective stories. She loves Michele Giuttari."

Irena stared at him in bewilderment. "Who's Cass?"

He felt his smile fade. "My wife. Your daughter-in-law. She lives here, remember?"

After a while he tried to kiss her cheek, but she ducked away. "Well, I'd better go. I'll bring you an azalea. It will look nice by the window."

He wasn't sure if she'd heard. She was humming an old tune *un baccio a mezzanotte.* She stopped, frowning. "What happened to that girl?"

"What girl?"

"She looked terrified. Tried to deny it. Said it was something she ate. I told her I might be old, but I'm not stupid. I didn't tell anyone. Has she had the baby?"

"You've lost me. I don't know who you mean."

She clicked her tongue. "Oh really, you never listen." And went back to humming the tune, oblivious to any more questions.

Chapter Fifty

1944

It was well after curfew. Standing on the balcony, Martina saw three men arrive at the priest's house directly below the villa in the middle of the night. An hour later, only two of them came back. They'd been carrying something when they arrived, but left empty-handed. Food, she supposed. And yet the priest still had the nerve to ask her for her apples and oil and gifts for the evacuee children.

In the early hours of the morning, another group left the priest's house, walking past the villa and up towards the ridge. One of them looked a bit familiar by the way he walked. For a moment she found herself hoping it might be Gianni coming back after all. But what would she and Gianni have to say to each other after all this time? Wasn't it likely the only reason he'd come back now would be to ask her to leave?

The men weren't close enough for her to make out their features, but from the height and build and the way they moved, she could tell as they got closer that Gianni wasn't one of them. A sudden fear gripped her. Were they enemies of Gianni coming to take out their revenge on his family for something he'd done? She retreated further into the shadows.

It wouldn't be so unusual. An elderly couple had been shot because they had patched up a wounded soldier they found on their land; a young woman hanged from a tree because she'd been seeing a German soldier. Another had her tongue cut out because she was seen talking to a partisan. The German soldiers would shoot partisans they caught, but not before gouging their eyes out.

She shrank back against the wall, feverishly assessing possible hiding places, listening for sounds of the men breaking in. They didn't come. As the footsteps died away, she wept with relief and then rage that she could be made to feel so vulnerable in her own home.

***

The sense of euphoria they felt when the Allies recaptured Rome in June 1944 gave way to an even greater fear as news spread of atrocities closer to home. At the end of June, German soldiers stormed into the village of San Pancrazio, south of Florence, at dawn following a clash between soldiers and partisans. They rounded up the men and boys and took them to a farmhouse cellar. The local priest pleaded for their lives. He was the first to be shot.

That same day, one hundred and seventy-three people in nearby villages were killed in a similar barbaric manner. In Santa Zita, the atmosphere was charged. People were on edge the whole time. It would only take one moment of madness to trigger something like that.

Martina had always known that the rumours about Gianni would eventually reach Cesare, but she had, if anything, underestimated his reaction. He came up from the piazza red-faced after overhearing something in the bar.

"You know what they're saying down there?" He searched her face for signs that she already knew. "He's alive."

She didn't know what to say. "Please don't get your hopes up."

But Cesare was pacing furiously round the room. "He's been fighting with the partisan scum near Florence. Now he's up in the hills around Santa Zita. Have you heard about this?"

"It's rumours," she said. "Someone probably made a mistake."

Her father-in-law shook his head. "It was the Giacomini lad. He's known Gianni for years. He was at school with him. He wouldn't make a mistake."

"But if he's alive, that's good, isn't it?"

Cesare was shaking all over. "How could he put us through this? Let us think he was dead? Three years we've been mourning him. We thought this was all we had left." He picked up the photograph off the piano and hurled it across the room. "And all this time he's been living like a savage."

Cesare's face was red, and his breath was coming out in rasps. "I just can't believe that my own son was prepared to undermine the government that his brother died for – it's worse than hearing he was dead. The grief nearly killed his mother. You know that?" he shouted. "What does this make him? A traitor. A coward. All the things he was brought up not to be. I just don't understand it."

He turned towards her, his eyes bloodshot and swollen. "Have you been in touch with him?"

"No. Nobody's heard from him. Nobody knows anything," Martina said. "Whatever you've heard, it's all speculation."

He didn't seem to hear her. "I tell you this, if I ever, *ever* set eyes on him, I will kill him with my own hands before his mother hears about any of this. At least she should be able to die believing her son had some honour."

There was no doubt that he was serious, in intention at least, although it was doubtful Cesare, in his state of health, could inflict much harm on a fit young man who had been trained in armed combat. He clutched his side as a spasm of pain crossed his face.

"No-one's seen him," she repeated, but Cesare refused to accept it.

"I'll kill him."

He was taken over by a coughing fit, rusty-coloured spit dribbling down his chin. The next thing she knew, he was struggling to breathe. He braced his back, fists on knees trying to get more oxygen, but it didn't seem to work. His

187

face was flushed and panicky, eyes bulging. She rushed to help him, loosened his shirt, and tried to calm him. A vision shot through of the old man dying in the piazza, the same helpless look in his eyes.

"I'll get someone," she said, jumping to her feet. Cesare barely made a response.

Chapter Fifty-One

Down in the piazza, the doctor's wife informed Martina that he was unable to come because he was ill himself, but he could send someone else in his place – a younger chap, very well-educated, knew his stuff. He'd be there as soon as he could. Martina ran back to check on Cesare, her mind too preoccupied to think about the implications. In her hurry, she forgot to close the kitchen door. Her father-in-law was lying on the floor where he'd fallen from the chair. He was trying to push himself up, struggling to breathe and panicking now.

"Someone's coming," she told him. "Try not to worry."

Footsteps in the doorway behind her made her lurch round. The face that greeted her in the open doorway was startled and disbelieving. He barely looked at her as he walked in, didn't use her name, just brushed her aside, asking about Cesare's symptoms. He nodded as he listened and crouched down to examine the patient, asking questions every so often and giving encouraging responses, all his energies focused on the patient.

"Can you help me lift him?" he asked. She assisted as he hoisted Cesare onto the sofa.

"Will he be all right?" she asked.

"The next few hours are crucial, but I think so."

She watched his hands as he worked. He gave orders quietly, with absolute confidence, and she responded. She wanted to lose herself in his warm certainty, his strength, and knowledge, and kindness, which he showed to anyone but her these days. At one point, she felt his hand brush hers and an electric current shot through her just as it had done years before in the cafe. He pulled back, seemingly unaware, but she felt herself blushing.

"It's bronco pneumonia," he said. "You'll need to keep an eye on him. The problem is I don't have anything to treat it with. There's a new serum that might help if I could get hold of it."

"We can pay."

She looked around her. What did they have left that they could sell?

From his expression, she could see it was pointless. As usual, money wasn't the problem. "We'll just have to wait until the fever breaks. Keep him sitting up. Lots of fluids. Brandy, if you have any. I've given him something to ease the pain and help him sleep."

She accompanied him to the door.

"I'll come back in the morning and see how he's doing," Roberto said. "If there's any change, come and get me."

"Thank you, Doctor." It seemed unnecessarily formal to address him in that way, as though she were laughing at him, but then it was easy to forget that she had no reason to be informal. He dropped his head, raised it, gave a flicker of a smile and turned to go.

Chapter Fifty-Two

"I came to see how the patient was."

"Of course."

What other reason would he be there for? Martina stood back to let Roberto pass. The way he spoke, it was as if he was addressing the housekeeper, someone he'd never met before. She led him through the house to the old couple's bedroom. He thanked her, spoke gently to Cesare, listened to his breathing, asked how he'd been in the night. He gave Elena some tablets, instructions and words of comfort, and then left them together.

"I'll see myself out."

"No, no. Martina will see you to the door," insisted Elena.

They walked briskly to minimise the awkwardness. There were only tiny sounds – the swish of her skirt, the crackle of her stockings, and the soft creaking of his shoe leather on the marble floor.

"You're very good to your father-in-law," he said at last.

She shrugged. It wasn't as if she had a choice.

Roberto had been back a couple of times and was always professional and courteous, but he seemed to have very little time for conversation, as though he couldn't wait to get out again. His questions always seemed to be addressed to someone standing beside her. His eyes rarely met hers, and when they did they flickered away to somewhere or someone else that was obviously of more interest. Was it so difficult for him to look at her and say something nice?

She barely looked at him either, sensing the disappointment would be too great. It had been like this ever since he'd come to Santa Zita. Try as she had to be bright and entertaining, he'd been impervious to her charms, deflecting her comments and inviting her to talk about other people but never herself. It was impossible now to imagine that that mouth, those lips... She felt the familiar anger welling up inside her.

Why couldn't he make more of an effort? He was barely civil. Was he so embarrassed by their first encounter in the town that day? Did he see it as such a terrible mistake? Did he really think she was spiteful enough to tell Irena? Or that Irena was that shallow? It had happened so long ago, well before Irena had met him. How could she hold it against either of them?

When they reached the door, she opened it, but he didn't leave. He turned to face her and stood there on the step, his hand on the door, looking at her quizzically.

"Have I done something to offend you?" he asked.

"Why would you think that?" And then without meaning to, she mumbled, "You couldn't make it any clearer that you can't stand being anywhere near me. You seem to go out of your way to avoid me."

He put his hands in his pockets, took a deep breath, and acknowledged the point with a nod. His voice came out sharply. "And why do you think that is?"

"I really have no idea."

He fixed his eyes directly on hers for the first time in as long as she could remember.

"Well, it's because I'm in love with you."

Martina opened her mouth to say something, although she had no idea what. But Elena's voice rang out from the drawing room. "Has he gone?"

The door was pulled closed in her face. She listened to his footsteps die away.

Chapter Fifty-Three

2018

Irena spoke softly into the machine. It was late, and she didn't want her son or his interfering wife to come and ask what she was doing. Someone had taken this thing the other day. She'd driven herself mad looking for it. Now she'd found it, she wasn't going to lose it again. She stopped and started a few times, unhappy with the way things came out. It was painful even now to remember.

I think if I'm honest, I did see something that evening when Martina came to the party. It wasn't anything major, nothing that was said or even an obvious silence or a look that passed between them - more of a tiny shift in the air, something you could never put your finger on, that should have alerted me.

I chose to ignore it. Told myself it was nothing. Of course, I wonder now, would things have worked out so differently if I had said something?

When Roberto and I were dancing, I asked him if he thought she was beautiful. I can't think why I did that now. I must have wanted to torture myself.

"She is," he said.

And yet the way he said it, he somehow managed to convey that he didn't of course mean it in that way, that she wasn't his type. And she so blatantly wasn't. They were chalk and cheese, he and Martina. He even implied he was paying her the compliment to please me, recognising how important she was to me. How was he able to that? I suppose the truth is I must have made it easy for him, because I understood what I wanted to in what he said.

I remember thinking how mature our relationship was despite it being so new. We were a union of minds, of souls, already secure enough together for him to be able to describe someone as beautiful and for me to understand and not feel threatened by it, not fly off the handle like other silly women. To understand that it was no more than an observation, like commenting on a piece of art.

Because our love wasn't like everyone else's. It was about so much more: philosophy, books, the way people think, the meaning of life. We came from the same families, Roberto and I; we had the same roots. There was nothing skin-deep about us. I think back then I even felt superior to others around us, believing they could never have what we had. As though they were paddling in shallow waters while we were riding the high waves.

God, what a naïve bloody fool I was.

I think I might have glimpsed a distraction in him that evening. I don't know – perhaps he wasn't holding me quite as closely or as carefully as he had done – but I didn't really take it in. I was too blinded by his presence and the simple fact that he'd chosen me to be with him, not just on that evening but forever.

I was only too ready to believe that what I'd seen was mutual admiration on a physical level, nothing more. I must admit, it gave me a certain pride knowing that for the first time Martina's life and mine had been reversed. It was she *who was envious of* me*. Because I did feel that. I sensed her looking at me as though she couldn't quite fathom how I'd done it, how I'd hooked this extraordinary person, and I did feel proud.*

If it had happened on a different night, if he hadn't just asked me to marry him, things might have been different. I might have been more anxious. But I truly believed we were going to spend the rest of our lives together, with Martina as our dear, loyal friend.

Oh, it sounds daft now. I even started to have this idea that after the war he and I would buy a house in the town, from which he'd operate his surgery and I'd have a school room, and perhaps we might rent rooms to Martina and Sonia. I had to get them away from Villa Leonida. It had nothing to offer them now, and if Cesare died, I couldn't bear to think of Martina on her own with Elena whom she'd never got on with.

I thought she could get some training, make something of herself – perhaps learn some secretarial skills. Then she could get a job and turn her life into something interesting. There'd be all sorts of opportunities after the war if we could just hang on until then. People were always talking about after the war – things would be so different. Of course, it wouldn't be easy being a single mother, but being a war widow wasn't unusual and I'd be able to keep an eye on Sonia at school. It was all taking shape in my head, you see.

And then everything shattered.

Irena switched off the machine, her hand shaking to match her voice.

Chapter Fifty-Four

1944

The next morning, when she opened the door to Roberto, Martina told him her father-in-law had had a more peaceful night. Her words were coming out too fast, tripping over each other.

"Actually, it wasn't him I came to see." He put down his doctor's bag with that same shrug of surrender she'd seen once before. All his anger, his coldness had gone. He looked vulnerable but also purposeful.

When she was younger, much younger, she used to climb the rocks by the river and dive off. She could still recall that feeling of having reached the top and be standing there with that sudden pang of fear in the pit of her stomach. Afraid to let go but knowing she couldn't turn back now. Did he feel the same?

Wordlessly, she showed Roberto through to the drawing room at the other end of the villa from Cesare's bedroom. Anyone seeing him turn up at the villa with his doctor's bag would have had no reason to be suspicious. It was well known that Cesare was ill. Several people had asked after him when she was down in the piazza that morning.

The villa was unbearably quiet. Cesare was asleep, and Elena had taken Sonia into the woods to find some cherries before the trees were picked clean.

"What I said yesterday," Roberto began, as though he were about to deny it in some way. His hair was ruffled where he had put his hand through it a moment ago.

She walked slowly towards him. The next moment they

were in each other's arms, feeling each other's kiss. She so wanted to abandon herself completely, but this was wrong, it was madness. She stopped, catching her breath.

"We shouldn't be doing this."

His face remained close, out of focus. A smile played around his lips. "You're right, we shouldn't." But he made no attempt to move away. "Did you really think I'd forgotten?" His lips found hers again.

She came to her senses and pushed him away.

He looked shocked. His arms dropped to his sides. He brought one back up to his head, clutching his hair.

"Did I misunderstand you? I thought…"

She turned away biting her lip. She had surprised herself. It went against everything she was feeling. She sat down, trying to ignore the tremble in her legs.

"You didn't misunderstand. It's what I want, too. But we can't, can we? I mean, you and Irena. You're engaged."

He looked wounded. He shook his head. Almost laughed. "I made a mistake, Martina, you know that. Any fool can see it. Have you never made a mistake?"

Of course she had. Her whole life seemed to be made up of them. And not so long ago she'd told herself that her biggest mistake of all had been falling in love with a man – no, the *idea* of a man – she'd met for a few moments, who could no longer remember her and was marrying her best friend.

"But I promised her…"

He nodded. "I promised her, too. And I meant every word. But we weren't to know, were we? I never expected to see you again or to fall in love with you when I did – but it's happened. It has, hasn't it?"

"You don't really know me," she said.

He laughed. "No, that's where you're wrong. I know everything about you. Probably much more than you want me to know. You're Irena's favourite subject. She talks about you all the bloody time. Perhaps you think I'm cruel for letting her, but I couldn't stop myself."

He sat down next to her and took hold of her hands

197

before she could snatch them away. He held them, studying them. She wished they weren't so rough and the veins didn't stick out.

"I've tried to ignore it," he said. "Tried to pretend it wasn't happening. I avoided you whenever I could. I tried everything – even tried to make myself hate you. But it didn't work."

She looked away. He brought his hand up to her face and gently twisted it back towards him. His eyes burned into hers, as though he were reading her thoughts. "You feel it, too. I've seen it. We can't go on like this. It will make us all miserable."

Perhaps this was enough. Just knowing what could have been. To know that she'd been right after all, that she hadn't imagined it all. It should be enough.

"Look, we've wasted so much time already," he said. "I've never forgotten you."

She looked at him, disbelieving.

"I was called up just after I saw you. I thought about you all the time I was away. I came up here during my first leave and asked about you."

Of course. The time she thought she saw him down in the piazza by the fountain.

"They told me you were married. Told me you lived up there in the big house with the most important family. I thought perhaps they were lying because I was an outsider, but then I saw you with a child. I'd sort of expected it, but I was still crushed. I didn't want to embarrass you, so I left. And I tried to forget you.

"I got on with my life. Never expected to see you again. But when you turned up at that party to celebrate the engagement, I couldn't believe my bloody bad luck. I recognised you straight away. It was excruciating, everyone congratulating me on the engagement just when I'd found you again. I tried to ignore the effect you had on me. I've been trying for weeks, but I can't do it any more."

The clock chimed. When she didn't reply, he went on.

"You must understand what it's been like for me out

198

there. Seeing people die every day – people who shouldn't be dying. Not being able to help them. Young men with… I'm sorry." He shut his eyes and stopped himself from saying any more.

"You get one chance at life, that's what I'm saying. One chance. That's what I learned out there. And I thought about this when I was out there. I thought, if I ever get back, I'm not going to be an observer any more, taking what life throws at me. From now on I'm going to make choices."

She thought about it, her heart racing. "But what can we say to Irena? It will break her heart."

"She doesn't have to know. We can go away from here. I know I'll never love anyone else."

Neither will I, she thought. *But neither will Irena.*

He must have thought she was hesitating for some other reason, because he took her hand again. "Face facts," he said gently. "Your husband's not coming back. For whatever reason. It's been three years. I know what people are saying, but even if it's true he wasn't killed at the start, he could have got in touch with you if he'd wanted to. You have to move on."

She bit her lip. On that at least she was clear. But what she said was, "I don't know if I can."

"You can." He almost shouted it. "This is your chance to change your life, or carry on the same for ever. What do you want to do, because it's your decision?"

She still didn't reply, a thousand thoughts running through her head. Seconds passed. It seemed like hours.

"Fine. I'll wait."

She processed his words. Laughed. She shouldn't have laughed. "I can't ask you to do that."

"No, but I will anyway."

"How long would you wait?"

"As long as it takes for you to change your mind."

"But how do you know I'll ever change it?"

That look again – so sure, so intense. "You will, when you decide to start living again."

The front door slammed, and they sprang apart. Sonia's

footsteps pounded down the hall. She appeared in the doorway, looking pleased with herself, clutching a handful of cherries that had stained her hands and dress dark red. Elena's steps went the other way, towards the bedroom. They could hear her chatting to Cesare, asking what the doctor had said. Roberto got up to talk to her about Cesare's condition.

"I'm going back to town tomorrow," he said to Martina before he left. "Doctor Serafini's better now. I'll be at the Caffé Napoleone in town on Thursday at 11. Meet me there if you want."

He wrote down the address on a scrap of paper and pressed it into her hand. Before she could answer, he said, "It's your choice. If you don't come, I'll be there again the following Thursday."

"Who was that man?" asked Sonia after he'd gone.

"He's a doctor," Martina said, lifting the child onto her lap and counting the berries with her, gasping at their jewel-like colours. "He's making Nonno better."

But the thought kept going through her mind: what in the world was she doing?

Chapter Fifty-Five

Martina clutched the address as she walked, pushing her bicycle along the last street. Her heels echoed on the paving stones and the bicycle wheels hissed through puddles. Fragments of conversation drifted past her from people walking by, a sea of faceless figures emerging out of the mist. With her swing coat and beret, she stood out among the shuffling, weary people in their drab clothes on their way to shops, banks or offices. She was alive with anticipation. Her mind was made up.

A piercing breeze swept along the street, sending dried blossom scuttling. The cold air stung her legs through her thin stockings. She passed boarded-up shops, ancient churches, and abandoned palaces. This city had escaped the air raids, its spirit bruised but intact. The buildings had seen so much history. It was hard to imagine that this day would be part of history, too. Today would be a turning point. The day she made a choice and stuck to it – not out of duty or guilt, but because it was what she wanted.

Deep in thought, she almost walked straight past the café. She stopped, craning her neck to read the engraved gold lettering. She was too early. Should she walk around outside for a bit longer? No, it was too cold for that. She propped the bicycle up against the wall opposite.

An immaculately dressed doorman greeted her. The dark interior smelled of wood and coffee. She realised she'd been here before with her grandmother as a child. Then the glass cabinets had groaned with cakes and biscuits, fruit boats made from light-as-feather pastry, pistachio macaroons and croissants filled with *gianduia*, but today they stood empty, save for some paper decorations.

He showed her to a table near the window, which gave a good view of the piazza. A waiter brought her tea with lemon. She twisted off the gloves and sipped the tea, making it last, glad to be inside a warm building. Her face smarted from the sharp wind. The cafe had a sense of permanence, of indestructibility. Once a popular meeting place for socialist artists and poets, it now served well-heeled businessmen and German soldiers. At tables all around her, deals were being struck, acquaintances made, reunions formed, all discreetly masked by the soft notes of the piano playing in the corner.

She felt conspicuous sitting there. What if he didn't come? She fumbled through her bag to make herself look busy. It wouldn't do for him to see her looking out for him. She studied her reflection in the large gilt mirror on the wall. It was a shock to see herself looking back. She'd expected to see someone exotic with a secret smile, the sort of woman who enjoys not one life but two, who was cherishing a delicious secret. But the face in the mirror was a theatrical mask – the rouge, red lips, and carefully lined arched brows barely concealing the hollow cheekbones and anxious look in her eyes.

Would he turn up?

But then he was there, strolling across the square, carving a path through the pigeons, his coat open, flapping in the wind that cut across the piazza. He held his hat on with one hand. He was beautiful, like an angel.

He was at the door. His eyes were searching for her, hungry and hopeful as he made his way to the table. She wanted to jump up and run into his arms, cling to him and cry like a baby, let go all the pent-up fears, frustrations, and missed opportunities of the last three years. Instead, she let him kiss her on the cheek.

"I wasn't sure if you'd come," he said.

"You shouldn't have doubted me," she replied with a smile, as though the decision had been that simple.

The waiter arrived, and Roberto ordered coffee. It tasted

202

almost as she remembered coffee. They talked about safe things – how cold it was outside, how they'd got there, how they'd spent the week, Cesare's health. Neither of them mentioned Irena. Martina jumped as she felt his knee brush hers under the table, but she didn't move hers away.

"How long can we keep this up?" he said at last. And it all came out in a rush. "I can't think about anything else but you. I can't get you out of my head. Look, I know it's wrong, but I'm never going to let you go again."

They left the café and walked down the road arm in arm, wheeling the bicycle between them just as they had in her imagination years before. She'd made a choice, made this happen. *It's a new world*, she thought, *and we're part of it.* He propped the bike against the wall of a building in a quiet street and unlocked the door. Wordlessly, they climbed the stairs, which smelled of damp and old stone and millipedes. He opened the door of the apartment.

She barely had time to take in its appearance before he was kissing her, drawing her towards him, pressing his body against hers, making up for all the time they'd lost. They made love as though nothing else in the world mattered, nothing else existed.

Their clothes lying in a heap on the floor, he traced his fingernails very gently over every part of her, making her shiver. She suddenly felt horribly aware that her shoulders stood up in points, her ribs stood out, and her throat was hollow above the collarbone. He should have been repelled but seemed not to be.

Afterwards, they lay wrapped in the crumpled sheet, feeling the breeze creep across them through the open window. They must have fallen asleep at some point, because when she was next aware the light in the room had changed.

The room was sparsely furnished with an old iron bed and a marble-topped dressing table. The clock face of a tower filled the window. Voices floated up from the street below, and they heard footsteps and the fizz of bicycles wheeling along the damp pavement. The air smelled of tobacco as they shared the last of the cigarettes she had been given by the German soldier.

"We can come here whenever we want," he said. "It belongs to a friend who's moved up into the hills because of the air raids. I've said I'd look after it for him. Will you remember where it is?"

She would remember every step. At last she swung her legs down onto the cold terrazzo floor. "I have to go."

"I know."

He smoked another cigarette as he watched her dress.

"Will you come again?" he asked, as he held the door open for her.

She said she would. She stepped out onto the street again, the same person and yet a changed one. Wrapping her coat around herself, she set off down the road, keeping her face down to avoid the biting air, carrying with her the touch of his lips on hers, his breath on her skin.

There could be no going back now.

Chapter Fifty-Six

Martina hadn't spoken to Irena for a couple of weeks. She hardly dared trust herself. Irena knew her so well she was sure to give something away, and besides, she was just too ashamed. It had been easy to avoid her while Cesare was ill. Irena would understand how busy she'd been. It was hot, and it had been hard to keep down Cesare's fever. He appeared to be getting better, but a few weeks later Elena woke in the middle of the night and they watched him for hours. But he died just before dawn.

Despite their differences, Martina had become fond of her father-in-law. How ironic that she and Elena, who'd never seen eye-to-eye, were now left together in Villa Leonida to bring up Sonia as best they could. It was so far from the life Martina had envisaged there, but in a funny way it made sense. Over the years they'd come to accept their differences.

There was nothing remarkable about the night Gianni came back. Not back from the dead, as the rumours had suggested, but as good as. There was no letter, no message. He just appeared, tapping softly at the kitchen door as though he'd only popped out to check on the fire in the chestnut tower.

It took a few moments to recognise him. Her first instinct was to slam the door. He stood there, bearded, gaunt, dishevelled, staring at her with an animal-like hunger that frightened her so that she shrunk back into the doorframe.

As though he read her intention, he lunged forward and put his hand over her mouth to stop her crying out.

"Missed me?"

He was hardly recognisable as the man she remembered. This couldn't be happening. Gianni coming back was her worst nightmare. She could only mumble in reply to his question, hiding her thoughts in an embrace. He drew back and ran his eyes over her, then pulled her towards him again. She twisted her head so that his lips met her cheek rather than her mouth, but he held her face so that she couldn't do it a second time.

She tried to ignore the unwashed smell, the coarseness of his skin, the scratchy beard, and the fact that he was probably crawling with lice. She shut her eyes, remembering the old Gianni, the one who'd left in that smart uniform with a glow in his eyes, such strong ideals even if they had been misguided. But in her head, all she was seeing was Roberto.

"Where have you been?" she asked to avoid answering his question.

He just laughed. His teeth were in an awful state. It kept running through her head, if anyone had to do a magic trick and reappear from the dead, why did it have to be Gianni? All those people who'd been left heartbroken by the deaths of their loved-ones – and he had to be the one who'd survived. Gianni pulled out a chair, wincing as he did so, bringing a hand to his shoulder.

"What happened?" she asked as he sat down.

He half smiled. "I got shot." The way he said it made the question seem stupid and pointless.

She closed her eyes. "I meant years ago."

He shrugged as though she couldn't be expected to understand. "It's a long story."

She removed his shirt, trying to disguise the shaking in her hands. She felt him looking at her and shuddered. What was he expecting from her? He was painfully thin. The wound in his shoulder had become infected and was a foul mess. So that was why he'd come back. That at any rate was a relief. She could cope with being a nurse. She'd cared for Cesare for a long time, and was much less easily repulsed by blood and vomit these days. Just as long as he wasn't

206

expecting her to behave like a wife.

"I can get a doctor," she said, her head still swimming with questions. "He's trustworthy."

Gianni shook his head. "No. I can't risk word getting around. I've put your life in danger coming here. You must be able to get me something for it, though. Most of all, I just want to sleep in a real bed."

She must talk to Roberto – get something to stop the infection spreading. He'd ask questions, of course, but she'd think of something. She ran a bath for Gianni, and he bathed and shaved. She cut his long hair and removed all the lice she could. Afterwards, he looked more like his old self, but there was something indefinably different about him. That hard extra layer he'd grown when they were on honeymoon was impenetrable now. Despite this being his family home, it seemed as if he was the intruder. Did he feel that, too?

Martina fetched fresh clothes for him from the drawers Elena had insisted on leaving untouched after he left. She examined the ones he'd taken off, wondering what to do with them and who'd worn them before. She felt herself colour as she realised he was watching.

"Where did you get these?" she asked.

"From someone who didn't need them any more."

She cooked him the meal she'd been planning for the following day – a soup with cabbage and beans. Somehow, she'd have to explain to Elena why they couldn't have it.

"How long will you stay?" she asked as he ate.

"A week or two. Until I can fight again. I'm no use to anyone at the moment, and there's not enough food for people who are no use. They might decide to shoot me like an old dog."

She looked at him appalled. "Would they do that?"

He gave a short laugh. "Why not? It's been done before. You can't trust anyone from one day to the next. We're all there for different reasons. Communists, Jews, foreigners, gypsies. People with beliefs and people with no beliefs. The only thing we have in common is that we've run out of choices."

She shook her head. "It's madness."

He snorted. "It's not perfect but it's better than the alternatives. I'm not going to prison, I'm not going to do slave labour in Germany, and I'm not going to join those Fascist bastards. I need to get better. Then I'll go back."

"But it doesn't make sense," she said. "You all want the same thing now, but afterwards – what then? What is it you believe in now?"

His dark eyes bore into her. "I believed in you. It was all I had left."

Her heart exploded. Surely he could have had no way of knowing about Roberto? And even if he did, what did he expect? It had been three years since he 'died', and he had done nothing to let her know he was alive. More worryingly, if he had heard something, how long would it be before Irena found out?

"Then why didn't you write to me? Tell me what was going on?" She couldn't keep the anger out of her voice.

He took a drink and wiped his mouth. "At first, I thought it would be tempting fate. Superstition, I suppose. Every time someone sent a letter back home they got killed the next day."

For a minute she thought she hadn't heard him properly. "And that's your reason for letting me think you were dead? It's been three years. Three bloody years."

The look he gave was sheepish, just a trace of the old Gianni there, the one who could win her round in any situation.

"I know I didn't send them. But I wrote them, didn't I? Alvaro gave them to you. He promised he would. He said he'd tell you everything."

Alvaro? How was that possible? She thought back to the day he'd come to Villa Leonida to tell them about how Gianni had died. His nervousness, his reluctance to look her in the eye, the way his Adam's apple bobbed up and down his scrawny neck, making him look like a gecko. Had it been anyone else, his nervousness might have struck her as suspicious, but Alvaro had always been odd.

"It's the first I've heard of any letters," she said. "Alvaro didn't tell me anything except that you were dead."

Had he hated her that much? Did he really still blame her for some silly trick she'd played when they were children? Had this been his way of getting his own back? Martina went over the conversation with him when he'd been standing right here in this house. He'd been afraid of her — that was obvious. She could tell he was holding something back. Was it because he was afraid she'd find him out? Know he was lying to her?

The look of bewilderment on Gianni's face seemed genuine. He didn't seem to know whether or not to believe her. But in a way, what did it really matter now whether Alvaro had told her or not? She'd heard the rumours anyway. But it had been so long ago. There must have been countless other occasions when Gianni could have got in touch.

"Why haven't I heard from you since?"

He stared into the fire. "I stayed away because it would have put you in danger. I'd deserted. Families get shot for that. I couldn't contact you."

"You could. Other people did."

They sat in silence for some moments. What was the use of going over it all now? He didn't seem to remember things the way she did.

"Your father died a few weeks ago," she told him. "I'm sorry."

He nodded, obviously already aware. Someone had been keeping him informed.

"How's my mother?"

"She's…your mother."

He grinned and nodded, then looked serious. "She can't know I'm here. Not even her."

Martina ran her hands down her face, then rested her chin in them. "Why did you do it? Why did you desert?"

He gave a short laugh. "Because I didn't want to die. Isn't that enough for you? Do I have to dress it up in fancy language?"

She waited.

He pushed his bowl away. "It wasn't for any political reason or personal principle, if that's what you're asking. I did it because I was terrified of being killed. That might sound feeble nowadays when everyone's supposed to be a hero, but I wasn't ready to become one."

"On our honeymoon," she began.

"On our honeymoon it was starting to sink in, what was expected of me. I knew that even if I survived, I'd probably lose all this," he said gesturing. "And you."

He tried to take her hand but she slid it away. "I'm sorry. I really am. I'm different now. I've changed, Martina. I've learned so much."

She couldn't keep the sharpness out of her voice. "Oh, so you're a hero after all now, are you?"

But she was thinking that she'd changed, too. It would be impossible for anyone not to have changed. Gianni ignored her.

"I owe my life to a Greek family who hid me after I deserted. When I first got there, I was in shock from what I'd seen and lost. I'd lost all faith in Fascism after seeing what they did to ordinary villagers. Everything I'd believed in was destroyed. I joined their partisans. Being with them taught me a lot."

She wondered if he'd fallen in love with a girl in the family, but couldn't think of a way to ask that wouldn't sound like an accusation.

"They died, the whole family...because of me."

"How awful. What happened?"

He shrugged, signalling he wasn't going to talk about it.

"What I've learned over these few years is that there are two types of fear. One that paralyses you, and one that makes you act even if you know it's hopeless. I gradually realised I had choices. I didn't have to wait to be rounded up and shot, or sent to a camp.

"And it's working. Florence is free. Lucca will be next. It won't be long before they get through the Gothic Line – some of those fortifications aren't as strong as they look.

The factories deliberately supplied the worst quality concrete. This is our war; the Allies don't know this territory like we do."

A wave of fear crashed over her.

"We've heard what it's like down south. Is that what's going to happen here? People forced to live in caves and cellars while their towns are flattened. Coming back to their homes and finding there's nothing left. And no water, no electricity. Children, grandmothers being raped by soldiers. Is that your idea of freedom?"

"It's war," he said sharply. He dropped his voice again. "It happens occasionally. Some soldiers get out of control. Their commanders shut their eyes to it all. They're savages. But we need the Allies' help. Once they've done their job, we can start to rebuild our lives."

"Can we?" It was getting harder and harder to envisage a future now that she wanted to be part of. And sharing that future with Gianni? No, that didn't make sense.

Her mind was reeling. Did he really expect to come back into her life and pick up all the pieces just as he'd left them? What would it be like having him back in the house after all this time? A stranger to Sonia. A stranger to her. And what about Roberto? Why should she give him up now she'd finally found him?

"I'm going to hell, Martina," Gianni said. His voice sounded strangely distant. "I've seen things – done things – I could never have imagined. But I have to go back up there and finish the job. If I stayed, I'd be putting your life in danger – and Sonia's."

Martina let out a sigh of relief at the news. She couldn't help it. She hoped to God he hadn't noticed. His look told her that he had. At the mention of Sonia's name, his voice broke slightly.

"Is she asleep?"

"Yes."

"Can I see her?"

She wanted to say no. She didn't want him anywhere near Sonia. Her heart squeezed at the thought of how clean her little girl had smelled lying in the bed when she kissed her goodnight. Normally she'd creep in beside Sonia and enjoy the warmth of her silky hair and her soft skin as she read her a story, feel her breathing slow as the little girl fell asleep.

"She thinks you're dead."

"Good. She mustn't know. I just want to see her."

Martina chewed her lip. The thought of him touching Sonia, breathing over her... but what could she do?

They climbed the stairs in silence. He faltered outside the room where Elena was sleeping but then passed on.

It was almost too dark to see. Martina lit the night light and he sat on Sonia's bed, gazing at her angelic face. He reached out and caressed her soft features. His eyes glistened. Sonia's cheek flickered. He backed away, leaving her sleeping.

There was nowhere else for Gianni to sleep but in the double bed with Martina. At least he didn't try to make love to her. He was feverish. He flinched in his sleep and grimaced from the pain in his shoulder when he tried to turn over. Martina lay awake, listening to the unfamiliar sound of his breathing and wondering how she could get out of this situation.

It was the first night she'd not had Sonia sleeping next to her, and she missed the warmth, the softness, and the smell of the child. In the middle of the night, Gianni cried like he'd done when he was a boy after losing a game. Martina took him into her arms, but she endured rather than enjoyed the experience of being with him, and couldn't get rid of the feeling that she was being unfaithful.

***

The weeks that followed were unbearable. Terror gripped Martina every time she left or entered the house, in case someone was watching her, questions being asked. It was an awful thing to conceal Gianni's presence from Elena, but he was adamant his mother mustn't know he was there. It was safer that way, and Martina had to bear in mind what Cesare had said, that his wife should be allowed to die believing what she wanted to about her son.

Martina set up a bed for Gianni in the cave inside the chestnut drying tower, insisting on it for safety reasons. It was too much of a risk, him being in the house. It was cold in the tower, but the conditions were probably better than he'd been used to. If anyone came looking for him, she could disguise the entrance with boxes and barrels. It wasn't perfect, but it would have to do. She told him not to come outside during the day. He said he wasn't stupid.

When he was well enough, she let him have sex when he asked for it. If she'd refused, he'd have wanted to know why. She couldn't think of it as making love. He drove into her as though he were reclaiming her. She sensed he knew how much she disliked it and that he was doing it mainly to punish her, to dare her to tell him why. And all the time she had no way of getting word to Roberto to explain her absence. He would be waiting for her in the café. Or perhaps he would have given up by now.

She wriggled away from Gianni's sleeping body. If only he would leave. And if he didn't leave, how could she make him?

Chapter Fifty-Seven

"It's snowing."

Giant white flakes buoyed by the wind floated around the piazza. Sonia tried to catch them as they danced around her. But it wasn't snow, only paper. Martina picked one up and read it.

"What does it say?" Sonia asked.

Martina felt her face tighten as she tried to smile. "Nothing important."

More threats. Last week they'd found leaflets from the Allies with a different set of rules. Either way, it was clear their lives were in greater danger than before.

The house was filled with piano music when they got in. Sonia hugged her grandmother and clambered up on the stool beside her, planting her hands on the keys until Elena told her which one to press and when.

"I saw Gianni last night," Elena said as she bent forwards over the piano and then away from it.

"I'm sorry?" Martina felt her face blanch.

Her mother-in-law continued to tickle the keys. "He was standing by my bed as large as life. He said, 'I'm fine, Mamma. Don't cry about me any more.' It felt so real. It almost felt as though if I reached out I would touch him."

Martina's heart squeezed tighter. "And did you?"

Elena frowned. "Did I what?"

"Did you touch him? Did you try to touch him?"

Her mother-in-law's glance was withering. "Of course I didn't. I was dreaming, not mad."

At the first opportunity, Martina ran to the chestnut tower. "What were you thinking of? You'll get us all killed."

He laughed. "She thought she was dreaming. Don't tell

me what to do."

But she suspected Sonia had seen him, too, because the little girl had started to ask questions about a strange man. Martina grabbed her chin and spoke close to her face.

"Don't you *ever* talk about this to anyone. That man is not real. He's in your imagination. Do you understand?"

Sonia nodded, tears sliding down her face. Martina pulled her towards her and enveloped her in a hug. She hated Gianni for doing this to them. She felt like killing him.

When eventually the wound was healing and the infection gone, he announced he was leaving.

"Will you come back?" she asked.

He looked at her with something close to hatred. "I don't think there's any point, do you?"

But when he got as far as the door, he stopped. "But I will when we've finished the job. After all, this is my house. And you are my wife."

Martina locked the door behind him and slumped to the ground. She wanted to hurl things, smash things, slice open his head with an axe. Instead, she bit her hand until she could taste blood and she couldn't bear the pain. How could she ever feel free in the villa again, knowing he was out there?

Chapter Fifty-Eight

SONIA

2018

After the cool, dark interior of Florence's cathedral, the solemnity of the Mass, and the priest's sonorous tone, Sonia stepped out into blinding sunshine and a cacophony of sound – voices, music, car horns, orders given by megaphone, and the bells from Giotto's campanile. A massive crowd had gathered around the piazza. People jostled and surged to get a better view, but were held back behind barriers by police with megaphones. Others watched from windows and roof terraces of nearby hotels and apartments.

Sonia, who hated crowds, was hemmed in on all sides, but she glimpsed the gleaming gold painted horns of the white oxen, and the garlands of flowers around their necks as they were led into the piazza pulling the famous, brightly painted cart towards the Baptistry.

On the stroke of noon, the priest released the sacred *colombina*, the dove-shaped rocket, which shot down the wire to the cart and ignited the fireworks, creating a spectacular display above the cathedral square, symbolising new life, new hope. After the fireworks there were processions in medieval costume, and a magnificent display of flag throwing.

"Beautiful!" Sonia concluded, despite herself. Francesca and Lorenzo exchanged a look that she knew was because she'd always refused to come to Florence for this event in the past.

In their own village of Santa Zita, the priest would be releasing real doves from the steps of the church, the piazza would smell of sweet pastries and chocolate as people picked up their beautifully packaged confectionery gifts from the bar, and everyone would be dressed up, especially the little girls in their white dresses and ribbons. The tables outside Carlo's restaurant would fill the square as people arrived for the Easter lunch, which would last most of the afternoon. And yet, she was relieved to be here, anonymous amid the tourist crush.

Making their way back to the flat for lunch was hard work, weaving in and out of groups that seemed to be in no hurry and stopped to take pictures every few minutes. She had to duck more than once to avoid being hit by selfie sticks. Crossing the bridge, they had to keep stopping to avoid being in other people's holiday snaps and weaving around artists, a beggar with a wretched-looking litter of puppies, and street vendors selling watches and sunglasses, poor quality prints of The Birth of Venus and smutty aprons featuring David's torso.

"Chaos," she murmured, and she saw the young couple look at each other again. Was she so predictable? She'd have to bite her tongue from now on.

Francesca carved a passage through the bodies, looking round at Sonia and motioning her to follow her. She looked lovely, Sonia thought as she followed, with her big, unselfconscious smile and her long chestnut hair swinging in the breeze. She looked so effortlessly smart in her silk dress amid all the jeans and shorts and trainers, her three-inch heels making her almost as tall as Lorenzo. He drew her close to him, aware of the admiring glances she was receiving from males and females alike.

It was a relief to get over the bridge and into a quieter district of the Oltrarno. They stopped at a little patisserie to pick up a dessert. The pain in Sonia's stomach was creeping back and she couldn't face eating, but she made appreciative noises and held Flavio's arm as she walked.

The lift was broken, so they puffed up the stairs, flights and flights. The flat at the top was very small, but the roof terrace had a charming view over a piazza where they could see people milling about, exchanging kisses and walking their dogs. A group of small boys booted a ball across the space.

"We won't be here forever," Lorenzo said. "We're going to be looking for somewhere bigger this year – and preferably with fewer stairs." He glanced conspiratorially at Francesca again, then back at his mother. "That was the thing I wanted to tell you about."

Of course. New life, new hope, Sonia realised with a smile. And then it hit her.

New lies.

Chapter Fifty-Nine

Sonia looked at her son, soon to be a father, uncorking the Prosecco on a rooftop in Florence, his black hair and white linen shirt ruffled by the breeze. It was one of those moments in life that would always be there. She just wished things weren't so complicated.

Lorenzo handed Francesca an orange juice and planted a kiss on her nose. For them, the future was exciting, happy, an adventure.

"I'm sorry we didn't tell you straight away," he said, turning back to his parents. That impish smile transported Sonia instantly back to those days when she had felt young and in control, looking into that little face. The grin that said *It wasn't me. I didn't do it. You can fix it, can't you?*

"We wanted to tell you in person, not just over the phone," he said, "and Francesca was really sick for the first few weeks, so she didn't feel like going anywhere."

Sonia threw her arms around Francesca and Lorenzo, not wanting to let her son go. She laughed away her emotional response, which was easy to do under the circumstances as even Flavio had tears in his eyes. He took her in his arms, laughing and scolding her, but squeezing her tenderly. She knew what was going through his mind.

All those pregnancies that had come to nothing. It had been agonising to lose one baby after another while all around the cheerful blue or pink rosettes appeared on neighbours' front doors announcing their good news. And they were so often the wrong people to be parents. Seeing the way they brought up their children had made her seethe. She shouldn't judge, but it was hard not to.

For so long it had been impossible to see past that stage.

They stopped talking about it, but time after time her hopes were raised and then dashed. Each time the bleeding started, she'd lie still for days with her legs raised, praying that it would stop, that this baby would be the one she held onto.

She tried to stay philosophical, but in her fragile state doubts started to take hold. If she couldn't find a sensible reason for the problem, she'd look for one that didn't make sense. She couldn't help thinking about what her mother had done. Couldn't help thinking that it might be nature's way – perhaps even God's way – of ensuring that nobody would inherit that bad blood.

Flavio tried to argue her out of this. He always knew when it was all over, although she tried to keep it from him. After all, he pointed out, her mother had given birth to her and she wasn't like her mother. But at the time she couldn't see. She'd wanted to apply some sort of rationale, no matter how far-fetched it seemed.

She couldn't believe how resilient she became. After the first couple were lost, Flavio had suggested they stop trying. It was too painful. She knew it made him feel helpless. But they'd embarked on a course they couldn't abandon, because that would mean that the pain they were enduring had no remedy. Until Lorenzo came along.

Like most new parents, they used to stare into their child's exquisite face for hours when he was asleep, marvelling at his soft eyelashes, perfect nose, mop of dark curls, as he lay there with hands up by his head, mouth slightly open, utterly content.

She knew she fussed over him more than she should. If he was out of sight for too long, she panicked. If he was slightly ill, she called the doctor, even if it was the middle of the night. Flavio tried to stop her, afraid they would be accused of crying wolf, but really, he was as concerned as she was.

And here Lorenzo was now, a grown man, about to be a father himself, laughing and joking, so pleased with himself and proud of Francesca. He had no idea that anything could be different from how it appeared.

"Thought of any names yet?" asked Flavio.

Francesca laughed. "We're always arguing about it. We don't agree on any so far. Lorenzo's choices are so old-fashioned. I want something special and different."

Lorenzo rolled his eyes. "Yours are all foreign celebrity names," he protested. "We want something traditional with a bit of class."

"Do we? Such as?"

"Pilade."

"Troy."

"Isabella."

"Elle."

"Lucrezia."

"Beyonce."

"Oh, for God's sake." He appealed to his parents, laughing. "You see the problem?"

Francesca looked at Sonia. "What would you choose?"

"How about Maria?" For one crazy moment she'd almost said Martina.

Lorenzo himself had shown no curiosity about his heritage as he was growing up, so Sonia hadn't had to tell him about his grandmother, although there had always been the worry that someone else would. But his baby being born in Florence would be free of all that.

And yet the impending birth opened up new anxieties. Francesca looked radiant, bubbling with excitement about being a mother, but who knew what genes she was carrying, what might be revealed later in a screening, and what questions would that lead to?

"Are you all right, Mamma?" Lorenzo asked, bringing her back to the roof terrace in Florence on Easter Day.

"Of course I am. I'm so happy for you. I was just thinking how quickly time flies."

"You looked like you were miles away."

If anyone could make her see the lighter side of a situation, it was Lorenzo. If only he could now. If only he had an idea where to begin. But it wasn't his problem. It must never be his problem. His life had been so wonderfully

221

simple and straightforward. Why should he be burdened with this knowledge? The old debate started up in her head. Wouldn't telling him really be a selfish act, more of a release for her than a help to him?

For the next couple of hours, she busied herself in the kitchen. This lunch, this Easter Day, could be their last together as the family they were. Who knew how things would be next year? She stabbed back the thought and forced herself to concentrate on cooking the lunch, refusing offers of help. After all, she had things to do.

As the laughter and chatter continued from the roof above, she slipped out of the kitchen and across the stairs to the bedroom. Her heart thumped as she pushed open the door, startling a tabby cat that leapt off the bed and rubbed against her legs.

She felt like a thief going through their belongings. How would she possibly explain if one of them popped back down to the room for something and found her?

Lorenzo's bedside cabinet had a stack of Scandinavian noir novels and a glorious picture of him and Francesca on a beach. Francesca's side was completely clear, but the dressing table smelled of her perfume, that distinctive mix of marine and herbal notes, and was crammed with bottles and jars.

A cat eyed her as she lifted the lid off a slim white box. Her fingers trembled as she picked through earrings of every description, a couple of gold bracelets, and various Murano glass pendants. From the town came the sounds of bands leading the processions before the Medieval football game.

Feverishly digging through, she lifted out a gold chain, but it wasn't the one she'd been looking for. Where else could it be?

Sliding open the lingerie drawer, she gingerly lifted garments, so pretty and so tiny – forcing back mental pictures of her daughter-in-law wearing these things or, worse, Lorenzo undressing her in this room.

Her heart leapt into her mouth as she heard footsteps on

the stairs. Francesca's voice. "Be right back."

She froze, her hand still in the drawer. But a door above her closed with a thunk. Francesca had only been going to the bathroom. Sonia released her breath. Her fingers closed around a scrap of tissue. Unfurling it, she held the shooting star pendant up to the light, watching the diamonds in its tail sparkle. She had a sudden vision of the girl in the church leaving the necklace on top of the baby before she ran away. And the television showing an identical one that had been found on one of the bodies discovered at Villa Leonida. If someone recognised the pendant, they could make the connection even now, and she couldn't risk that.

"Mamma?"

Her heart catapulted. She stuffed the pendant into her pocket. Lorenzo's face, as he came through the door, was full of surprise.

"What are you doing?"

"Your cat was stuck in here," she said, reaching down to stroke the tabby as it wound itself through her legs. "Isn't she lovely?"

Her son grinned and scooped up the cat. "She is, isn't she? I don't know how she'll take to the baby. She's used to being queen around here."

Sonia's hands curled around the pendant inside her pocket. Stealing from your own child was an awful thing to do, even if it was technically stealing back, but it had to be done. Perhaps some time in the future when the talk had died down again, she'd be able to slip it back in among Francesca's belongings.

Getting into the car at the end of the day, she felt her stomach contract with pain once more. It felt as though a shard of glass was stuck inside her. If Lorenzo were to find out the truth about his birth, this could be the last occasion he'd want anything to do with her. Francesca, too. She'd wonder what sort of family she was marrying into. She might even change her mind.

Although nobody could be good enough for Lorenzo, Sonia had found it impossible to dislike Francesca, who was wise and generous enough not to try and monopolise her son when they were together.

"Look after yourself," she managed to say.

Francesca, patting her stomach, had laughed and said, "Don't worry, I will."

There were jokes about how she was planning to make the most of it and spend the next few months with her feet up, being waited on, taking advantage of every opportunity to pamper herself. Then they were gone, Lorenzo and Francesca, strolling along the road back to the flat, hand-in-hand, blissfully ignorant.

Sonia lay awake staring into the darkness. It was hardly a surprise that the girl had come back again in her dream, finding her way into the house and taking the baby. Only this time she spoke, too.

"I'll tell."

Next to Sonia, Flavio snored heavily, blissfully ignorant of her fears. He'd never had trouble sleeping, in all the years she had known him. She reached out and touched him, and he automatically drew her towards him. She felt the warmth of his body, his broad chest rising rhythmically, and he folded his large, solid hands around her. Could it really be said that you love someone if you lied to them about something so important, or at least hid the truth?

Chapter Sixty

Martina found the door of the building open. She pushed it back and clattered up the stairs, her heart racing. Roberto was waiting for her at the top, standing in the doorway, his head resting on an arm that was leaning on the frame. He must have watched her coming down the street from the window. He pulled her inside, kicking the door shut.

He kept talking as they were kissing and undressing.

"For God's sake, where have you been? I thought you'd changed your mind. I've been going out of my mind thinking about you. About doing this. And this."

She couldn't tell him about Gianni, so she talked about needing to be there for Cesare. She felt bad lying to him, but in the end it would be safer for all of them.

"In a way, I was glad," he said. "I don't know how much longer it's safe to stay down here with these air raids. There are so many alarms and mostly they don't come to anything, but you never know. It would be safer if I came up to Santa Zita again."

"No." She'd rather take the risk of being bombed down here by the coast than set tongues wagging in the village, with all the heartache that would cause. And besides, now that Gianni was stronger, she feared for both of their lives if he saw them together.

It was the same the next week and the next. There was so much time to make up for. If they'd known that final day that it would be their last, would they have spent it any differently? What would they have said to each other? She would always wonder.

"It won't always be like this," he said, letting her hair run through his fingers as he lay with her head on his chest. "I

225

want us to be together properly."

"I couldn't leave without Sonia."

He smiled as though that was understood. "I mean with Sonia, of course."

It all seemed so easy. She no longer had any doubts. She still didn't know him as well as she thought she should, but that only added to the attraction, and there would be so much time to get to know everything about each other when the war was over.

Outside on the street, she looked back up to the window. He blew a kiss and mouthed something. Was it 'I love you'?

The plane roared above her. Probably one that had strayed off course heading further up the coast. No, the sound was getting louder, so loud she couldn't think. In that second as she looked up, she saw Roberto's face at the window filled with a brilliant whiteness, his eyes silver, his smile frozen. She didn't so much hear as feel the blast, caught up in an explosion of white as the buildings erupted. She felt herself being lifted through the air and hurled across the street, crashing through a million fragments, falling into darkness.

In a split second, everything had changed. She was lying on the ground in a dark world, choking on dust. The darkness was so intense that when she first opened her eyes it made no difference, and she thought she must have been blinded. Her nostrils were filled with dust and another smell she couldn't quite identify. She couldn't breathe. For some moments, she thought she was stuck in a dream. She lay there waiting for it all to stop. But the realisation gradually came that she couldn't wake up. This was reality and it was worse than the worst nightmare she'd ever experienced.

In the dense darkness that swirled around her, she went over in her mind what she'd been doing before she found herself here. She'd been in the apartment with Roberto. They'd made love. They'd talked about everything. She'd seen Roberto's face light up. Then the world had disintegrated.

Where was he?

She cried out but couldn't make herself heard over the ringing in her ears. It bored into her head like a physical pain. For a long time, she thought she was alone. How would anyone find her? But as the dust began to settle and she was able to see more clearly, she could make out shapes of people moving, stumbling about, hauling wreckage away, as though in a silent film. As her ears popped, she noticed that this film had a backing track – a constant chorus of moans and screams. Was one of the voices hers?

Her cheek hurt. When she touched it, she found it was slippery, coated in something viscous. At the same time as she began to feel the pain, she realised her hand was soaked with blood. She must have cut it on a piece of masonry or the metal bolt of a window.

Gradually, the picture became clearer. Part of a building had collapsed on top of her, but she wasn't crushed. She wasn't trapped. She could get up, get away.

I can't die here.

She tried to get to her feet. Pain shot through her ankle, as if it had snapped. She sank back down. No, she couldn't stay here. With a gargantuan effort, she forced herself up again, calling out for Roberto although she already knew it was hopeless.

She kicked something by accident. Looking down, she saw it was an arm lying there on its own. For a while she stood staring at it, transfixed. She could make out the body of a woman with red hair, lying twisted at a grotesque angle, and an old man except that part of his face was missing. Someone said something about a building being unsafe. She must get away.

A ghost was walking towards her. She stopped, staring, running a hand bewilderedly through her hair. The ghost stopped, too. She found herself staring past her own figure caked in dust, to a café interior. Seeing her, the waiter rushed out and sat her down and brought her a glass of water.

"A whole house has disappeared. Luckily the owner's

away."

Thoughts raced through her mind. Nobody knew Roberto was using the house, but they'd find his body in the wreckage. Would they know she'd been there, too? *I have to get back. I have to get away from here. I can't let anyone know I was here.* But the words started to slide as everything went dark.

Chapter Sixty-One

IRENA

1945

Irena rummaged for the machine. Thoughts had been swirling round her head for days. She had to get them out.

Martina knew. She knew how much he meant to me. She of all people knew that he was my first, my only, love. It wasn't as though I had a different boy every week and could think, oh well I'll just find another. He was everything to me. And she took him. Simply because she could.

Instead of planning for my wedding, I found myself at my fiancé's funeral. I so hoped Martina would come with me but was told she'd had an accident, some kind of fall, and was recovering in bed. I was too distraught and bound up in my own grief to find it odd. I hadn't seen much of her lately, what with her father-in-law being ill and all the stuff they'd had to sort out afterwards. It never occurred to me for a moment that she'd been there in the town that day, with Roberto.

I should be even angrier with him. He painted himself as this deep and trustworthy person but turned out to be shallower than the rest of them. He proposed to me one night, fell in love with my best friend the next.

And yet I always saw hers as the greater betrayal. After all, she'd known me for years. And he, of course, paid the price. You can't heap that much hatred onto someone who died that way, can you?"

Carlo turned up the volume. He sensed he was getting

close now.

It happened on such an ordinary day. I can't even remember what we were doing or what the weather was like. There was some incident down in the town. Some German soldiers had beaten up a shopkeeper for swearing at them. Later that day, one of the partisans retaliated by shooting a soldier. We knew they weren't going to overlook it.

The Nazis were aware the partisans were up in the hills, but they hadn't been able to find out where they were hiding. That incident changed everything.

It was Dieter who told us about the reward. They were offering money - a substantial amount - for information on the group. He urged us to tell them anything we'd heard. "We know there's a partisan cell around here. We just need to know where they are," he said.

He was very persistent. Anxious even. I got the impression he wanted to persuade us for our sakes as well as theirs.

"You know you'd be putting German lives at risk by not telling," he said. "You know how seriously that would be taken. I don't want to see any harm come to you."

But we both denied all knowledge of it, of course. He gave Sonia some chocolate before he left. He looked behind him several times as he went, giving us the chance to change our minds, but we still said we had nothing to tell.

For a few days, nothing happened. We went about our business, but it was always there, an undercurrent running through everything we did, every conversation we had. We were all holding our breath, wondering who'd be the one to break. I still couldn't tell if Dieter had said what he did out of concern or as a threat, but we weren't stupid. We knew if they didn't get their information through bribery, they had other methods. And we knew it was only a matter of time before their patience ran out.

"It's Gianni's fault," Martina said, as we sat on the wall of the fountain in the deserted piazza. "As long as they're up there above the village doing stupid things, they're

230

making us a target for revenge. We need to get them to go.'

I'd never seen her like that. She hated Gianni for bringing this to us. If the Nazis found the partisans, perhaps they'd deal with them and leave our village alone. Someone had to explain to the Germans that we'd never asked them to come, they were nothing to do with us. Then they might realise there was no sense in taking it out on us.

If Gianni was gone, Martina wouldn't have to worry about her future any more. Or Sonia's future. Or Villa Leonida.

Carlo felt a trickle of fear between his shoulder blades as he sensed what was coming.

Chapter Sixty-Two

The muffled roar of engines grew louder as the Germans proceeded through the town below and along the valley. From the balcony at Villa Leonida, Martina saw them before she heard them. It was rare for there to be so many vehicles. In the piazza, people gathered to watch, then dispersed and disappeared.

It looked at first as though the convoy would carry on past the turning to Santa Zita, through the valley to a village further north where there had been lots of trouble. But it stopped. Martina held her breath. The vehicles were turning round. They filed back along the road towards the town. One by one they disappeared from the road and she could tell by the revving and stalling that they were swinging around the first bend that led up to Santa Zita.

As the engines grew louder, shutters banged closed. People called their children inside and retreated into the shadows of their homes. Some figures ran across the piazza and up into the hills. Others tumbled out into the fields.

By the time the soldiers arrived, the place looked deserted. The engines cut. A couple of men went into the bar, where they were used to singing and exchanging a joke with Bernardo the barman. They came out with him in silence. He looked up towards the villa and Martina retreated from the balcony and closed the French doors.

Between the slats of the shutters she could see the soldiers spreading out, knocking on doors. Some of them started coming on foot up the hill towards the house. This was going to be worse, so much worse, than she'd expected.

She ran to Elena's room. "We need to go," she said.

Elena was sitting in bed, her mouth set firm. "I'm not

going anywhere. Where would we go?"

"We need to hide. One of the barns or the chestnut tower."

Her mother-in-law refused to move. "This is our house. We've done nothing wrong."

"Do you honestly think that makes a difference?"

"You go if you want to. I'm not going to hide like some common criminal. They're looking for those fools up in the hills. They won't harm us."

"When are you going to realise? They don't care what we've done or what we haven't."

Martina ran back to the window. She could see the young, broad face and silver eyes of the first soldier. It was Dieter, the one who'd given sweets to Sonia. He had been trying to warn them, of course he had. She heard someone giving orders in the familiar clipped accent. She closed her eyes. It couldn't be happening. Not like this.

She waited, pressed against the wall. Perhaps Elena was right. They had nothing to fear. And if they were caught running, it would look as though they had something to hide.

The soldiers passed. More steps, a blur of bodies moving close enough for her to reach out and touch them, boots clattering on the cobblestones. Then, for a very long time nothing. She knew where they were headed. It wouldn't be long now. It was too late for anyone to get a warning to the men up there. If they tried, they'd be shot or hanged.

From a long way off Martina thought she heard a sudden shout and a shot. Then another. Then a volley of shots and shouting. After that, things happened very quickly. Perhaps the soldiers had walked into a trap and the partisans were shooting at them, or perhaps the partisans had been overpowered. She thought briefly of Gianni. Would he be lucky this time?

Below, someone left the priest's house and ran down into the woods. Another shot. Shouting, rushing feet, more orders delivered in German. Something had gone horribly wrong.

"Mamma?" Sonia's voice was soft. She knew something was going on. "Can we play cards?"

Martina scooped the child in her arms, hugging her close, savouring the feel of her soft hair, the orangey scent of her skin. "Let's play hide-and-seek instead. But it's different this time. We'll hide together. Show me your very best hiding place, Sonia."

"But who'll find us?" asked the child, puzzled.

"Nobody. That's the point. Nobody must find us."

"Can *Nonna* play, too?" Sonia asked.

Martina shut her eyes for a moment and shook her head, remembering Elena lying in bed. They couldn't afford to be held up. "*Nonna*'s asleep. We mustn't wake her."

Surely anyone could see a grandmother was no threat? Dieter and his friends had always been respectful of her when they'd seen Elena in the piazza. And one glance around the house would show framed pictures of the King and Mussolini, evidence of her loyalty to the Fascist state.

"I know a great place," Sonia whispered with an impish smile. "No-one will ever find us there."

Sonia took her mother's hand and led her to the chestnut tower.

At the back, where the tower had been built up against the rock, was the cave the family had used as a cantina for their wine in former years, and where Gianni had slept recently. If she could rearrange some things in front of the entrance, it might just work.

"Quickly," Martina urged. She grimaced as she shunted some boxes.

"Not here," said Sonia. She pointed above her head. "Up there."

Martina looked up. There was a ledge above her and a narrow, dark space like a chimney. Sonia climbed up with ease. Martina nearly fainted.

"You go up. I can't. But stay there, Sonia. Stay there until I call you. Don't come out for anyone else."

Where could she go now? There wasn't time. If she left the building, someone might see her.

Sonia poked her head back out. "You can do it, Mamma. It's bigger once you get up here. Look."

"How did you know about this?" Martina whispered.

"The man showed me. The one with the beard who lived in my imagination, the one you said I was never allowed to talk about."

Martina's heart twisted at the thought of what Gianni had done for them, making plans for an event like this – and what she'd done. But there wasn't time to think about it now. If Gianni could make it into that restricted space, she must be able to. She had to try. She'd been so angry when she discovered he'd been out of the tower visiting Elena at night and talking to Sonia, but it was just possible that in showing her this place he'd saved their lives. Sick dread trickled through her as she thought of the danger he was in, that they were all in.

She heaved herself up, slipping back twice, bruising her shin and taking the skin off her shoulder. There was room enough to sit with her legs drawn up, but the space was very small. How long would the air last? How long could they stand being here? She'd dragged the box back across the opening to the cave, but she tried to stamp out the thought that kept sweeping through her. In doing so, had she sealed them into a coffin?

Even as a small child Martina had been afraid of the dark and panicked in tight spaces. The more she thought about it, the harder it was to breathe. Hours passed. It was impossible to say how long. She heard Elena calling. She didn't reply. Sonia looked at her quizzically, asking permission to shout, but Martina shook her head firmly, making ready if necessary to clamp her hand over her daughter's mouth.

Engines revved below them. Reinforcements must have arrived. There was noise, movement everywhere. The soldiers must be making their way through the village, house by house. Martina shrank as she heard doors being kicked in, windows smashing, people screaming. She could picture the scene, though she didn't want to. She'd heard enough accounts from elsewhere. Old people being dragged out of bed, children pulled out of hiding places. Houses set on fire, and soldiers standing outside to gun people down as they tried to escape the flames. Others coming out of their homes voluntarily, knowing it was only a matter of time and wanting to preserve as much as they could of their dignity and their possessions. Made to gather in the piazza....

"This isn't a game, is it, Mamma?" Sonia whispered. Her eyes were huge and luminous in the dark space. "What will they do to us if they find us? Will they take us away, like the Palmieris?"

Martina buried her face in the child's hair. "I love you," she whispered over and over again, like a mantra. And, "I'm sorry, I'm so sorry."

Their hearts jolted as they heard their own front door being pounded. There was no sound from Elena. Surely the men would leave her once they'd established she was alone, an infirm, elderly widow? Shouts. Boots. Elena whimpering. She must have tried to get out of the house after all. Someone must have spotted her running away. Martina hugged Sonia to her more closely to shield her ears.

Furniture being hurled out of the windows. Elena pleading. At least she couldn't tell them where her daughter-in-law and granddaughter were, but Martina wouldn't let herself imagine what they were doing to her. More noise and movement, and then something very quiet.

So quiet she almost thought she had misheard. The exchange of weight from one foot to another. An inhalation. Her heart sank like a stone. Someone was standing in the chestnut drying tower. They hadn't heard him come in.

Could he sense that people were here, even without seeing them? Were they trained in the army to tell such things? Had Martina left some sign, some stupid infantile clue like a trail of footprints across the floor? Her heart thumped as she relived those feverish moments when Sonia still thought it was a game. Had they dropped something? One of Sonia's toys?

The feet slipped slowly into the room, heel-toe, heel-toe, moving systematically around the tower. The rustle of a great coat against jack boots, the grating sound of boxes being shifted aside. A light was cast beneath them. It swung around, presumably catching different parts of the room in its glow. *Do they know we're here?* she thought. *Are they just waiting for us to come out?*

A slow grinding sound as more wine flasks and boxes were moved. So quietly done. Another beam of light. Then a voice chillingly soft: "Come out. I've seen you."

She almost fell for it. For a moment she just wanted it all to be over. But even if she had wanted to move, she couldn't. She'd lost all feeling in her legs in those cramped conditions. Someone would have to drag her. Or shoot her.

More footsteps. "Anyone?" asked a second voice. Martina had picked up just enough German from the time she'd spent with Dieter and his friends to understand what they were saying, or at least the gist of it.

"Rats," replied the first. "Come on."

"Someone's been here. It smells of piss," said the other.

For the first time, Martina noticed that she'd lost control, as well as Sonia. She'd thought she was simply bathed in sweat. Now she was terrified that it had trickled down the wall and would be as visible as any signpost.

The other laughed. "You and your fucking smells. Well, they're not here now. That old cow probably tipped them off. She's not as ill as she makes out." The feet moved away, and she heard them going back over to the house. There was a brief exchange with some others. A gun was fired. Silence.

Sonia's face was frozen into a mask of horror. It must mirror her own. Martina had forgotten how to breathe. Then something extraordinary. The sound of their piano being played. Quite well. These men who had quite probably killed Elena were now playing her piano as though they had popped in on a Sunday visit.

Martina and Sonia stayed in the hiding place for hours, even after the piano stopped. She suspected another trick and was too terrified of what they might see when they came out. They clung to the only certainty they had, which was each other. Sonia seemed asleep, she was so still. Only the rhythmic movement of her ribcage against Martina's assured her that her little girl was still alive.

More time passed. Martina was in such excruciating discomfort crouched in the suffocating space that she thought she'd pass out. If she were on her own, she'd give in to it. But then what would happen to Sonia?

Eventually, she stretched a limb. Sonia started to scramble down. A noise from outside made them freeze.

They heard more footsteps coming up towards the house, more orders being given. "Keep walking. Shut up. Look where you're going."

She grabbed Sonia and hauled her back up to the ledge. The idea of being back there was unbearable, but the alternative was worse.

It was starting to sink in. "I'm sorry," she whispered again into Sonia's hair.

Then the screaming. She couldn't work out where it was coming from, but it was real, and it was terrible.

Powerless to do anything now, Martina covered Sonia's ears, but she couldn't drown out the noise. She could hear the cries of a baby long after the rest had fallen silent, and the air was filled with the smell of burning. The cries must have stopped at some point, but she already knew she'd never stop hearing them. What had she done?

Chapter Sixty-Three

IRENA

I was in the school when the soldiers came. We heard the vans draw up outside; heard the whispers that were going round. We'd been expecting trouble ever since the German officer had been shot in the town, but this still seemed to come from out of the blue.

I told the class to close their books. We'd sing songs instead. I just kept thinking they wouldn't do it, not to children, especially not ones who were singing patriotic songs.

The door burst open. Some of the parents rushed into the room to get to their children. Those who were left clung to me, wanting to know what was happening and where their own parents were. I still didn't think we were in immediate danger, but thought they might see something upsetting or get caught up in something distressing, so I urged the children to hide. But before they all had the chance, a soldier came in and ordered us all to get out and join the others in the piazza. They checked under desks and in cupboards, dragging out any children they found hiding, and pushed them out, too.

I think it was going through all of our minds then: would we ever be coming back?

Chapter Sixty-Four

People filed like robots out into the piazza. There were some moments of confusion as an armoured vehicle had to be moved out of the square in order to accommodate them all, and a silence – a strange formality among the people as they gathered. A ripple of movement crept through the crowd as people pushed their way along the lines, trying to get into a preferred position or be with people they knew – swapping places over and over, as though taking part in some bizarre silent dance. A command was shouted. All movement stopped.

The Nazi officer in charge read out a statement conveying his disappointment and anger that this village had chosen to obstruct them in their quest. His voice was measured, reasonable, the tone injured.

Someone had been so arrogant as to think they could pick an argument with no less than the Fuhrer. And someone had shot dead a fine and noble German soldier. For that, everyone must surely understand, a price would have to be paid.

It wasn't as if they didn't know – it had been well enough publicised, the co-operation expected by the Italian people, and that cooperation had been left wanting here.

There was silence as he read. People looked down, looked away, looked straight ahead, terrified to in any way antagonise the soldiers or draw attention to themselves. They had an idea of what was coming.

At last, Irena stepped forward, pleading for the lives of the schoolchildren to be spared.

"Shut up," shouted an officer.

Someone pulled her back into the crowd. She stood trembling, unable to believe that an exception couldn't be made for children. The soldiers moved along the crowd, picking out people at random. First, Bernardo from the bar, then the two brothers from the restaurant. Some went defiantly, most shuffled; some broke down.

A teenage boy burst out of the crowd.

"Not her. Not my mother. You can't take her."

The officer turned to him. "Have you finished?"

He nodded.

"Good."

A shot rang out. The boy slumped to the floor. There was an intake of breath and a muffled cry of anguish from his mother who tried to tend to him, but she was pushed roughly on.

Irena watched the blood spill onto the cobbles. She couldn't take in what she had just seen. She felt her knees give way as she was the last to be picked. She wrested her hand out of her mother's – it wasn't worth them both being killed – then stepped out, her head down. How was she going to be able to walk?

She was shoved forward, and they made their way up the path, barely aware of who was among them. As they were ordered up the little path that led towards the villa, she found herself being pulled back by one of the soldiers.

"Wait."

He said it so quietly it could have been in her head. Irena looked up. It was Dieter. His eyes were fixed ahead, his body blocking the view of the rest of the people as they continued up the path. He indicated the alleyway to his left. "Down there. Go."

She went without a word, not daring to thank him or even knowing if she should. Slipping down the cobbles, she waited all the time for a bullet in her back. It didn't come. She rounded the bend and flattened herself against the wall, her breath coming in stabs as she tried to shut out the sounds of the rest of the party moving on up the hill. Then she sank down to the floor, hugging her knees. Perhaps

Dieter would come back for her. Or perhaps he had something worse in mind.

In the little courtyard behind the chapel, the residents of Santa Zita must have realised there was no chance of making a run for it. All they could do was wait. The odd thing was that Irena, slumped on the steps several levels below Villa Leonida, thought she could hear music – a piano being played beautifully from somewhere up above her. An order was given. Bullets pumped. She shut her eyes. Human beings turned to a heap of rubble.

Chapter Sixty-Five

IRENA

Gianni was hanged in front of us in the piazza, along with the two other partisans they'd captured. I was only glad his parents weren't there to see it.

Carlo was sitting in the empty restaurant. The Easter rush had fallen off a bit, but takings this lunchtime had still been good. He poured himself a brandy and drank it too quickly.

At first, I just didn't believe she'd started all this. His mother's voice was frail and bewildered. *She was my friend. I trusted her. We'd known each other since we were babies in our prams. We told each other everything. I didn't speak to her for a long time after. It was too painful to look at her and think about what she'd done. You want to know why, don't you?*

The air crackled as she sighed. *The thing is, amore, you don't have to be a bad person to do a terrible thing.*

Carlo stared at the device, willing her to go on but at the same time afraid of what he was going to hear.

They promised us they would guarantee our safety if we told them where Gianni and the rest were hiding. Martina trusted Dieter. I think at that time she meant to be generous with the money – thought it would benefit all of us. We were all starving, you see.

Her voice dropped almost to a whisper.

But that's hard to accept, of course, when your family and so many good neighbours have been slaughtered.

***

Carlo sat staring at the machine. There was something about his mother's story that didn't ring true. He didn't want to confront it, but he had to.

He found her in the living room in her usual chair. She was sitting with her back to him, looking out at the cloud formation over the mountains opposite. A sixth sense must have alerted her to his presence because she swung round.

"What is it? What do you want?"

He was trying not to brandish the device at her and put her on the defensive, but he caught the startled look on her face as she spotted it in his hand.

"I told you not to touch that. It's mine. You had no right." But her tone was resigned rather than fiercely indignant like last time.

He played the last section back to her. They sat together and listened to it, not looking at one another. He pressed the back of his fist against his lips. Tears leaked down her cheeks, pooling in the contours and crevices of her skin.

"Was it really Martina who talked to the Nazis?" he asked.

Irena's eyes glistened as she gripped his hand. She shook her head. All these years, and she was finally on the point of letting go of the truth.

"I didn't think they would do it to us," she whispered. "I trusted them. I was stupid. I wanted vengeance for what she'd done to me, but not like that. Not like that."

It took a while to absorb what he'd just heard. Outside in the piazza came the sound of laughter and footsteps – a group of teenagers walking through, the new generation keeping Santa Zita alive.

"It was you, wasn't it?" he said. "You who told them about the partisans and where they were hiding. That's why they let you go." He wanted to get it clear in his own mind. "But *why?*"

She looked at him aghast. Her voice shook with anger and indignation. For a moment he thought she was going to slap his face. "It wasn't me. I did not tell them."

He shut his eyes. Was this one of those conversations that

was going to go round in circles? He tried to control his voice, but there was a sharpness to his tone he couldn't suppress.

"Well, if it wasn't you, who was it?"

After a while she said, "It was Alvaro."

"*Alvaro?*"

"Yes, don't you remember? The boy she bullied at school."

"Of course I remember, but what did he have to do with it?"

His mother smiled and shook her head. "You see, what you and so many people don't understand is that often it isn't one little thing that leads to an act of hate. It's dozens of little things that add up over the years.

"Gianni was no better than Martina. He lied to Alvaro. Promised him all sorts of rewards for covering for him when he deserted. But Alvaro certainly didn't get anything that I'm aware of."

No wonder he resented both Martina and Gianni for the way they'd treated him.

But even so… Carlo shook his head in confusion. "It still doesn't make sense."

"He was so messed up by then," she continued, "and so addicted to stuff, he must have been easy to bribe. He probably didn't even know what he was saying. And he'd become invisible to just about everyone; no-one noticed him. I saw it, but I understood too late. I spotted him talking to the Germans that evening, sitting on the bench outside the school. I'd gone back to get some books. There was a little knot of soldiers around him.

"Dieter lifted his head, and I saw something in his expression. Something died in his eyes. And I knew then something very bad was going to happen."

Carlo digested this. "So why didn't you tell people? Give them the chance to escape? Or at least hide?"

His mother looked at him as though he were a child. "There was nowhere to escape, *amore*. Nowhere to hide. Where would we have gone? If I'd tried to organise a mass exodus, things would have ended up even worse than they did. Dieter had seen me. He would have guessed I'd overheard. And I didn't know exactly what would happen, or when, or how. We were all expecting something, remember."

She sighed and drew her cardigan around her shoulders. Her mouth hardened. "And to tell the truth, I thought things might work out for the best."

Carlo felt he was talking to a stranger. "How can you even say that?"

Irena didn't seem to hear him. She got to her feet, her arms shaking as she leant on the sides of the chair for support. He watched but didn't help her. She walked over to the window and started rearranging the ornaments.

"I wanted her to know what it felt like. To have something, someone, of hers taken away from her." She was as calm as if she had been discussing what to put on her shopping list. "Taking Roberto from me. Getting him killed. She destroyed me."

She moved the azalea, knocking over a china figurine, which crashed to the floor. She looked out of the window, probably at some remembered scene, while her reflection continued to address Carlo.

"I wasn't thinking clearly. I just wanted to hurt Martina as much as she'd hurt me. I knew Gianni was up there with them, leaving her free to eye up other men and ruin other people's lives. I heard rumours that he'd been staying with her down at the villa, not that she ever told me.

"You see, she and Gianni didn't care about anyone but themselves."

Her arms, gripping the window frame, shook.

"I wanted him to be frightened. And her to be frightened for him. It was both of them, you see, who'd destroyed me. Gianni fooling about with the partisans and Martina helping herself to Roberto.

"I wanted justice. But not like that. I didn't think it would end the way it did."

Carlo shook his head. "But you said it was Alvaro. If he

246

was the one who told them…"

She looked back at him over her shoulder and smiled. "Then what was my vengeance? What did I say? The answer is, nothing at all. Let's just say I heard someone and then someone else say that it could have been Martina who talked. That she'd been seeing another man, she'd been flirting with a German officer, and that she wanted to keep the villa but not Gianni. I heard the rumours spread. And I never set the record straight."

Carlo felt sick. All those years his mother had stood back and let her best friend be treated as a pariah.

"What happened to Alvaro?"

She shrugged. "I never saw him after the massacre. Perhaps he's living in a grand villa on the Riviera, smoking fat cigars and drinking fine wine, surrounded by the things he bought with the reward money. But it's just as likely he died that day. His house was burned to the ground, like so many others."

She was silent for a while, probably going over the events again in her head.

"How did you find out Martina was seeing Roberto?" Carlo asked at last.

Irena laughed softly. "Someone saw them together. Someone always does, don't they? The waiter from the café where the two of them used to meet helped Martina after the blast. He lived in the road where the bomb went off. He was dating a girl from Santa Zita, and word got round.

"You know, losing Roberto was unspeakably painful. But finding out that the two people I believed closest to me in the world had been together at the time, was even worse. It made a mockery of my feelings for Roberto and what we had had. We did have something before she took it. We did."

She looked out of the window again to where a young couple on a motor scooter weaved their way through the piazza, and a group of girls sat eating ice creams on the wall of the fountain, while her reflection continued to address Carlo.

"I wished it was Martina, not Roberto, who died. The only thing that gives me comfort is that they didn't die together. They didn't deserve to have that privilege."

"For God's sake."

She turned to face him again. "As it was, she had that scar for the rest of her life, disfiguring her face so that people forgot she'd ever been beautiful. They say you get the face you deserve by middle age, don't they? Well, she certainly did. Her appearance was an accurate reflection of her soul: ugly and twisted. She left me with nothing."

Carlo got to his feet. "That's enough. I can't hear any more of this."

Irena had an odd smile on her face. He couldn't look at her, suspecting but not wanting to hear what came next.

"Except for one thing. What neither of them knew, of course, was that I was expecting Roberto's baby."

He froze halfway to the door. He should have guessed. Perhaps he'd known for a long time but never let himself acknowledge it. The face in the photograph. Irena reached out towards him, but he pulled back. She was suddenly very composed. Almost frightening.

"So, in a sense you see, I feel I never lost him."

Carlo walked back slowly and sank down in the chair. "Why did people believe the rumours? Why were they so ready to believe it was Martina who'd betrayed the partisans?"

Irena laughed and waved her arm dismissively. "Oh, they knew what she was like. She made it easy for me. The obvious choice, when you think about it. They knew she'd been abandoned by Gianni. They'd seen her talking to the Germans in the town, Sonia accepting sweets from Dieter, him passing her little gifts.

"And, of course, Martina was unharmed in the massacre. No-one saw her. She turned up the following day in the piazza, holding Sonia by the hand, as right as rain except for the injury to her face, and that was starting to heal. I'll never forget it. They were greeted like long-lost heroes, kisses from everyone. Two more survivors. A miracle.

"It was only gradually, in the days and weeks afterwards, that people started asking why they hadn't been found at the villa by the Germans? Why hadn't they been killed like Elena? And everyone knew Martina and Elena didn't get on."

"You let her take the blame all those years?" he said, appalled.

For a while he didn't think she was going to answer.

"The thing is, *amore*, I think she wanted to."

"Really? How do you make that out?" He wanted to shake her, his own mother.

"She could have defended herself, pointed the finger at me. But I think she wanted to atone for what she had done to me. That was the way I saw it."

He dropped his head, staring between parted fingers at her slippers, of all things: pink, velour, so at odds with her coldness.

"And you never spoke to her since?"

She turned her mouth down. "Barely. We avoided each other if we could. Once, we came close to talking about it, but she said something like, 'As far as I'm concerned you don't exist any more'."

Carlo was at a loss for words. He didn't trust himself to say too much. "What about Sonia?" he asked finally. "Didn't you think she had a right to know?"

Irena eyed him steadily. "I still think that Martina was responsible for what happened. What I did was a result of what she did. That's why she took the blame. She understood. I'm sorry for Sonia, of course I am. I loved her as a child, I'd have done anything for her. But I don't owe her anything."

"You don't *owe her anything?*" Carlo could barely look at her. "What about having to grow up as the daughter of a traitor? What about—"

"I've made it up to Sonia in my own way," his mother said. "I've kept a secret for her for many years, probably the one that means more to her than anything else in her life. Do you really think Lorenzo's Sonia's child?"

249

Carlo shook his head. Perhaps this had to do with that pregnant girl his mother had been talking about last time. But what business was it of anyone's if Sonia's miracle birth was really the result of some surrogate arrangement? He couldn't listen to her any longer. He had to get out.

Chapter Sixty-Six

2018

Sonia climbed the stone steps to the doctor's surgery. She was in no hurry to reach the top. The tiled staircase was dark and cool after the warmth of the piazza, and smelled of cleaning fluid. She pushed open the door at the top and chose a seat by the window. This was a formality, as far as she was concerned. It would be no less than confirmation of what she already knew.

It was terminal, sure to be by now. She'd ignored the symptoms too long. First the gnawing pain, then the dark, tarry stools, the distended stomach, the weight loss and confusion. Now the retching producing that dark red granular stuff. All the time, she'd mistaken it for stress – God's final cruel joke. The discovery of the bodies last year, and the villa coming up for sale again this year, had only masked the signs. Perhaps it had been lying dormant for years just waiting for the trigger.

Stupid. So stupid. She should have faced up to it sooner. Now she just wanted to get the diagnosis out of the way. She sat in the little waiting room overlooking the park, watching the fir trees dancing in the breeze, trying to fix her thoughts on immediate things, not daring to look into the future. She was only vaguely aware of the clicking of knitting needles, the rustling of pages of a magazine, a mother reading quietly to a small child, and the child's legs swinging against the chair,

"Who's next?" the doctor asked, popping his head out of the door.

A cold fear crept over Sonia, chaining her to her seat.

The young mother nodded in her direction, but Sonia shook her head. "No, no – after you." The doctor raised his eyebrows at Sonia. She couldn't make herself move. She smiled and waved her hand, indicating she was in no hurry and the child was obviously growing restless.

When the door closed, she got up and made her way quietly down the stairs.

Not today; she couldn't cope with hearing it today.

Back home, she rummaged for writing paper and a pen. Sitting on the balcony at the back of the house, she wrote the letter that had been forming in her mind for weeks. It seemed strangely formal to be writing to her son. When had she last done so? It must have been when he was at school camp. It had probably been a brief description of her day and some words of affection and encouragement, a reminder to wash his hair in the shower and use the deodorant she'd packed for him. Thinking about it now, she'd never talked to him about anything very serious.

Whichever way I say this, it's going to come as a shock. But you need to know that we are not your biological parents. I always meant to tell you, but it never seemed to be the right time, and I'd come to believe that it was irrelevant anyway. We couldn't have loved you any more than we have, and although I wish that I'd given birth to you, I wouldn't have wanted you different in any tiny detail. You were always, as far as I am concerned, our son.

It isn't a straightforward situation. I'm not a baby-snatcher. In all those years of waiting and hoping and having my hopes dashed, I never looked at anyone else's child and felt the urge to take it. I wanted my own. But when I saw you there, given up to God, it was as though I was being given a gift. One thing I'm absolutely sure of is that you would have died if you'd been left there. You were very weak as it was.

I know it will be hard for you to understand, and I so wish you didn't have to be hurt by the knowledge. I'd have chosen never to tell you, although I know you have a right to know. But times have changed, and science has made it necessary for you to have the information in case it's ever needed. Not that I can give you the details of either parent. All I can assure you is that the girl was very young, far too young to be a mother, and in all probability your father never even knew you existed. I doubt she'd have told him. I've always hoped what I did gave her a second chance at life, as well as you. I wish I could pretend you were conceived in better circumstances.

I believed genuinely at the time that she'd abandoned you and had left you in the hope that someone would adopt you. I felt I was that person, called upon by God. It fitted perfectly with everything I'd prayed for.

It's something that's haunted me ever since the bodies were found at the villa last year. All I know is that after what she must have gone through the girl clearly couldn't have been mentally stable and wasn't capable of looking after a baby.

I don't know if she came back to look for you or if the father did, or if someone else at the villa found out about it – but it was clearly a violent household, and I hate to think what might have happened to you if you had grown up there.

I know this will come as a shock for you, but what makes me really ashamed is the fact that I was too cowardly to tell you in person. That I'm not there to comfort you as you read this, or to answer your questions. But I thought I had so much time, and suddenly I realise I haven't any more. I hope you can understand this, and one day forgive me…

It was hardly adequate but would have to do. She read it through several times, sealed the envelope and wrote his name on the front, but put no address. She set off downstairs to the cantina where she kept the box of small treasures she'd packed away when he was small, and that contained some of his hair, his first tooth, first shoes, and of course the locket she'd stolen back from Francesca. Nobody would look in there until well after she was gone.

The door slammed. She bit her lip as she heard Flavio calling her name. No chance of going down there now without making him suspicious. She shoved the letter in her handbag and greeted Flavio with a smile, banishing imagined scenes of father and son reading the letter while grieving.

Now that she'd written it, she felt curiously relieved, released from the burden she'd imposed on herself for so long. *In the end, you just had to trust*, she told herself. And if she couldn't trust Lorenzo, what was the point of any of it?

Chapter Sixty-Seven

SONIA

Sonia woke in the night, the sheets around her soaked in sweat. Her stomach was on fire. The pain was so intense she could barely breathe.

"What is it?" Flavio's voice was full of concern.

She couldn't reply. At first, she lay curled in a foetal position, concentrating on taking shallow breaths without causing more pain. She was vaguely aware of him helping her to the bathroom, but the movement made the pain worse. The accidental touch of his hand on her stomach made her scream, although she was barely aware the noise came from her.

His voice sounded far away and unfamiliar. Something about "Be right back. Calling the doctor." But she couldn't really tell if he was still in the room. She had to retch. The next moment she was aware of, she was staring into a basin full of blood – so much of it, shockingly red against the white china.

She didn't know how she ended up in the ambulance, but became aware of the cool air on her face as she was carried out on the stretcher. She thought she was alone, but then Flavio was beside her.

His face was full of fear and she could hear the pleading in his voice as he spoke to the medical team, but not the words. She wanted to reassure him, but she couldn't. A kaleidoscope of images crowded her mind: scenes of happiness – riding along a coastal road on a Vespa with Flavio in their courting days; Lorenzo as she'd seen him most recently on the roof terrace of his apartment; and then as a small boy wrapped in a towel, still pink from his bath, hair sticking up in tufts, those serious dark eyes looking into hers; his hug, the smell of his skin, the feel of his kiss planted so determinedly, his little hands clasped around her head.

Now she was back at Villa Leonida, dancing with her mother on the moonlit terrace to an old tune on the gramophone, being whirled around and feeling her skirt spin out about her. Looking up and seeing the sky peppered with stars. She saw a young girl in the bar. The girl handed her a baby. But it wasn't Lorenzo – it was Lorenzo's baby.

No, that wasn't right. How could it be Lorenzo's baby? That was a memory that hadn't yet happened. She wanted so much to be around to see her grandchild. So very, very much. She had to hold on. The images were crowding in on her, then going their own way, dissolving and changing. Slipping away.

***

Gradually, sounds permeated through to her, and blocks of light reformed themselves into shapes. How long had she been in limbo, not knowing if she was alive or dead? She became aware of touch, of Flavio's hand around hers, warm and knobbly. She heard his voice, smelled the familiar cigarettes and coffee on his breath, and the wood smoke on his shirt. As his face came into focus, she saw he had tears in his eyes. Recently, especially since his heart attack, she'd thought he looked old, but now she felt much older than him, and at the same time as young and helpless as a baby.

"How long have I been here?"

"Four days. God, you had us all worried. But you're going to be fine," he told her, stroking her hair. "It was an ulcer. Perforated your stomach. If only we'd known earlier; that heartburn you kept talking about."

It took some time to process. An ulcer. Not cancer?

She didn't really hear the rest of his words: something

about infection, major surgery, antibiotics, very serious. It was all words. She noticed the flowers, beautiful colours. It took a while to sink in – she wasn't dying.

But the girl. She had seen her, hadn't she? Standing by her bed, holding Lorenzo's baby. Had she really been there? Did it actually happen, or was it one of those dreamlike fragments of thought she'd experienced as she slipped in and out of consciousness?

Over the next few days, Flavio sat by Sonia's bed waiting for her to get stronger. He kept her up-to-date with the news, both local and global, brought messages from Lorenzo, and a copy of her favourite magazine. They laughed together over pictures of a show-jumping cow, and a philandering film star caught out by the paparazzi with his secretary in Milan while his wife and children were holidaying on the coast.

She began to glimpse a future. Perhaps things would be all right after all. There was no need for Flavio to know. Her time with him was too precious to throw away.

"By the way, I had to check through your bag for your phone to see if you'd had any messages and appointments I needed to cancel," he said. "There was a letter in there for Lorenzo."

Oh God. The letter. Her heart stopped. She waited.

"Don't worry. I sent it on to him."

No! She wrenched herself up on her elbows. She must get up. Must phone Lorenzo, tell him not to open it. But a new wave of exhaustion and nausea hit her. She sank back and closed her eyes. It was finished. She was too tired to keep down the truth any longer.

Flavio kissed her head. "I'll leave you to sleep."

Chapter Sixty-Eight

SONIA

Flavio was sitting by her bed again. He had the letter in his hands, the one she'd written to Lorenzo. Lorenzo must have read it and shown it to his father.

Here it comes.

Best to get it over with. Lying there in the hospital, she'd had time – too much time – to think about it. Yes, Flavio must be angry. Hurt. He might hate her. But it was the practicalities that mattered now. Could he live with the truth? Or more importantly, because this was what mattered, could he live with the fact that she'd deceived him and Lorenzo? Could he live with her? After all, they were both old. They needed each other. It was too late to turn back the clock. She couldn't expect forgiveness, not now, but couldn't they stay together and support each other, despite what she'd done?

"You silly girl," Flavio whispered, squeezing her hand. "Did you really think I didn't know all this time? I've always known."

The words swirled round her head. "You *knew?*"

He nodded. "Almost from the first moment I saw him. I thought it was something we silently agreed never to talk about."

"I didn't snatch him," she said. She had to make him understand that at least. "He was abandoned. At least, I thought so... at the time, I truly believed..."

"I know," he said. "And I know who by. I saw her – the young girl from the villa, stumbling along the path towards the church carrying a bundle. I was up in the trees. It didn't really click then what she had in her arms. It was only later that I made the connection."

His words took a while to sink in. All this time he'd kept the secret for her. Allowed her to lie to him, to everyone, been complicit in the crime of covering up Lorenzo's real identity, and without ever saying a word to her.

"And you know, I've got a lot more to feel guilty about than you, my love."

What was he talking about? Had he understood this thing at all?

"Those bodies at the villa," he said in her ear. "Why do you think they weren't discovered until last year? Who do you think hid them?"

Sonia felt a chill pass through her. Surely Flavio hadn't been mixed up in whatever awful event took place at Villa Leonida on the same night she took Lorenzo from the church?

"What are you talking about?"

Flavio sat with his elbows on the bed, hands clasped as if in prayer, pressed against his mouth. Eventually, he said, "I was working in the woods around the villa as usual the day after you brought Lorenzo home. I knew he wasn't ours – how could he be? But I tried not to think about that. I put all my energy into logging and clearing. I just kept telling myself it must be real, even if it didn't seem to be. I'd lost count of how many times you'd got pregnant and lost the baby over the years, and I thought we'd missed our time, but I told myself it must be right.

"I was felling trees up by the waterfall or I probably would have heard the commotion. It started raining, so I had to give up using the chainsaw. On the way back, I spotted some strange marks on the stones outside the drying tower. When I got closer, I could see it was blood – lots of it, turning the stones pink.

"I could tell something awful had happened before I got inside the tower."

He pushed his thumb and forefinger into the space above

his eyes. "God, it was a gruesome sight. Terrible. Those poor people."

He paused, recollecting. "I examined the bodies – or what was left of them. There was nothing anyone could have done. I saw a baby's dummy on the floor, and a pile of nappies. But no sign of a baby.

"I backed away and ran to the house. I hammered on the doors and windows but got no reply. I forced the French doors open. I was shouting, running through the rooms, looking for the rest of the family. There was no-one."

"Why didn't you go to the police?"

He nodded. "That was my first thought. But I started to panic. What if they thought I'd done it? I had no way of proving I hadn't. The one who discovers the bodies is always the first suspect, aren't they?"

All those detective programmes they'd watched together. And all these years she'd had no idea what he knew or what he'd done.

Sonia felt her head snap up. "You didn't think I could have killed them?"

He laughed at the implausibility, squeezing her hands more tightly than ever. "Of course not. I know you'd never harm anyone. But I thought, supposing the girl had brought the baby to you? Asked you to get him out of the way and keep him safe?

"You'd have taken him. Of course you would. He was alive, he had a chance. Whatever terrible thing had happened to his parents, nobody could give him a better home than us. I understand, Sonia. You rescued him from hell."

"But…"

"If you remember, there was trouble with some hawkers at the time. I thought it was probably they who'd killed the people at the villa. But if we went to the police and told them what we'd found, they'd take the baby away from us and place him with some young couple they deemed more suitable. And I couldn't bear that to happen, knowing what it would do to you."

It was starting to make sense. "So, you moved the bodies?"

"I had to. I couldn't risk them being found and our secret being discovered."

She stared at him, incredulous. What he must have gone through – how could she not have known? How could she have been living with him, sleeping in the same bed, and not have had any idea? But then it came to her.

Because of Lorenzo, that was why. In those early weeks, lost in the fog of feeds, nappy changes, dressing and soothing, she'd swung between euphoria and exhaustion. The world could have ended, and she wouldn't have noticed.

"I burned all the clothes and things. Then I hosed everything down as best I could, went home and got straight in the shower. It wouldn't have struck you as odd because that's what I always did after being in the woods. I was always filthy."

She nodded. He had been.

"It took me days to get rid of all their things from the house, but I had days. I had weeks. Nobody ever went there. It was months, perhaps years, before anyone mentioned the people at the villa – said they must have moved on. It didn't surprise anyone. That was the sort of people they were."

Sonia cupped Flavio's face with her hand. She couldn't stop the tears. So, he had known – known more than she did. But in any case, she told him her story from beginning to end – how she'd found the baby in the church, not in the chestnut tower; how she'd known nothing about the bodies until last year; had had no idea that anybody else knew about the baby, although she'd always dreaded the truth coming out.

"I know just how you feel,' he said. "When I heard about the bodies being discovered at the villa last year, I thought the stress would kill me. The police questioned me about whether I'd seen anything, and I kept thinking that at any moment they'd connect the baby to the bodies, but it didn't happen. Then just as I thought it had all gone away, I heard

261

a rumour that the villa was for sale again. It was too much."

Of course, the reason for his heart attack. The agonies he must have gone through.

"I can't believe we were both going through this together but alone," she said. He kissed away her tears and they stayed in each other's arms for a long time.

"What about Lorenzo?" she asked, hauled back to the present. "Has he read the letter?"

Flavio nodded. "He has. I'm sorry, I had no idea what it was, or I wouldn't have sent it to him. Not like that. But perhaps it's for the best. It was a shock, obviously. Might take him a while to come to terms with it, but he'll be fine." He must have seen her doubts in her face, because he added, "Come on, Sonia, you know Lorenzo – he's our son."

Chapter Sixty-Nine

"We'll take it."

When Cass brought her new clients into the restaurant after showing them the villa, Carlo almost asked the couple to repeat what they'd said. He'd assumed they were just another set of curious people adding Villa Leonida to their list of things to see that holiday, but from their faces he could see they needed no persuasion. It was the right house in the right location and they were getting it at a good price. Their offer was low, but Cass had little doubt the owners would accept it. They'd be fools not to.

She made the phone call on their behalf to the owners in Switzerland, and the couple sat with Carlo in the restaurant while waiting for the answer. The older man drummed his fingers on the table, his partner twisted his hair nervously. When the answer came, Carlo opened a bottle of Prosecco, which they insisted he share with them. Cass went to get the paperwork, and he ran through the buying process. The last of the lunch crowd had gone, so Carlo was in no hurry for them to leave.

"Carlo, it's your mother," said Cass, running back out from the kitchen. "I'm so sorry. I think she's had a stroke."

He made his excuses and ran to the door. Cass had already called the ambulance and he could hear the siren clanging as he reached her room.

Irena looked shrunken and pale. One side of her face had slipped, but otherwise she looked peaceful. Carlo had barely spoken to her since she told him the truth about Martina – he'd felt too angry. But looking at her now, it was hard to stay angry.

Later in hospital, he sat by the bed, held her hand, and talked to her for many hours about the good things he remembered from his childhood. And for want of filling the silence, he recounted many of the stories she'd told him over the years. Speech was difficult for her, but he hoped she understood. The doctor had said she would. At times she looked as though she was going to add a detail, or contradict him like she usually did, but it was beyond her and she closed her eyes, listening to him.

He only hoped that her mind was alive with scenes being replayed from the stories he was telling, but with the benefit of familiar faces and voices, truer colour, smells and sensations than he knew how to portray.

"I'm so sorry," whispered Cass. "You were right. I shouldn't have tried to stop you making those recordings. It's good that you've spent so much time with her recently. I know how much she appreciated it."

He loved her for not saying what she could have done – that making Irena confront these memories was what had brought this on. Couldn't he have left the past alone?

On the fourth or fifth morning when he arrived, Irena was agitated, and it was obvious she had something on her mind. Despite her inability to speak, she was able to indicate the Dictaphone.

"What do you want me to do with it?" Carlo asked.

By asking a series of questions, he was able to ascertain that she wanted him to give it to Sonia. Perhaps she guessed the end was near and she wanted to do this one thing before it came.

"Are you sure?"

She groaned in assent. He turned the device over and over in his hands, knowing it must contain her confession, perhaps even a plea for forgiveness. Probably the last thing she'd done before having the stroke. He kissed her cheek and assured her he would do it. She looked more peaceful when he left. Although there was no reason to be certain, he knew he wouldn't see her again.

Driving away from the hospital, he switched on the radio

and found it was playing his mother's old favourite, *Un Bacio a Mezzanotte*. He imagined her dancing to it with Roberto when she'd still believed everything was perfect and they would have a future together. Carlo turned the music up loud enough to drown his emotion.

Questions crowded his head as he swung his car up through the bends and took the road that followed the river. How would it really help Sonia now to know the truth about what happened? Apparently, she was very sick, in the same hospital as Irena, and might not even make it herself. Did she really need the added stress of being reminded about the past?

But Irena had trusted him. She'd faced up to what she'd done. How could he let her down?

Memories make us what we are. If memories were what defined people, where did that leave Sonia, whose whole life up until now had been built on false memories? Yet, she'd survived, and found a way of muddling through. Why embarrass her now by bringing it all back up?

When he got as far as the arched bridge, he made a decision, pulled over, walked until midway over the river, and looked down at the green water, as smooth as glass. He considered for a few moments. Of course, he should give the recording to Sonia. It was the right thing to do. But then he reminded himself, he wasn't perfect. Sometimes the right thing was just too difficult. He raised his arm, ready to hurl the device into the water.

No. At the last moment, he stopped himself. He'd come back to Santa Zita to get to the truth. Now that he'd found it, he had to face it... however difficult. Something Cass had said came back to him: *It's our choices that make us who we are.*

Carlo put the Dictaphone back in his pocket and got back in the car.

Chapter Seventy

Baby Graziella was born on October 1st, weighing a healthy 3.6 kilos. Holding her for the first time, Sonia was transported back to that evening in the church of Santa Maria del Soccorso when she'd watched the girl with the plaits setting down the baby in front of the picture of the angry Madonna. All those years of guilt, but she knew for sure now that if she had to make the same decision, knowing what she knew, knowing Lorenzo as she did, she'd still have made it.

Graziella opened her eyes and turned her unfocused gaze on Sonia. This was such a different baby – plump and strong, born to loving parents, a happy home.

Since the villa had been sold, talk about its past had been superseded by discussion of other things that were going on in the world – an earthquake, a political scandal, a shooting spree in an American school. The talk would return to Villa Leonida, of course. Perhaps Lorenzo would one day want to find out about his birth mother, why she'd abandoned him, and what had happened to her afterwards. But for now, he said he had enough on his plate looking after a baby. A baby who'd grow up free of the guilt Sonia had carried for so long. It was time to put it to rest. Perhaps someone one day would make the connection, but that was a problem for another day.

"She's got your nose." Lorenzo checked himself, remembering that wasn't possible. And yet she did.

Sonia handed him back the little box containing the pendant that Francesca had agreed they must give Graziella when she was old enough.

The past was what it was; they couldn't change it. But they could move forward together.

THE END

Fantastic Books
Great Authors

CROOKED
CAT

Meet our authors and discover
our exciting range:

- Gripping Thrillers
- Cosy Mysteries
- Romantic Chick-Lit
- Fascinating Historicals
- Exciting Fantasy
- Young Adult and Children's
  Adventures

Visit us at:
www.crookedcatbooks.com

Join us on facebook:
www.facebook.com/crookedcatbooks

Printed in Great Britain
by Amazon